CAPTIVE
RIVAL
CAPTIVE SERIES BOOK TWO

paige press

CAPTIVE RIVAL

CAPTIVE SERIES BOOK TWO

STELLA GRAY

Paige Press
Leander, TX 78641

Ebook:
ISBN: 978-1-957647-39-5

Paperback:
ISBN: 978-1-957647-46-3

Editing: Erica Russikoff at Erica Edits
Proofing: Michele Ficht

ALSO BY STELLA GRAY

———

ABOUT THIS BOOK

I thought I could walk away...but Armani Bellanti wants me for keeps.

My intentions were good.
I thought I was on the side of angels.
But all my plans led me straight to hell.

There's nowhere for me to turn.
My whole world is his cage.
I have no one.
No one but him.

He silences me with cruel kisses.
I taunt him with his desire for me.

We don't trust each other, but we can use each other.

Armani can take what he wants from me.

And I can keep pretending I'm not falling for the devil.

CANDI

PEOPLE ARE GOING to be talking about my wedding celebration for a very, very long time.

Just not in the way that Armani and I had intended.

Our extravagant reception at Bellanti Vineyards was abruptly cut short after a group of armed Bruno soldiers burst in during our cake cutting, guns on display, effectively dispersing most of our guests. Some quietly excused themselves, some ran, and the ones who froze in terror or tried to stick around to rubberneck were soon hastily escorted off the winery grounds by Bellanti security. I'm just grateful no weapons were discharged. The volley of rounds exchanged between my husband and the leader of the Brunos' men was strictly a verbal one.

After Armani hustled me back to the main house, he left me with a few guards for protection and then returned to the reception area to circle back with his brothers. I haven't stopped worrying since, my ears straining for the sound of gunshots or screams or squealing tires on gravel.

I'm currently glued to the front window with my eyes

on the string lights that still glow softly around the perimeter of the party space. From here, I can see a few tables knocked over, trampled flowers on the ground, an upended punch bowl, a single high-heeled shoe left behind in the mad rush to get away.

The scene of a fairy tale turned into a nightmare.

A sick, nauseous feeling twists in my gut, and I realize I'm shaking. I sink into one of the chairs by the window and reach for the hot tea that one of the kitchen staff brought out on a tray for me. But the cup rattles against the saucer so badly, I end up spilling half of it before I can even take a sip.

"Mrs. Bellanti?" one of the guards says gently from the doorway of the sitting room.

"I'm fine," I snap, the tremor in my voice loud and clear. I take a breath and set the tea back on the tray. "I'm going to my room."

"We'll come with you," the guard says.

Upstairs in the lounge area of the bedroom, I find my cat, Mr. Sprinkles, and cradle him in my arms for emotional support. I should change out of this ridiculous satin dress, take a hot shower, climb in bed and burrow under the blankets—but I can't do any of that. Not until my husband returns in one piece.

I start trembling again, and I pull a blanket around my shoulders, but it doesn't banish the cold inside me. The horrified looks on our guests' faces are still riveted in my mind. Their initial hushed shock and confusion at the symbolic blood-red liquid running out of the white frosted wedding cake when Armani and I cut through it with the knife. The rising murmurs of fear when those Bruno thugs sauntered into the tent like they owned the place.

I'd known this would be a night to remember...but now I wish it was something I could forget.

Finally, after what feels like an eternity, I hear footsteps echoing on the stairs, down the hall, and then my heart leaps when I catch the low rumble of Armani's voice as he converses with the guards outside the door. I get up off the sofa just as he steps into the room wearing his trademark scowl.

"Armani."

Relief nearly overwhelms me as I rush to meet him, even though the hard set of his jaw tells me his anger has not cooled. Unless—maybe something else happened.

"What did you find? Are the Brunos all gone? Did anyone get hurt? Are you okay?" I babble.

He strides across the room, away from me, barely giving me a second glance.

"There was nothing to find," is all he says.

I follow him into the bedroom, where he's working his tie loose.

"I don't understand," I say. I'm still reeling, and I can't stop asking questions. "Why did the Brunos send those men here with guns? Just to intimidate us? What was the point? And the cake—"

"The cake turned out exactly as expected," he says, nodding in self-satisfaction.

"What? The *bleeding* cake? It was horrible."

"It was a test, Candi," he says coolly.

"A test of what? For who? And why do you seem so damn pleased about the whole thing?"

He shrugs out of his suit jacket and lays it over a chair. The X of his shoulder holster makes a stark contrast against

3

the white of his dress shirt, the dark leather crisscrossing over his back. He has two guns strapped to his body that I can see, and I'm sure there's a third tucked away somewhere. Armed and dangerous as hell, as usual, and yet all I can think about is ripping off his clothes.

"When you ordered that cake, you gave the Brunos an opportunity to make us feel small," he says. "They took it. Thanks to you."

"But...I just ordered the cake you asked for, from the bakery you wanted," I say, shaking my head. "I had nothing to do with how it turned out."

"You had everything to do with how it turned out," he says, walking toward me. "But don't worry your pretty little head about it. The grown-ups are taking care of business now."

"How can you tell me not to worry when they put *blood* in our wedding cake?"

"It wasn't real blood."

His nonchalance only fuels my panic even more.

"That's beside the point, Armani. The Brunos threw down the fucking gauntlet. They just restarted the war, and you're acting like you've been given a gift."

"Don't be naïve. The war never ended. As their mole, you should know that better than anyone," he says, disappearing into the closet.

My cheeks burn at the rebuke. I can't even defend myself. I *was* the Brunos' mole, there's no denying it. But that doesn't mean I was privy to any of their plans. Especially not concerning their moves against Armani's family.

To the Brunos, I was nothing more than a tool to be used, not a member of their clan. My role was solely to

glean information from the Bellantis and feed it back to Juliana and her uncle, the Bruno patriarch. I had no idea what I was getting into when I agreed to help my best friend. No inkling about the scope of the war between these two mafia families. But now that I've been forced to switch sides and act as Armani's pawn—and his wife—I deserve to know what the hell is going on.

I'm so lost. And frustrated. And I'm getting angrier by the second.

Armani walks out of the closet in dark jeans and tactical boots, his guns strapped over a fresh shirt. My stomach clenches. He's going somewhere, and I still don't know anything.

"Just tell me. What the fuck. Is going on," I grind out. "You can't expect me to keep on helping you when you leave me completely in the dark like this."

It's a threat, but a weak one. The dirt Armani has on my brothers is what's keeping me obedient. As long as my own family is still in danger, I have no grounds to be throwing out demands or issuing ultimatums. But my words seem to have some kind of effect, because Armani looks me in the eye and seems to weigh what he's about to say.

"The bakery you ordered the cake from, in Santa Rosa—it's a Bruno owned business," he says.

"Okay..." I'm not following. It makes no sense. Why would he contract with the enemy?

"And when you placed that order," he goes on, "you gave them all the information they needed to crash our reception. Date, time, location, even the number of guests."

"But why would you want them to crash our..." And then it clicks. "You baited them."

He smiles cruelly. "No. *You did*. You're their mole, Candi. When you made that call, it looked like a message from you."

I sink onto the bed, my eyes closing, my ears ringing. Of course he's right. I called the Brunos and essentially offered them a goddamn invitation to infiltrate a gathering of their sworn enemies. And they delivered. And now this mafia war has unstoppably entered its next deadly chapter.

This is all my fault.

Armani set me up—or, more accurately, he used me to set the Brunos up. And I walked right into that trap like a fool, completely ignorant, playing my part once again as the perfect fucking pawn.

"I still can't believe you didn't figure out the bakery was theirs right off the bat," he says. "Though I can't be too surprised. You don't have the best track record of thinking for yourself."

"I can't believe you did this to me," I whisper, glaring at him through stinging eyes.

"Did what? Use you for your intended purpose? Don't forget why you're here, Candi."

My heart and my mind are breaking all at once. I'm so shattered, I can't even drum up a response as he walks away from me. When the door shuts behind him, I fall back onto the bed and cover my face, letting the tears fall. I have no idea where he's going, or why, but I'm too upset to chase after him and grovel for more answers—not that he'd give them to me anyway.

Armani used me. He manipulated me. Moved me around like a chess piece on his own private gameboard, and even though the signs were there all along, I was too

stupid to realize it. Because deep down, I was still holding on to the pathetic hope that he might actually care about me. About us. About our future together.

When in reality, all he cared about was restarting a mafia war.

ARMANI

I'VE CALLED an emergency meeting in the war room, aka the library, to strategize a plan of attack against the Bruno clan.

My brother-in-law Clayton slouches by the window, a glass of Irish whiskey in his meaty fist. Dante, meanwhile, is pacing, the hard line between his brows etched deep. As the head of the family, my older brother carries the constant weight of the world on his shoulders. I've never envied him that. He's also technically the man in charge, but since I'm the Bellanti war general, this is my area of expertise—ergo, I'll be running point. My younger brother Marco is the last to arrive.

As soon as he locks the door behind him, we gather around the long table in the center of the room. I'm the only one of us not still wearing party clothes, and the only one who doesn't look both disheveled and agitated. The tension is thick. But I'm in my element.

I already filled them in earlier on what happened with Candi and the Bruno bakery. They were none too pleased

to have been left out of the loop of my little scheme, given how quickly things escalated with the Bruno thugs who crashed the reception. But no matter. My brothers might not understand my secrecy or exactly why I'm playing my chess pieces the way I am, but they don't have to. I'm the master of this game. I will orchestrate our every movement.

"I'm sure you've guessed why I called you here. We need to implement a war plan," I say, cutting right to the chase. None of them look happy about my words.

Not that I care. The situation we're in with the Brunos was always an inevitability—a matter of when, not if. Now it's up to me to make certain we destroy our enemies as cleanly and quickly as possible. Slice the head off the snake and crush it under our boot heel. It's the only way to ensure this feud doesn't drag on indefinitely, a never-ending cycle of devastation, retaliation, kidnapping, violence, murder. Tit for tat, bullet for bullet. We can't just keep killing each other.

I need to put a stop to this once and for good.

"I see no viable alternative," Dante concedes, nodding at me. "We'll move against them in full force. Where do we begin?"

"I'd like to start by delegating the duties, make sure we're all on the same page," I say. "There are a lot of moving parts to this, and if we're not unified in our actions, the Brunos will home in on that weakness and exploit it. It's a risk we can't take. No more half measures, no more pretenses of civility, no more long game. It's time to end this. So if anyone here needs to back out, for any reason, do it now. I need 100% commitment and 100% follow-through until this is finished."

"You can count me in," Dante says.

"But the baby—" I start.

"I'm doing this *for her*," he interrupts. "I'm the boss, I'm responsible for all of us, and I won't hide behind my wife and daughter while the rest of you put everything on the line for this family."

"Fine. How about you, Marco?" I ask.

"I'm in," he says without hesitating.

"Me too. Always," Clayton adds. "Family first."

I nod. "Good. Here's what you need to know. I'm taking Candi to the island for a honeymoon—"

"Wait wait wait. Seriously, bro?" Marco scoffs. "You're gonna run off and diddle your backstabbing mole wife on the beach? How exactly does that constitute a war plan?"

"Marco," Dante warns.

"It's not a real honeymoon. It's how I'm going to get her off the grid and neutralize her," I say.

My great-grandfather purchased a small island off the coast of Morocco many years ago. It's out in the middle of nowhere, so tiny it's not on any map, and all but forgotten. I can't honestly remember the last time any of the Bellantis visited. The property—including the house, the landscaping, and the beachfront—is maintained seasonally by trusted staff who have been on our payroll for generations, and they know the name of the game is discretion. Every so often, a family ally will use the place as a safehouse or a neutral meeting zone, but it's currently empty with no upcoming visitors. It's the perfect hiding spot. And an excellent location to conduct a little underhanded business.

"Right now, thanks to the intel Candi passed along with the wedding cake order, Sergio Bruno thinks she's the

perfect mole," I go on. "That means he's going to get greedy. He's going to want more intel, and soon. If she doesn't give it to him, she'll lose her value. They may even stop trusting her."

"Bruno will get suspicious fast if she doesn't cooperate," Clayton agrees. "He's paranoid enough about employee loyalty as it is. Speaking as a former employee."

"Exactly my point," I agree. "If he thinks she's been compromised, we lose our edge. We can't have that. I don't want to give him any reason to question which side she's working for. Which is why I'm taking her out of the equation completely."

"If she's out of the country, she has an excuse not to have any info," Dante says.

"Correct," I say. "And the Brunos will still trust anything that comes out of her mouth whenever we do return from our trip. She's our tool now. I have to keep her sharp."

"Makes sense," Marco says begrudgingly. "So what about the rest of us?"

"You," I say, pointing at him, "don't make any more stupid moves. Or moves at all. And no fucking bets, either. As far as you're concerned, it's business as usual for you and Karina. Just lay low."

He's not smiling, but he gives me a terse nod.

"Clayton," I continue, "I need you to do your usual intel gathering. You're my eyes and ears no matter which continent I'm on."

Clayton raises his glass to me and says, "Alwa

"And Dante—" I turn to my big brother last. " ⌐ of Frankie and Lili."

He's silent for a moment before saying, "So our jobs are to do nothing. You want us to just sit here with our thumbs up our asses and wait for you and Candi to come back from your vacation."

"That's the gist of it," I say. "Though I'm not trying to tell you what to do with your thumbs."

Dante looks at me skeptically. The shadows under his eyes speak to how little he's been sleeping since he and Frankie brought the baby home from the hospital. He's barely come into the Bellanti offices since Lili was born, working remotely so he can stay close to his family. I'm not complaining—I'm glad to see Dante leaning into his new parenting role. I just need him to stay there.

"I don't like it," Dante finally says. He sighs and runs a hand through his hair. "We're all sitting ducks. Those fuckers are itching to pounce. To be honest, if I had known you were going to use Candi to trick the Brunos into crashing your reception, I would have put a stop to it. You basically welcomed them right back into the boxing ring."

"They never left it. All I did was test them," I say. "They failed."

He frowns. "You didn't need to test them. We already know they had no intention of honoring the peace treaty. They set our warehouse on fire, they put a hit out on you in Vegas, and Clayton's heard more than enough from Italy to corroborate the rumors that they're plotting to run us out of Napa. But for some reason, you still went behind my back and sent your wife to them with spoon-fed intel—"

"Intel that Sergio Bruno was more than happy to gobble up!" I point out. "Proving that they still trust Candi, that her role as a spy hasn't been compromised. That's something we can use against them, and catastrophically at that. She's a chess piece still in play. I'm going to take advantage of it. But I can't do that if they think she's turned, which is why I have to take her out of the country right now. If we stay here, we risk tipping our hand. Are we in agreement?"

His eyes flash. "We are."

I lock eyes with him. "Good to know we're on the same page."

What's unspoken between us is that my mind is already made up about taking Candi to the island. He knows it. I know it. But it's not a good look for me to be sidestepping his authority at every turn. It's something I have no right to do as his subordinate. Something I could easily be punished —or even killed—for. Hence this little dance between us, where I pretend to ask his permission before I do something and he pretends to give it.

Not that Dante would ever lay a finger on me even if I did disobey him. That's not how our family operates, not since our father died and took his bloodthirsty legacy with him. The truth is, I've been defying my older brother for years, in ways big and small. My behavior is permitted for one reason and one reason alone: in all my time as our head of security, intelligence, and both defensive and offensive operations, I've kept our family safe. I've done the dirty work. I've *won*.

Even still, my headstrong nature—stubborn, but never impulsive—and my self-direction have been near-constant sources of conflict between me and Dante. I'm well aware of that. But this is no time to walk on eggshells. I'm going to execute this plan, with his blessing or without it.

"Before I go, I need to know that I can trust all of you to

handle things in my absence," I tell them. "And precisely according to my instructions. You might be sitting pretty now, but things could change at any moment. Which is why I'll need you all locked and loaded."

"It might not be my place to say so, but I think you should nix the island," Clayton says, knocking his glass against the table.

Dante and Marco look over at our brother-in-law with mild surprise. Clayton's an impeccable soldier. He's never challenged me before.

"I don't recall asking for your opinion on the matter," I deadpan.

Clayton shakes his head. "No, you didn't. But I've fought alongside you all long enough now that I hope you'll at least consider my input."

"Very well. Speak," I say, impatience creeping into my tone.

"I just don't see the sense in leaving when we have the chance to finish this now and be done with it. Besides which, there's no guarantee you'll be safe where you're going. There could be other leaks among our ranks."

The back of my neck prickles. Clayton is an absolute bloodhound when it comes to finding information. There is no man that he can't track down, no name or piece of intel that can hide from him. He is an incredible investigator. Initially, it was difficult to get over my reservations about welcoming a former Bruno operative into the innermost circle of my family, but over time I've grown to trust him implicitly.

"What leaks among our ranks? What do you know?" I prod, my blood pressure spiking.

"Nothing at present," Clayton admits. "I'm just taking worst-case scenarios into account. But if I'm right, you won't want to be trapped on some remote island when the shit hits the fan. I think we should be planning an attack, not setting up more of these cat and mouse games while you're overseas. We need to cut their knees out from under them so bad, they won't be able to stand up again afterward. Once the Brunos find out you've left the US, they might decide it's the best time to strike."

"They won't. Because they know I'd instantly respond in kind, and with all the power of the Bellanti allies at my back. Sergio Bruno might be reckless, but he's not that stupid. He won't make a move until he thinks he can wipe out all of us in one fell swoop. Me included. Me especially."

"Maybe you're right," Clayton says uneasily.

"I am right. We need to bide our time, not act on our impulses," I tell him. "The best way to win this war is to get Sergio to play into our hands, to do exactly what we want him to. Don't you get it? Without Candi in our pocket, the Brunos' offensive maneuvers will be too unpredictable. The retaliation will just continue, unchecked. With her, we can predict their moves. We're doing this my way."

Clayton frowns, and then says, "All right. Then consider taking your wife to Italy instead. We have plenty of contacts and allies there. It's safer. And you'll be aware of what's happening—"

"Who says I'm not aware?" I interrupt. "Everything's under control. I'm not worried."

The Brunos have their claws in plenty of old Italian mafia families, true enough, but Clayton has spent a significant amount of time and effort monitoring their conversations and activities—not to mention greasing palms when necessary and maintaining "beneficial" mob relationships of his own—so the Brunos and their friends are able to keep very few secrets from us. We're well-connected and well-resourced in our own right. Plus, I also have my own Italian sources, though I keep them to myself.

Clayton looks at me dubiously. "Very well. The island it is, then. I've said my piece."

"Excellent. Any further objections?" I ask Dante and Marco.

They shake their heads.

I let everyone mull things over while I pour myself a drink and drop into a chair. Everything I've just told my brothers is true, but there is one thing I've left out. I'm not taking Candi away from Napa solely to protect her as a Bellanti asset. I'm also taking her away because I need to get her out of my system once and for all. I can no longer lie to myself about the fact that she's become a distraction to me.

And if I don't remedy the issue, I'll never get my head back in the game.

Which is why I plan to use her good and hard, until I've had my fill.

"I really hope you know what you're doing, bro," Marco says with an edge to his voice that pulls me from my train of thought. "I'm getting real sick of living this life. Karina and I just want to move on. End this once and for all."

I take a slow drink of my scotch, relishing the burn of it in my throat. I have the urge to pat my little brother on top of the head and tell him not to worry, but that would really rile him up.

"Believe me, I am going to end this," I tell him. "Which

is why I need to maintain complete control of our every move. The Brunos won't make it through what I have planned. Not this time."

I finish the rest of my drink, then slam my glass down on the table.

"You're all free to go," I say, standing up. "I'll send word once I've reached the island."

"*Viaggi sicuri*," Dante tells me. Safe travels.

"Always," I say in response.

And then I walk out.

3

CANDI

It's still dark when I wake to the sound of Armani unzipping two suitcases at the foot of our bed.

I sit up, my eyes slowly adjusting to the predawn gloom, watching him fill the luggage with clothes and make back and forth trips from the closet, the bathroom, and his chest of drawers.

"Where are you going?" I ask sleepily.

He doesn't answer me, but my heart starts racing as I realize he isn't just packing for himself. He's packing for me, too. At six in the morning and with a quick efficiency, as if he's in a hurry to get out of here. A little red flag waves in my brain. We're fleeing. Did something happen? Are we in danger?

"Is it the Brunos? Why are we running away?" I ask, sliding out of bed.

"God, Candi. Don't be so melodramatic. We're not running away. We're taking a trip."

That's no kind of answer at all.

I move to the foot of the bed and block the suitcases,

folding my arms over my chest. Armani pulls up short in front of me with an armload of my shoes.

He lets out a huff of annoyance. "Move."

"Not until you tell me what's going on," I tell him. "And by the way, you're not packing my Jimmy Choo sandals. It's almost winter."

But when I try to grab them, he steps back, out of my reach. "Trust me. You'll want them."

"Because we're going to..." I coax, hoping he'll fill in the blank with someplace good.

"Be gone for a while," he finishes, darting around me and dumping the shoes in a suitcase. "And before you ask, yes, Mr. Sprinkles will be well taken care of. Your favorite cat is staying with your favorite chef's assistant for the duration of our trip. Becca was quite happy to offer her services as kittysitter again, thanks to the generous bonus I paid her last time."

He goes back into the closet and returns with a bunch of my dresses, still on their hangers, and then proceeds to shove them into the suitcase in one big lump.

"Okay, I've had enough," I say. "You're going to wrinkle up everything in there. Let me do it."

With that, I pull out the pile of dresses and lay them flat on the bed. As I start to remove them from their hangers, Armani comes around the bed to where I'm standing. As I catch the scent of his cologne, my adrenaline races.

"I never said I needed your help. Go back to sleep, princess," he says.

I frown. "But you're destroying my clothes."

"Where we're going, you won't need them anyway."

Instantly, visions of sex flash before my eyes, and I'm

rendered speechless. Armani is standing mere inches away in sweatpants and a tight white T-shirt, and my gaze drops to that low-slung waistband hugging his hips, because how the hell can I not stare? There's something undeniably delicious about a man in sweatpants and no underwear. I barely get a second to enjoy it though, as he takes me by the shoulders and pushes me back on the mattress. I yelp, but he lifts my ankles and tosses my feet onto the bed, then whips the covers back over me.

"Rest up. I'll be back at eight to fetch you for your spa appointment."

"I have a spa appointment?"

He slams one suitcase closed, zips it, and tosses it on to the floor. "Stop asking questions. I'm in charge. You obey."

A shiver goes over me, but it's not from fear.

───────

NOT TWO HOURS LATER, Armani and I are sitting in the back seat of a luxury SUV as Donovan, the Bellantis' driver, takes us on an outing that I'm starting to think of as the mafia hostage version of the *Pretty Woman* makeover. Because I have zero say in any of this, and apparently, the spa isn't the only thing Armani scheduled for me today. Oh, no. I've got to go shopping as well. I guess whatever this mystery trip turns out to be, I need new clothes for it. Which I would normally enjoy, honestly, but I'm not exactly a willing participant this time around.

Since my spa appointment is first, I'm in yoga pants and a hoodie, so at least I'm comfortable. But my mood is crap. I'm still sleepy after my rude awakening this morning, and

Armani has been nothing but shady, refusing to answer any of my questions about our upcoming trip. He's wearing pressed slacks, a dark dress shirt with the sleeves rolled up over his strong forearms, and a silk tie. Irritatingly scrumptious, though I do my best to not ogle him openly. He doesn't deserve the attention.

Scowling over the rim of my to-go cup of coffee, I tell him, "I'm not a child, you know. You didn't have to skip work just to chaperone me."

"I'm not comfortable having you out of my sight on your own all day," he says coolly.

"I wouldn't be on my own. Donovan would be with me," I point out.

"You're a flight risk, a liar, and a mole," he reminds me cruelly. "I don't trust you. I don't trust the Brunos, either. They've got a bad track record when it comes to kidnapping Bellanti women."

"Fine. Have it your way then," I say shortly, glaring at him.

A smile plays at his lips, and he slides his sunglasses on. "Oh, I intend to."

I take that as my cue to be quiet.

When we get dropped off at the spa in Nob Hill, we walk in through the smoked glass entry doors to find the place empty, save for one employee who greets us from behind the front desk.

"Good morning, Mrs. Bellanti," she says serenely. "You have the place to yourself this morning."

"I do?"

"Per my arrangement," Armani murmurs beside me.

"Oh. Right."

Was he afraid there might be an ambush at the spa?

I'm suddenly a little afraid to be inside.

The employee comes around the desk and gestures for me to follow her. "This way, please. We'll get that Brazilian taken care of first."

Pulling up short, I look over at Armani, my eyes narrowing. "Another arrangement of yours? Yeah, no. Not happening."

The employee pauses and looks between Armani and me. "Of course, we can certainly skip—"

"Oh, but I insist," Armani says, flashing me a grin. "After all, it's my treat. Wife."

I smile back, hoping he can see the threat in it. He will pay for this later. "Fine. Husband."

"Wonderful," he says. "I'll be waiting."

"How nice for you." Turning back to the employee, I tell her, "Lead on."

We go back to a private room with mood lighting, a cushy treatment table draped in fresh linens, and the scent of eucalyptus and lemongrass heavy in the air. I'm left with a soft cotton robe and told to undress and get comfortable. Once I'm lying down on the table, however, all I can do is mentally prepare myself for torture. This isn't the first time I've been waxed within an inch of my life—I got a Brazilian when I was in college, after Juliana convinced me to go with her—but I swore I'd never do it again.

And yet here we are.

The ambiance is much better this time, at least. Relaxing New Age music plays from hidden speakers, and the table is comfortable and pleasantly warm against my back. Just when I start to think I might actually fall asleep, the door opens and an older woman bustles in wearing a pale green uniform.

The second she puts me in The Position, the soothing effect of the ambiance disappears. No amount of essential oils or ethereal flute song can make me forget what's about to happen. I take a deep breath and remind myself that I survived my first Brazilian, and I can survive this one, too.

Much to my shock, the pain is nowhere near what I thought I remembered. Not that it's a walk in the park, exactly. But it's definitely bearable. And during my hot stone massage afterward, I actually do fall asleep. Then I get a facial, a mani-pedi, and some kind of acupressure scalp massage that has me practically floating on a cloud. Almost four hours have passed by the time I walk out of there.

I'm surprised to find Armani working on his iPad in the waiting area. I assumed he'd still be up the street at the coffee shop. He quickly puts his tablet away when he sees me.

"Shall we go to lunch?"

"You tell me. You're the boss, aren't you?" I say sarcastically.

Yes, my vulva is silky smooth, but it stings like a son of a bitch. It's going to take a lot more than an excellent massage and a lunch date to make me warm up to Armani again.

"I know a great Italian place," he says.

"I'm actually sick of Italian at the moment," I say sourly.

He throws his head back and laughs, which only boils my blood more.

"Then we'll do French. Come on."

With that, he takes my arm and leads me out to the curb, where Donovan is waiting for us.

Admittedly, the restaurant Armani takes me to is superb. There's a fig and goat cheese tart, a lobster salad, and a croque madame made with the best bechamel sauce I've ever tasted. But I keep my thoughts to myself, eating just enough to be polite, refusing to let my guard down for even a second.

"Dessert?" Armani asks as our plates are being cleared.

I stare at the wall behind his head. "Pass."

"Are you just going to be pissy all day?" he says after a moment.

"Are you just going to treat me like a prisoner all day?"

"I hardly think this counts as prison," he says, gesturing at the fancy décor around us.

"Perhaps you're unfamiliar with the term 'gilded cage,'" I shoot back. "I didn't ask for any of this, nor do I want it. What I want is some answers."

Armani's impassive expression remains unchanged.

"You're going to want some new things for this trip."

I throw my hands up. "Oh, yes. For the vacation that I'm not allowed to know anything about."

"It's not a vacation."

My cheeks grow hot with frustration. I don't even bother asking for the millionth time what this trip is about, because I know he won't tell me shit. As soon as the bill is paid, I stalk out of the restaurant. But I know better than to get too far ahead of Armani. Invisible or not, my leash is a short one.

Our final stop is a very posh boutique, so self-important that its front windows are full of spiny air plants and blown glass vessels suspended from wires instead of actual cloth-ing. Just like the spa, I walk in to find we are the only guests inside the store. A stylist greets us as we enter and casually locks the door behind us. I shoot Armani a raised brow, but he doesn't acknowledge me.

"Welcome, Mrs. Bellanti. Please follow me."

I ignore the smug expression on my husband's face.

She shows me to a fitting room area that's furnished with a velvet covered fainting sofa, a wall of ornate antique mirrors, and a beautiful three-tier chandelier hanging from the ceiling.

"Wow," I can't help murmuring. This place looks like a palace.

"We've prepared a selection of items based on your husband's recommendations, but please let me know if I can find anything else for you," the stylist says warmly, gesturing at a dressing room curtain that's been pulled halfway open for me. "I'm Natalie. Just give a shout if you need me."

"I will, and thank you so much."

She leaves, and my eyes grow wide when I step into the dressing room and see what's waiting there: two elegant clothing racks loaded with flimsy lingerie, baby doll night-gowns, and silky robes.

Crossing my arms over my chest, I consider my options. I am in no mood to try on sexy things for Armani. I am in no mood for any of this. I'm terrified of what's going to happen with the Brunos, and I still can't erase from my mind the image of those armed men who showed up during my wedding celebration. A storm is brewing, and Armani's acting like we're about to jet off on some sexcapade.

The curtain is suddenly pulled back and there he is, taking up space I don't want him to take up.

"I'd appreciate some privacy," I say coldly.

He grabs my chin and levels my eyes to his. "You know, it was cute at first, but I'm getting tired of the attitude, Candi. If I didn't know any better, I'd think you were asking me to punish you."

A delicious shiver goes over me. "What kind of punishment did you have in mind?"

His gaze drops to my lips and I have to fight the urge to lean into him.

"I'm going to help you," he says.

Huh? "Help me w—"

But I don't get to finish my sentence before he pushes me back against the wall. As I glare up at him, one side of his mouth pulls into a sneer.

"Help you try on some of these things," he says. "We don't have all day."

"I don't need your help," I snap, annoyed now.

"Clearly you do."

My nostrils flare as he proceeds to roughly undress me. I don't bother helping whatsoever. Instead, I just stand there like a mannequin even as hot bolts of desire shoot through my body. Once I'm naked, he pulls me against him and looks down at me.

"What will you try on first?" he asks.

"I don't care."

He cocks a brow. "I find that hard to believe. You're usually so opinionated."

I suck in a breath at the sudden brush of his crisp cotton shirt against my peaked, aching nipples. He's doing this on purpose. Humiliated by my own horniness, I turn my head so he won't see the lust in my eyes, even as my brain silently screams at him, *Kiss my neck. Grab my ass. Run your tongue and teeth over my skin. Do it.*

"Black or red?" he prods.

"Black," I murmur, unable to keep myself from giving in.

"Good girl."

His hot breath caresses my throat as he speaks, and I let out a sigh when one of his shirt buttons scrapes my nipple, cool and hard, sending a zap of pleasure bursting through me.

"Don't move," he orders.

Clenching my thighs together, I breathe heavier as my anticipation grows. But instead of kissing me, he tugs something off the clothing rack and then drops to one knee before me. He nudges my right leg until I lift my foot, then slides something over it, then does the same on the other side, finally pulling a pair of black satin and lace panties up over my hips.

"How do they feel?" he asks, looking up at me.

It takes all my willpower not to grab his head and shove it between my thighs. "Fine."

Armani stands up again and runs a hand between my legs, pressing the fabric against my pubic bone. The feel of the soft satin and his warm hand against my freshly waxed skin jacks my desire.

"Now the garter belt," he says.

All I can do is glare at him as he dresses me in a matching satin and lace garter belt and sheer black nylon thigh-highs, expertly attaching the garter straps to the top of the stockings. When he's done, he steps back to admire his work. I glance in the mirror behind him and the first thing I notice about my reflection is how pissed off I look. The second thing I notice is how hot this garter set is.

Almost as if I'm under a spell, I run my hands down my breasts, along the curve of my waist, my hips, and then I give the elastic straps a little snap. I barely register the sound of Armani's groan before he's shoving me against the wall, his hot hands gliding up the backs of my thighs, his nose pressed into the soft skin below my ear. Gasping, I loop an arm around his neck.

And then I realize what we're doing.

"Stop," I whisper harshly. "We can't do this in here."

He ignores me and dips a finger inside the panties—which is when I realize they're actually crotchless—and then runs his fingertip along my seam, making me whimper.

"Yes we can," he says.

"Armani—"

I try to push him away but he pushes his finger inside me, so deep and delicious that I instantly go weak in the knees, sagging against him.

"Tell me to stop," he teases me cruelly, pumping faster, curling his finger inside me to press against my G-spot.

But I can't. He knows I can't. I'm soaking wet and throbbing already, and he's fingering me so good that I can't bear denying myself. So I close my eyes and give in, riding the pleasure. My anger at him is only fueling my lust, and by now Armani is extremely well versed in exactly the right moves to get me off. His other hand slides over the base of my throat as he leans his chest harder against my breasts, trapping me completely against the wall.

"More," I pant, my hips jerking in time with every pump of his expert fingers.

He rubs my clit with his thumb, his teeth nipping at my earlobe, working me faster, harder. God, how does he do this? His fingers feel like an actual cock, the pump and glide so perfect I can almost pretend we're actually fucking. A moan escapes me and I bite down on my lip, the thought of the store employees listening to us making me both ashamed and turned on in equal measure. I'm going to—

"Yes," I whisper breathlessly, feeling my climax approaching. "Yes, yes, y—"

"Oh, no you don't," he says, pulling his hand away.

No, no, no.

"What the hell?" I yelp, stumbling as he steps back.

"That's enough for now," he says.

"Um, excuse me?" I say, incredulous.

"Nice smooth pussy," he calls over his shoulder as he walks out of the dressing room.

Bastard.

4

CANDI

AFTER THE INCIDENT in the dressing room, I refused to try on anything else. It didn't make a difference. By the time I got my clothes back on, Armani had already told the stylist that we'd take every single piece of fancy lingerie she'd picked out for me. I anticipated a very silent, very tense hour on the ride back home. When we got back into the car, however, Donovan didn't drive us to Napa.

He drove us to the airport.

After we get dropped off and taken through a VIP security checkpoint, we're driven to a hangar where a private jet is waiting. When we get on board, I quickly realize that Armani, a single flight attendant, and the two pilots in the cockpit are going to be my only companions for the duration of the journey. There are eight seats in total, all singles, all window seats of course, and they're all empty.

"You chartered this plane just for us?" I ask incredulously. I can't imagine how expensive it was.

"No. My family owns this jet," Armani says nonchalantly, sliding into a seat.

Hot damn. I didn't realize the Bellantis had a private plane. It's as high end and fancy as I'd expect, nothing but leather and polished wood everywhere, but try as I might, I can't get comfortable in my plush seat. Nor can I bring myself to sip the red wine the flight attendant hands me. She also gives me a sleeping mask, a pillow, a pair of sherpa slippers, and a very luxurious blanket, all of which suggest that this is going to be a long flight indeed...but I'm not in a napping mood.

Armani seems to have no trouble settling into his seat across the aisle. His eyes close the second we start to taxi down the runway, and once we're in the air, he downs a glass of scotch while reading an actual physical newspaper before reclining his chair into bed mode and dozing right off. I still have a million unanswered questions for my husband-slash-kidnapper, but I don't ask any of them as we wing off to our unknown destination.

Unknown to me, anyway.

Hours pass. The view outside my window does nothing to calm me. We fly over mountain ranges, vast brown and green plains, the geometric shapes of farmland, through piles of puffy white clouds, through time zones. The afternoon light starts to fade as the sun drops lower on the horizon behind us, and I can see on the flight map that we're getting close to Chicago, but there is no indication from the pilot or the flight attendant that we're anywhere near our end point.

Where the hell are we going, then? New York City? Miami? Toronto? I'd love to annoy my so-called husband with my random guesses—hell, maybe he'd eventually crack and tell me where we're *really* going—but he's still asleep. I'd probably be sleeping too, if I were him. He never came to bed last night. God only knows what he was doing all that time. Plotting against the Brunos, I'm sure. This feud is all he ever thinks about. Lately, it's all I ever think about as well.

My frustration has reached the point of no return. As slowly and quietly as I can, I unbuckle my seat belt, slide my pillow and blanket to the floor, and tiptoe to the front of the cabin where the flight attendant is sitting. She looks up from her magazine—*National Geographic*, with a photo of Mars on the cover—as I approach.

"Can I help you with something, Mrs. Bellanti?" she asks warmly.

"You can, actually," I say.

She's already out of her seat, reaching for a clean wine-glass, but it's not a drink that I'm after.

"Oh, um, that's okay—I'm good on the wine," I tell her. "I just wanted to know where we're flying to. You do know our itinerary, right?"

Her smile falters.

"Mr. Bellanti said the flight plan was confidential," she says apologetically.

"I get that, but I'm his wife, so...do you think you can make an exception? He's trying to surprise me, but I'm not really into surprises. I'm not even sure how long we're supposed to be in the air for, and honestly I'm starting to feel a little air sick."

"Oh! I'm so sorry, Mrs. Bellanti. Let me take care of that," she says, sounding relieved as she busies herself whipping up a glass of Alka Seltzer with a slice of lime.

"Please—" I beg, pulling the glass out of her hand. "Please, tell me where we're going."

She bites her lip and drops her eyes. "I apologize, but I can't. It's a matter of security."

"Fuck," I whisper. "I'm being kidnapped, aren't I? Maybe I need that wine after all."

With that, I chug down the Alka Seltzer in my hand as the flight attendant watches me, her brows knit together in concern.

"I wish I could help you, but I'd lose my job," she says quietly.

"It's fine," I sigh, handing the empty glass back to her.

"The flight time is eleven hours, forty-eight minutes," she says softly. "We will be landing in the time zone of Greenwich Mean Time plus one. This is all I can say."

"Thank you," I murmur. It's not a lot to go on, but it's better than nothing. And at least I know we're not going to be making our final descent for another seven hours or so.

Tiptoeing back down the aisle, I see that Armani is still passed out in his seat pod. The jerk. Sleeping like a baby while I have marathon panic attacks. Must be nice to be in control of everything.

I exhale, drop into my seat, and stare out the window again. The further east we fly, the darker it gets, and the more tiny city lights I can see winking on below us. A twelve-hour flight and GMT+1 puts us where? Pulling out my phone, I connect to the jet's Wi-Fi and try to get my map app working so I can see exactly where we are. Except it isn't working. Of course it's not. I mess with the settings, trying to get my phone's GPS to kick in, but nothing that should show me my current location is functioning. Fuck.

Frustrated but undeterred, I do a little Googling. Okay. GMT+1 time zone. We're talking either Scandinavia, Europe, or central Africa. It has to be Italy we're going to, right? Where else would Armani go to hide out? The Bellantis have allies there, and probably extended family. People willing to take us in.

Except that Italy is the first place anyone would look. It's way too obvious. Unless...is it so obvious that it's actually the *last* place anyone would look?

I'm back at square one. I know nothing. My best guess at the moment is that this trip has to be Bruno related. We have to be running from them. It's the only explanation for our abrupt departure and the secrecy surrounding it. Maybe Armani found out about an attack they were planning. A raid, a bomb, something. But then, why are the rest of the Bellantis staying in Napa?

Although, maybe they're not. Maybe the family has agreed to scatter across the globe to hide out in separate, secret locations so that the Brunos can't wipe them all out in one fell swoop. It would make sense, considering the way the rival mafia clan sent their thugs to infiltrate my wedding celebration—a warning of things to come. The more I think about it, the more I feel certain that we're going into hiding.

But that theory doesn't totally make sense. Armani isn't the type of man to run from a threat. He would much rather fight fire with fire, and swiftly. But if we're not running, then what *are* we doing?

I can't stand that he's being so secretive. My insides have been tied in a knot since he started packing our suitcases this morning, and my anxiety is half the reason I've been so bitchy toward Armani all day. Did Dante order me and Armani to leave for our own safety, or did Armani decide to take me away? What if we've been banished from Napa, or kicked out of the family for some reason? Or maybe the rest of the Bellantis are going to meet up with us later...

Before I can spiral further, the flight attendant appears and gives me a little nod. I watch her gently wake Armani from his nap to tell him that dinner will be served shortly. Apparently the menu includes some kind of lentil soup, lamb kebabs, vegetable tagine, and couscous. I realize that my mouth is watering despite the terrible day I've been having. Lunch was hours ago.

"Sleep well?" I say coolly as the flight attendant walks off to prepare our food and my husband returns his seat from lay-flat mode to its original upright position.

"I did, thank you," he answers, seemingly unbothered by my tone.

"So. Since we're literally *in the air* and I can't possibly back out of this trip now, do you think it might be a good time to let me know where in the hell we're going?" I say.

He shrugs. "We'll be staying on a private island property. More of an isle, really."

"An isle?" I sputter. Leave it to Armani Bellanti to rent himself an entire private island just so he can loll around in luxury while he's evading homicidal mobsters. "And where is this alleged isle?"

"Does it matter? The location isn't as important as what we'll be doing there."

"Hiding out, you mean?" I say.

He narrows his eyes. "I mean I'll be using this time to decide if you're still useful."

My mouth instantly goes dry as Armani's unspoken threat jacks my pulse. If I'm no longer useful, does that mean I won't leave the island—isle—alive? How long will it take for someone to even realize I'm missing? The Bellantis would cover for Armani if the cops start asking questions, I'm sure of it. And if I did disappear off the face of the earth, I doubt anyone would ever find my body.

I can feel my blood running cold, but I remind myself that I'm going into this trip fully aware of the danger Armani poses to me. He might be deadly, but he won't take me by surprise—because I am never going to let my guard down around him. And if it comes down to it, I'll fight back. I'll run. I'll hide. I'll do whatever it takes to survive, and I'll make this asshole wish he'd never underestimated me.

"Welcome to your honeymoon," he adds with a smirk.

"Honeymoon. Right. More like my jail sentence."

"You aren't a prisoner."

"Of course I am. I'm *your* prisoner," I point out.

That smirk spreads into a lazy grin as a flash of interest lights his eyes. He shifts in his seat, adjusting his pants in a way that makes it obvious he's physically turned on by the idea. He wants to trap me, hold me down, restrain me. He wants to own me. And as much as I hate to admit it, I want him to.

Visions of handcuffs and black leather and blindfolds flit through my mind, a corresponding rush of excitement pulsing between my legs. I think back to the way he fingered me in the fitting room earlier, the feel of him lightly choking me, the thump of my heart as I almost came in his hand. As much as I hate him, I can't deny that something about the man just...does it for me. Every time. Damn him.

Folding my arms over my chest, I swivel my seat toward the window, away from his diabolical hotness, just as the flight attendant rolls her cart out of the galley. I continue to ignore my husband as the attendant sets up a full-size dining table in the aisle between me and Armani. The food smells amazing, spicy and fragrant and savory. Unfortunately, I've lost my appetite and I have to force myself to smile politely as I'm served. Once she's gone, I glare at Armani across the table.

In between bites of lamb and couscous, he picks up the conversation where we left off.

"Although we'll be the only guests staying at the villa, you'll need to follow some rules."

"Why are you making rules if no one else is going to be there to catch me breaking them?"

"*Because,*" he goes on, "there will be a full staff there to attend to us, and while they've been thoroughly vetted, I don't know any of these people well enough to trust them. Chef, cleaning staff, butler, groundskeepers—that's a lot of potentially loose lips, and the last thing we need is someone leaking information to our enemies. So. You'll need to play the loving bride for the duration."

"Oh, of course. Because, per usual, we have to sell this bullshit marriage so that no one suspects you're only keeping me around to feed fake intel to the Brunos."

"Precisely," he says. "If it got back to Sergio Bruno that we're not madly in love, he'd immediately start to wonder why we went through the motions of eloping in Vegas in the first place. It wouldn't take him long to put the pieces together and realize that you're double-crossing him."

"Fine. I'll play the part," I say curtly, lifting my chin.

"But you don't get to touch me. I don't want you to lay a single finger on me the entire time we're on the island."

My words are a bluff—or an attempt to regain some semblance of control, really. Whether or not I'll be able to stay strong and stick to my boundary is another story.

Still, drawing a line in the sand right now sends a message that I'm not going to just sit around on this trip compliantly letting Armani boss me around however he likes. In fact, this no-touching rule might be the only way I can fight off my horrible attraction to him. If he doesn't touch me, maybe I can find some willpower. The willpower that usually flies out the window whenever I'm around him.

Armani nods, takes a long drink of his wine, and then says, "I will do my utmost to respect your wishes. Within reason. We don't know who might be watching at any given moment, or what they might be overhearing. We can't give anyone any ammunition."

"Okay. So if there *is* someone in the vicinity, you may engage in *limited* acts of PDA in the interest of keeping up appearances," I concede. "Beyond that, we will not be physically intimate."

"Understood."

What he doesn't know is that I fully intend to use my body as a weapon against him. Making him lust after me won't give me enough of an upper hand enough to call the shots, of course, but at least it'll give me an edge. I won't be entirely defenseless. And considering the pile of new lingerie now at my disposal, it shouldn't be too difficult to get him to play by some of my rules.

"In addition to keeping up the appearance of being a

deliriously happy newlywed, you will also need to agree not to leave the grounds," Armani says.

"I imagine I won't be able to, since it's a friggin' island," I sass.

"Should you attempt to leave the property by yourself, the perimeter guards have been instructed to do whatever is necessary to restrain you and return you directly to me. You'll go nowhere without my express permission."

Rolling my eyes, I pick a pomegranate seed out of the couscous and pop it in my mouth. "Mm. twenty-four-hour surveillance. How romantic. I can hardly wait."

"You'll also have no contact with the outside while we're away. For your own safety."

"Wow. Sounds super fun," I say, my words dripping with sarcasm.

"Honestly, Candi, your attitude is boring me," he says dryly. "I suggest you keep your comments to a minimum and eat your dinner. I'll be working for the rest of the flight, so enjoy amusing yourself."

With that, he tosses back the rest of his wine, stands to pull his laptop bag from the overhead compartment, and heads toward the back of the plane, where a sliding door leads to a small office.

What an asshole.

As soon as the door closes, I grab my fork and attack the food. Not because I'm hungry, but because I need to keep up my strength.

If Armani Bellanti wants to start a war with me, I'm going to be ready for it.

5

CANDI

It's noon local time when we disembark the plane. Unfortunately, my body—which is still firmly on California time—thinks it's the middle of the night. I barely slept, and I feel like shit. But honestly, I'm not hating the view as I make my way down the aircraft's stairs. This place looks like paradise.

Deep blue water surrounds the island. Green, rocky hills rise all around us, the landscape dense with foliage and flowers. I recognize the familiar shapes and scents of eucalyptus and citrus trees spreading out along the runway. The air is warm and inviting with a kiss of salty ocean dampness on the breeze ruffling my hair.

"Wow," I murmur, taking a deep breath.

But I'm barely able to appreciate my surroundings before Armani ushers me across the tarmac, through the small, makeshift airport building—obviously built for one private plane to use at a time—and into the car that's already waiting for us. The driver smiles at me in the rearview mirror as Armani helps the flight attendant from our plane load our bags into the trunk.

"Welcome to Yallah Island, Mrs. Bellanti," the driver says.

"Yallah—what does that mean? And where exactly are we?" I ask quietly, hoping to glean some information before Armani gets in the car.

"It means 'Let's go,' in Arabic," he says, sounding amused. "Good name for a vacation spot, no? We're located less than ten miles off the coast of Morocco, off the northern tip of Africa."

"Thank you," I say, grateful to finally be getting a few more tiny pieces of the puzzle.

Morocco—of course. The meal on the plane suddenly makes perfect sense. I should have guessed. My heart sinks at the location, though. Even if I was a strong swimmer out in open water, I'd never make it so many miles to the mainland. So much for swimming my way to freedom. Maybe I can make myself a raft out of palm fronds and tree trunks. It's possible, right?

Suddenly the trunk slams hard, making me jump. A second later, Armani flings open the passenger door and slides into the seat next to the driver, leaving me in the back all by myself. Just as well. I'm more than happy to have some space, and relieved I don't have to play a happy newlywed yet.

Minutes later, we pull up to a property that's hidden behind tropical trees and an imposing iron fence. The driver stops at the front gate to punch a code into the keypad of a high-tech looking box. The light on the box goes from red to green and then the gate swings open to reveal a wide gravel path that winds through the trees. We slowly drive down the path, seemingly into nothing but jungle. Glancing out the rear window, I watch the gates close tightly behind us. That's when I notice the tower to the left of the gate, partially hidden in the trees. A guard perches there with an automatic weapon in his hands.

I whip back around in my seat, gasping. Armani looks over his shoulder at me but shows no emotion when our eyes meet, even though I'm sure I look exactly as uneasy and overwhelmed as I feel. I say nothing. Neither does he.

Outside my window, the greenery passes in a blur until suddenly a palatial home looms before us. It's practically glowing. The Bellanti estate back in Napa is imposing and huge, of course, but this place is...something else. I've never seen anything like it outside of travel magazines or the internet.

The two-story villa is all white stucco, with arches and pillars and intricate geometric patterns as far as the eye can see, while a Moroccan tiled fountain in the shape of an eight-pointed star splashes in the center of the circular driveway. Subtle accents of cobalt blue and sea glass green around the windows are a feast for my eyes. Date palms and hot pink bougainvillea abound, thick vines climbing the ornamented portico over the massive wooden front doors. Lacy swaths of shade cover the tiled courtyard.

"What do you think, my precious love?" Armani asks from the front seat, turning to face me.

I shoot him an eye roll at the term of endearment. He's laying it on a little thick.

"It's beautiful," I tell him honestly. "Not what I was expecting at all."

He raises his brows at me, tilting his head toward the driver to remind me that I'm supposed to be fawning over my new husband a bit more noticeably.

"Um, I just can't believe I'm so lucky to have a husband like you to bring me here and spoil me," I add. I reach over to cup his face in my hand, squeezing his cheek a bit harder than necessary. "And I can't wait to see the bedroom."

"That will be our first stop then," he flirts back.

The driver laughs at that, so mission accomplished, I suppose.

Once we park, Armani gets out of the car and then opens my door for me. Meanwhile, a few black-clad house staff file out the front doors and walk over to greet us. One of them—the butler?—even steps forward and gives a half bow.

"Welcome back, Mr. Bellanti. I hope you'll find everything perfectly in order."

Welcome *back*? When's the last time Armani was here? And with whom? Another woman, or was he here on mafia business? Neither possibility makes me feel comforted in the least.

"Thank you." Armani tucks his arm around my waist and pulls me against him. "This is my new wife, Cassandra."

"Candi," I correct, smiling through my gritted teeth.

"*Magnifique*," the butler says, nodding at me. "I am Omar."

"Pleasure to meet you," I say.

After instructing the rest of the staff to get our luggage from the trunk and take it into the house, Omar immediately starts talking to Armani about rooms and meals and accommodations. Everyone seems to be ignoring me amidst the flurry of activity, which thankfully gives me a moment to breathe. I wriggle out of Armani's grasp and stare up at the villa, taking in my new prison. As gorgeous as it is, I can't suppress a shudder.

We go inside, where I'm surprised to find the décor is minimal and modern. The architectural theme continues, of course, and there are touches of traditional Moroccan design—carved wood, brass lanterns with stamped patterns, handwoven rugs—but overall, it's a lot of cream and charcoal and natural fibers. It makes sense, I guess. I'm sure the villa is meant to give off a light, airy, neutral vibe and appeal to the broadest range of wealthy guests looking to rent the place. It's actually very much in line with Armani's personal style, come to think of it, but I bet most rich people love this luxury hotel style too.

Some of the staff come up to me and introduce themselves again, but I'm still stuck on the whole "welcome back" thing I heard outside from Omar. Is this where Armani brings all his women? Or is the jungle riddled with the shallow graves of mobsters?

"So...how often do you come here?" I ask Armani, trying to draw him out a little.

But he doesn't even acknowledge the question as he urges me up the stairs. The maid ahead of us begins rattling off information for me, which room is where, when meals are served, the location of the heated pool, but it's a jumble of words in my mind. Still, I find the villa to be quite charming. It would be a wonderful place to rest and recharge if the circumstances were different.

As it is, there will be no relaxing on my part. There's at

least one fully armed guard, locked iron gates, and the watchful eyes of my husband. Not to mention the security personnel that Armani mentioned would be babysitting me. This is no kind of honeymoon I'd ever want.

The maid shows us to the master bedroom at the end of the hall, gesturing at the king size bed draped in white muslin and our luggage, which has been deposited outside the walk-in closet.

"We'd be happy to unpack your things and hang them in the closet right away," she's saying.

"No. I'll call down later for that," Armani says. "For now, we need a little privacy."

Her cheeks color. "Of course, Mr. Bellanti. And please let us know if we can do anything."

With a curtsy, she takes her leave, closing the door softly behind her.

The moment we're alone, Armani pulls me to him. My heart starts thumping in my chest. His hands slide from my waist to the backs of my thighs, skimming over my ass, but just as I'm about to remind him about the no-touching rule, he suddenly steps back with a look of irritation on his face.

"Where is it?" he says impatiently.

"Huh?"

He extends his hand. "Your cell phone. Give it to me."

My jaw drops, a trickle of fear sliding down my spine. "Excuse me?"

"I told you, you aren't to have contact with anyone on the outside while we're here."

He's right, but I didn't really process the full import of that until right now. He's essentially cutting me off from the world while I'm thousands and thousands of miles away from everything and everyone I know.

"Please. I'll be good," I beg. "You can disable my text messages and block my incoming calls. I just need to have it for emergencies."

"Sorry, but no. It'll be transmitting a signal and I don't want you traceable," he says. "And if you have any kind of emergency, you'll be very well taken care of."

Clutching my purse to my chest, I shake my head. "But the Brunos will be expecting me to check in. They'll get suspicious if I just go radio silent, so if you want to sell this happy little honeymoon ruse then I'm going to have to call them at some point and tell them that we're—"

"On what honeymoon would the bride sneak away from her husband to go make contact?" he scoffs. "That wouldn't even make sense. Trust me, they'll have nothing to be suspicious about."

"You don't know what Sergio Bruno is like," I insist. "He barely trusts me as it is."

"I know *exactly* what Sergio Bruno is like," Armani says coldly. "Now give me the phone."

"No."

I realize it's pointless to fight him on this, since he'll have me physically restrained if I do refuse to hand the phone over, but some instinctive part of me is silently kicking and screaming about having to give up my one reliable tether to the real world.

He sighs impatiently. "There's no cell service on the island, Candi. Even if you tried to make a call, it wouldn't go through. All you'd be able to do is drain your battery and possibly compromise our location in the event that a cell tower somewhere on the mainland is able to catch your signal."

He raises his brows at me and holds his hand out again.

"If there's no service, then why do you need to take it?" I prod.

"Because sometimes, you can catch a bar of service if you climb to the top of Mount Verde, and I wouldn't put it past you to try it. However, I encourage you to remember what I said about the guards watching you. And the instructions they've been given to keep you on the property at all costs."

My stomach sinks. I'm going to be utterly trapped here. With no way to contact the outside world, no one to talk to. And if all the friends and family we have think we're off on some romantic honeymoon, no one will suspect I'm actually being held here against my will.

And what about Juliana? My (former?) best friend knows that I eloped, but I didn't invite her to the reception at the Bellanti estate and I definitely didn't tell her that I was going on a honeymoon. Although even if I could reach her, I can't very well tell her what's *really* going on. She still thinks I'm playing spy games for her uncle Sergio Bruno, that I conned Armani into marrying me to ingratiate myself even further with the Bellantis so I could dig up more intel. I can't do or say anything to make her think otherwise, especially not admitting that I've been forced to go to an island—and take part in this marriage—against my will. If she knows I'm compromised, the Brunos have no reason not to kill me.

Reluctantly, I take my phone out of my bag and squeeze it tightly, all hope rapidly crumbling.

"Okay, you can have it," I say, "but at least let me text

my friends first. They'll be worried sick once they realize I've dropped off the face of the earth. Even people in jail get a phone call."

I give Armani my most pleadingest look, searching his eyes for some hint of compassion. If I can just talk to Juliana for even two minutes and tell her where I am (approximately), there's a chance of me getting rescued. Or if not rescued, then at least avenged later if I do end up in a shallow jungle grave.

Armani huffs out an impatient breath. "I told you. There's no service here."

My eyes drop to my phone, and sure enough, it says No Service in the top corner of the screen.

"I can still send a text using the house Wi-Fi," I protest.

"No. This is for your own safety," he says sternly, ripping the phone out of my hands and tucking it into his pocket. "It's not a punishment."

"I see."

Taking a slow breath, I move closer to him and reach for his tie. My fingers slide down the length of the silk before pressing flat against his abdomen. I never said that I wasn't allowed to touch *him*.

"The thing is, I just...really don't want my friends to worry," I purr, running my hands up his arms and then gently squeezing his biceps. "I'm sure you can understand that."

I start to massage his shoulders. Tracking my gaze up to his eyes, I smile, stepping even closer, until our hips are touching. I can feel the bulge of my phone in his pants pocket. So close, yet so far away.

"Just one tiny little text?" I whisper seductively. "Please?"

I lean in to kiss him. Honestly, I can't help it. I knew the minute I reached for his tie that I would come undone at the feel of him under my hands.

But Armani leans away from me, grabbing my wrists and pulling my hands off him.

"I don't have time for this," he says. "I have work to attend to."

His tone is so cold and detached, it's like getting a bucket of ice water dumped over me.

"Work? On what kind of honeymoon would the husband abandon his wife to go work?" I scoff, throwing his own words back at him.

"On mine," he says.

And with that, he turns his back on me and walks out the door.

6

CANDI

I'M so exhausted from travel—and, honestly, from arguing with Armani about my phone—that I crawl on top of the bed to take a "short" nap. Hours later, I wake with a start, temporarily disoriented by my unfamiliar surroundings.

It all comes back in a flash: the hours on the plane, the drive across the island to this posh villa, the fight with my husband. I feel groggy and sweaty and gross, so I get in the shower and clean myself up as quickly as I can. Surely Armani and I have dinner plans. This is our honeymoon, after all. Real or not, we have to keep up appearances.

But when I stroll out of the bathroom in my robe, a cloud of coconut-vanilla bodywash enveloping me, Armani is pacing the room like he's been waiting for me for hours. He's in a freshly pressed dark suit and he smells like his rich, velvety going-out cologne.

"*Finally*," he says. "Hurry up and pack an overnight bag. And then get dressed. We're late."

"Late for what? And if you wanted me to be ready at a certain time, you should have told me."

"Just pack the bag, sweetheart," he says peevishly.

"With what? Are we going to be hiking, biking, ballroom dancing?"

"You should look classy and hot. We'll be having dinner on a boat. I'll be back in twenty."

"Thanks for including me in your plans," I call after him sarcastically as he walks out.

Damn him.

I pack in a frenzy, grabbing silk pajamas, a floral designer sundress for tomorrow, and a handful of new lingerie. Then I dig my makeup bag out of my carry-on and plunk myself in front of the vanity to give myself a five-minute makeover. I swipe on some BB cream, two coats of mascara, and a hint of blush and then assess myself in the mirror. Yeah, nope. I'm giving off wholesome college girl vibes. But since there's no time for an elaborate glamour routine, I'm going to have to let my lips do the talking.

My secret weapon comes out—a deep, dark plum lipstick that Juliana always swears makes me look sophisticated and mysterious. As for my damp hair, I just scrunch it with a bit of anti-frizz cream and hope it dries nicely. Adrenaline pumping, I drop my robe and wiggle into a clingy black satin dress that's floor length with a scandalous slit up the side. Hopefully it's classy and hot enough for Armani.

I'm looking for a clock in the room just as I hear a knock at the door, and then Armani is stepping back inside to collect me and my bag.

"Well? How do I look?" I ask as he hustles me down the stairs.

"It'll do," he says distractedly.

Infuriated, I say nothing else as we get back into the car that brought us here. Armani sits beside me this time, but he gives no further details about our dinner date as we're driven down the hillside. When we reach the coast, a small boat is waiting to ferry us to a gleaming white yacht anchored offshore. A little gasp escapes me. The yacht is so huge, it makes Armani's yacht in Napa look like a bath toy.

At first, I think the evening is shaping up to be some kind of romantic callback to our first date on Armani's yacht in California. A chance to rekindle that white-hot flame between us. No wonder he'd been so secretive about where we were going—he was trying to surprise me.

And I *am* surprised. I'm also kind of excited to be going on an overnight cruise, honestly. I'm even feeling a sudden flicker of warmth toward my husband. But as soon as we board, my heart sinks.

We are not alone.

The yacht's huge deck is a cocktail party in full swing, complete with giggling, barefoot young women in skimpy spandex dresses, each of the girls sporting some variation of long, glossy hair, plump lip injections, mile-long legs, and a spray tan. I feel very out of place—almost matronly, in fact—in my long black gown and heels. As for the three men on board, they're all in stiff suits and ties. They're also wearing sunglasses, heavy gold watches, and the kind of scowls I thought Armani had trademarked.

"Who are these people?" I whisper through my clenched smile.

"Just some associates," Armani answers nonchalantly.

"Like, other winery owners?"

"Not exactly."

A steward appears to take our bags. After he departs, I notice one of the suited men taking his shades off to give me a brazen eye-fucking from across the deck. My skin crawls, and I instinctively move closer to my husband. As the men head toward me and Armani like a shiver of sharks, I start to pick up on a tense vibe. There's no mistaking the bulge of guns under the jackets of the men, and their frowns have me ill at ease. That's when I realize: these aren't just regular business associates.

They're mob men.

Which means my so-called honeymoon is nothing more than a cover for Armani so he can engage in criminal activity. It has to be. No wonder the staff at the villa was so familiar with him. He probably comes here all the time to meet with other underworld bosses and make shady deals.

Except that doesn't explain the scantily clad women lounging around the deck like pampered cats. They're obviously not here on mafia business. Are they part of the cover story too, or mere window dressing? But no, that's not right —they're not just here to be looked at, are they? They're probably the goddamn party favors.

My stomach turns.

"I want to go back to the villa," I say quietly.

"Not a chance in hell," Armani says through a clench-jawed smile directed at his "friends."

He briefly touches his hand to my back, pushing me forward as the three men circle us.

"Gentlemen, I'm glad you could make it," he says. "I'd like to introduce my new wife, Candi."

Not a single man looks at me, not even the one with the roving eyes. Instead, they all congratulate Armani, toasting him with their drinks and making jokes about how his glory days are over. Charming.

The tallest gestures to the yacht's cabin with a tip of his head. "Shall we head below deck? I have a bottle of scotch I paid a quarter of a million dollars for waiting for us."

"It's what we're all here for, isn't it?" Armani says.

"The scotch, or the business?" one of the other men jokes.

They all laugh, and then Armani walks off with them, leaving me alone on the deck with the other women. What the hell am I supposed to do? I look over and see a few of the girls taking a selfie together, and suddenly it occurs to me that they have phones. All of them have phones. I start walking toward them, friendly smile plastered on my face, preparing a lie about a tragically broken phone and how I'm desperate to call my BFF to wish her a happy birthday. But just as I reach the first woman, one of the men comes back out on the deck.

"Ladies," he calls out. "Please join us!"

There goes my brilliant plan. I'll never get away with borrowing a phone from one of these girls as long as Armani is close enough to keep an eye on me. Damn.

When we get to the lower deck, we find the rest of the men seated around a blackjack table, drinks in hand. Mirrors cover every wall, and brassy Cuban jazz plays from hidden speakers. The lights are dim, the scent of recently smoked cigars thick in the air. I see a row of slot machines, a pool table, an entertainment center with two rows of black leather reclining chairs in front of it. This is obviously the boat version of a man cave. A bow-tied server waits patiently behind the bar in the corner.

"Ladies, help yourself to some more drinks!" the man who fetched us says. "Play some cards, stay the hell out of the way, and for God's sake, shut up."

Well, well, well. Don't I feel special? So much for having a romantic dinner on a yacht.

I glare at my husband, but it's wasted on him because his back is to me. He's laughing, chatting up one of the other men, razzing his choice of cigar. When my husband asks the dealer for another card, I get a view of Armani's maddeningly good profile, and I can't help the rush of wings in my gut. The other men have removed their sunglasses now, and not a single one holds a candle to Armani. He's broad shouldered and shredded, effortlessly commanding, and devilishly good looking. He takes my breath away. I still hate him, but there's no denying the physical effect he has on me.

Forcing myself to walk around the room, I ignore the hushed gossip of the boat Barbies and browse a collection of black and white photographs on one wall. I recognize a handful of celebrities, politicians, and actors, but for the most part it's just mob men and occasionally their wives, laughing and drinking and having a good time. Must be nice.

I hear a set of heels clicking down the stairs. Glancing over my shoulder, I see a new woman coming to join us, and I freeze. She's breathtaking; tall and regal with striking cheekbones. I can only assume she's a model, her tanned olive skin contrasting beautifully with her white bodycon dress. Her black hair gleams as it sways loose around her waist. I wonder which of these men she belongs to.

My eyes widen as she strides straight over to Armani on her six-inch fuck-me stilettos. Narrowing my eyes, I bite the inside of my lower lip as I watch him light up at her approach.

"Esme!" he says.

"*Mani!*" she coos back.

Pushing his chair away from the table, he starts to rise to greet her. But instead of accepting his open arms, she forces him back into his seat and then lowers herself directly onto his thigh, wrapping one of her arms around his neck. The other men acknowledge her with cool familiarity. After she briefly greets them, she tilts her head against Armani's. The two of them immediately start speaking in expressive Italian to each other, Esme's body language screaming that she's one of Armani's former lovers. I'd give anything to have the pocket-size Italian-English dictionary I packed in my hand right now.

My face flames, my gut burning with jealousy. The conversation of the women behind me dries up, and I have no doubt they're watching this entire scene unfold like it's a soap opera. As she speaks, Esme presses her fingers to Armani's chest for emphasis and then makes a surprised face. Suddenly she's pawing at his biceps and abs, oohing and ahhing over him. I'm not sure exactly what she's saying, but it's very obviously something about how his body has gotten even better since the last time she enjoyed it.

She's feeling him up with her whole hand now, running it along the back of his shoulders and up his neck. She licks her lips slowly, her eyelids dropping halfway. I think she's staring at his mouth, but I can't really tell. And then I catch the end of something—*nel mio letto*. It's one of the few

Italian phrases I'm familiar with. It means, *in my bed*. But she didn't phrase it like a statement. It was a question.

There's a low ringing in my ears. Did she just *proposition* my husband right in front of me? But of course she did. I think of the sprawling, gorgeous villa and this luxurious little yacht. Armani's been here before. No doubt with her. I'm sure they've fucked on every possible surface.

But then Armani holds up his left hand and says, switching to English, "I have new jewelry now," pointing at the wedding band glinting on his ring finger.

The men at the table all laugh and start ribbing Armani, making references to his "ball and chain," aka his wife, aka the fun killer, aka me. Esme, however, seems completely unfazed by the ring.

Batting her eyes, she says, "It's a lovely ring. It will look even lovelier on my bedside table next to my panties."

Again, the men roar with laughter. My hairline begins to itch, my face getting hot, my hands clenching into fists at my sides.

She glances down at herself. "Oh, I forgot—I'm not wearing any panties!"

I am beyond enraged, beyond humiliated. I've never wanted to throttle my husband more.

He doesn't respond, but slowly drags his gaze away from Esme and looks at me, full-on. His expression says that he's challenging me to make a scene, to butt in on the conversation, to do something. And then, like the asshole he is, he smiles at me. Not in an encouraging way, but with the snarky, superior effect that comes so effortlessly for him. He's enjoying my discomfort at having his ex sitting on his lap.

"Esme," the tallest man says, slapping his hand of cards down on the table, "as much as I love you in that dress, us boys need to talk shop now. Why don't you go get yourself a drink and play cards with the other girls?"

She pouts and rolls her eyes, but nods at the command. Slowly detangling herself from my husband, making sure he gets an eyeful of her cleavage as she stands, she shoots me a smirk. Then she sashays over to join the other women at their table. They begin chatting again, whispering. I can feel their eyes on me. But I feel Armani's eyes on me even more potently.

He must be watching for my reaction, probably for his own amusement. Well, he won't get it. Lifting my chin, I casually saunter over to the bar. I order a Long Island Iced Tea, the strongest cocktail I can think of, and then make my way back to the stairs, gliding past Armani and his associates without even a glance, expecting someone to stop me. But no one does.

I'm alone on the sundeck as I sip my drink at the rail, watching the ocean ripple around me. The sun is starting to go down, casting sparkling diamonds over the surface of the turquoise water, but I'm so sick with jealousy and disappointment and humiliation that I can't enjoy the scenery.

What was I thinking, expecting Armani to wine and dine me? I should have known better. This isn't a real honeymoon anyway, and I know that. I also know *Armani*. He plays his own games, by his own rules, without a single care as to how anyone else feels about it. I'm just his accessory.

I finish my drink and realize that the yacht is slowing down. From the left, I see the outline of another boat approaching us. A much smaller vessel. As it gets closer, I spot two men on the deck. Suits, sunglasses, and one of them is holding a briefcase. Just wonderful. More mob men.

We slow down even more as the boat gets closer, closer. Suddenly, they're in line with us. There's a clanking sound on the side of the yacht as a ramp lowers, and a moment later, the men climb aboard. Little alarm bells start going off in my brain. They look rougher than the men downstairs, their body language more edgy and paranoid. One of them has a large scar running over his cheekbone and down his jaw. He looks like he's perpetually angry. His cohort is a very large man, built like a brick house, his ill-fitting blazer stretched taut across his massive shoulders. His thick hands could probably crack my skull in two, and I bet he'd enjoy doing it. They say something to each other and then a steward appears and leads them below deck with the others.

This makes six mafiosos total on board. What the hell is going on? The part of me that was groomed to source information from the Bellantis is still alive and kicking—I'm so used to keeping my ear to the ground, I can't quite kick the habit—and now flashing neon signs are going off in my brain.

Something is up. Something big.

I know without a doubt that it has to do with the Brunos. There's no other reason Armani would be meeting with so many people when he's supposed to be laying low. My husband is plotting something. And these men...these dangerous, murderous looking men...they're going to help him. A shiver passes over me. I need to find out anything and everything I can. I can't afford to be in the dark right now.

Before I can talk myself out of it, I go back downstairs, surveying the room when I reach the bottom of the steps. The newcomers are standing with Armani, all of them laughing like long-lost friends. Esme is still in her seat. She ignores me as I move past her and go to the bar for a second Long Island.

The presence of all these mob men has my teeth on edge. I wish I knew what Armani was planning. Whatever it is, it has to be about the Brunos. We fled Napa after a direct threat from them, and now here we are, hiding out on some island and having international business meetings with mobsters. It doesn't take much to put two and two together and get four.

Sipping my drink, I pretend to rest my head on my fist while subtly cupping my hand around my ear—the better to eavesdrop on Armani and his associates. It's difficult to pick out their hushed conversation with the music and the gossiping women and the clink of ice in glasses, but I concentrate on sorting out the sounds until I can isolate the familiar tone of Armani's voice threading through the din.

"So what do you think?" he's saying to one of the other men. "I know you're a connoisseur."

"She's incredibly attractive," the man answers. "You undersold her when we spoke last week."

My heart lurches into my throat. Are they talking about me? Leaning slightly on my stool, I strain my ears to follow their exchange.

The other man adds, "In fact, I'd like to take her out for a little trial run."

I can feel the blood drain from my face, disgust rising in me.

"I'm flattered," Armani says, "but she's mine."

"Of course she is," the man says placatingly. "I'm talking temporary, just a week or two..."

There's a pause, and I swear my heart is going to pound out of my chest.

"No. There's no room for negotiation on that," Armani says firmly. "I don't share my toys."

Toys?

"What about a weekend rental situation? I'm prepared to be very generous."

"Persistent, are we?" Armani laughs. "And again, it's a no, but thank you."

I lose the thread of the conversation as one of the other men throws down a hand of cards that has the others howling and tossing poker chips across the table and razzing the dealer for taking bribes. When it finally calms down, I catch the other man picking up the thread of where he and Armani left off.

"You're not gonna keep her around forever," he wheedles. "Let's make a deal for when the time comes. I'll take care of her, you know."

Take care of her? What the hell does that mean? Does it mean what I think it means, or—

"Okay, okay. I'll entertain your offer. What kind of deal we talking?" my husband says.

My gut sinks with dread. Is Armani actually contemplating this? Loaning me out like he's some kind of pimp? Is that what he did with his ex-girlfriends?

Or is he just pretending to consider it to be diplomatic? I know as well as anyone that maintaining good relations with mafia people requires a person to step lightly. But what if Armani is serious?

"Ahh, you see!" the other man crows. "I knew you were a man of sense!"

The eagerness in his voice makes me want to vomit. My hands are shaking, the remainder of my Long Island sloshing in its glass.

Trying not to look too obvious, I glance across the room at the men's table trying to figure out which one Armani is talking to. But before I can figure it out, the man with the scar calls the other women over to the men's table. They obey eagerly, each of them finding someone to drape over. Esme, of course, wastes no time settling herself on Armani's leg again.

"Candi! Come here," he says, whipping his head over his shoulder to look at me.

Slowly, I walk toward him, my drink held tight in my hand. I'm tempted to throw it in his face, or dump it down Esme's dress. Instead, I stop a few feet away and give him an icy glare.

"Do you need something?" I ask coolly.

"No. But this part of the meeting isn't for your eyes, so you'd better go to your room," he says.

There's a derisive chuckle from the men around the table.

Armani grins easily and adds, "Unless you want to join in?"

Fuck no. No, I do not wish to take part in a gangbang on my honeymoon.

A few of the girls giggle, all of them watching me stand

there silently, my rage simmering. I ignore their gazes, ignore Armani's invitation, and stalk up the stairs to the main deck in a hot fury. The sound of laughter follows me as I go.

7

CANDI

THE MATTRESS SINKS with the weight of Armani dropping onto the bed next to me.

The room is dark, so I can't see his face, but the scent of his cologne gives him away. A rush of power surges through me, because he came to me after all. He may have talked a big game around his associates, but when it came down to it, he left those other women in the dust. I roll over and look up at him, glad I wore my lacy new babydoll nightie and matching thong to bed.

Suddenly, his lips are on me, kissing me everywhere. My neck, my lips, my breasts. His hands run over me, easily removing my underwear with one rough tug before pushing up my nightdress and whisking it over my head. He positions his body over mine and then takes his time swirling his tongue around each of my nipples, pulling with hard little zings exactly the way I like. My whole body is instantly awake, my desire rising hot and fierce. Opening my legs, I welcome his hand as he gives my pussy a firm squeeze, knowing exactly how to use his thumb to circle my clit.

"So wet for me already?" he teases, and then he plunges his fingers inside me.

I buck to meet the thrust, urging him on, softly begging for more, which he delivers like the expert he is. Breathless with want, I grapple with his clothing, clawing at the buttons of his shirt, but he fends me off, grabbing my wrists with his free hand and pinning them over my head. I struggle against his grip, but it's mostly for show. There's no place I'd rather be than right where I am.

"Tsk, tsk. Not so fast," he growls.

His fingers pump into me harder, deeper, and it's so delicious I just relax against the pillow and give in to him. Closing my eyes, moaning softly, I trace my bare foot across his thigh. Slowly, I inch my way toward his crotch until my toes make contact through the fabric of his pants. His cock is hard, standing straight up and straining at his zipper. Mmm. Exactly what I wanted.

"So hard for me already?" I tease back, using the sole of my foot to stroke his erection.

He presses himself into the bottom of my foot, but remains where he is, doggedly working between my legs until I feel the first stirring of an orgasm start to take hold. In this moment, it's easy to forget that I'm angry with him, forget how he treated me in front of his friends. In fact I forget everything except the flutter of excitement in my lower belly, the hot pulse at my core, how good my husband is with his hands. Besides, he owes me for leaving me high and dry in the fitting room at that boutique. I'm simply collecting what I'm due. I can be mad at him again afterward.

The pleasure builds stronger and higher, the buzz

inside me heightening with every finger thrust. I'm so wet I can feel the fluid leaking out of me, my whole body strung tight as the sweet tension increases, the pump and glide of Armani's expert fingers pushing me closer by the second. He finally lets my wrists go and pushes my foot off his crotch, repositioning himself over me so he can wrap one hand around my throat while his other hand continues to fuck me.

He chokes me lightly, constricting my airway just enough to flood my nerve endings with a fresh wave of adrenaline and arousal. I'm close—so close. But I don't want to come like this. I want to come around his cock in hard, clenching waves, hear the sound of his groans as he releases inside me.

I reach for him again, grabbing his shirt, pulling him toward me. He doesn't budge. Groaning in frustration, I pull harder, growing confused as the fabric fills my hands while Armani only seems to move further away from me. I grapple with his shirt, tugging and tugging, but it settles over my head like a sheet and then Armani is gone. I thrash against the fabric covering me, losing the golden thread of my approaching orgasm as I snap awake, tangled up in the bedsheets I'm sleeping in all by myself.

Jolting into a sitting position with a gasp, heart pounding, I blink in the dim light and confirm that Armani isn't in the bed. In fact, the pillow beside mine is smooth and untouched, making it clear that he never went to bed at all. At least, not with me.

I rub my hands over my eyes, reality slowly sinking in. It was just a dream. A frustrating sex dream—one that *didn't even get me off*—about the man I'm still incredibly pissed at.

After Armani had banished me from his "meeting" last night, I had nursed my cocktail on the upper deck alone, angry and panicking that my husband might be planning to loan me out to one of his associates like chattel. Just as the sun started to set in a blaze of glory, a steward had appeared and politely but forcefully steered me to my quarters. When I got to the modestly sized but handsomely appointed room, I found a sumptuous meal of braised fish and vegetables in a harissa marinade was waiting for me on a tray. Along with a single set of cutlery.

"Dinner on a boat," Armani had said. Not technically a lie, was it? How infuriating. As if he wasn't showing the ugliness of his true colors enough.

Still, I was starving. I fell on the food and then realized how exhausted I still was from the long flight and my lack of sleep, so I'd changed into my nightie and climbed into bed. The last thing I remember is staring up at the ceiling, my thoughts in a knot as music and the intermittent smell of cigar smoke rose from the deck below. I wonder if everyone is still down there now, doing God knows what.

Pulling back the curtain, I glance out the small port window and realize we're not moving. We must have docked at some point in the night. Sunrise dances over the crystalline water, the sky streaked with pastel colors, still shaking off the cool blue of pre-dawn. It's early, but I have no idea how early.

I look around, but I don't see any alarm clocks or even electronics with digital numbers to tell me what the hour is. I also find no evidence that Armani even set foot inside this room at any point last night, not even to grab his leather duffle bag. My lips tingle as I realize that, if he didn't come to me last night, he's probably with *her*. Esme. And, who knows, maybe a few other women thrown in for good measure.

Kicking back the sheets, I pull off my stupid, pointless lingerie ensemble and slip into the designer sundress that I packed. Then I slip on my sandals and go looking for my husband. I am fully prepared to find him in the card room, drunk and draped in women, but it's empty in there now. My stomach sinks. That means he did go to bed last night. Likely with company. And I certainly can't go around knocking on the other bedroom doors and asking if anyone has seen my wayward husband.

What a damn hypocrite.

Not that Armani ever promised to care about me. No, that's not the type of relationship we have. But he *is* supposed to be presenting himself as a united front with me when we're around others. Does he seriously expect me to play the doting, loving wife while he runs around acting like a horny frat boy who can't keep it in his pants? I am well aware that our marriage is a fake one, but to think that he actually spent the first night of our honeymoon with other women hurts me on a level I never thought possible.

Gathering my composure, I head up to the sundeck for some fresh air. It's claustrophobic down here, and the sick pang of jealousy and rejection in my gut is making me feel even worse.

But once I'm topside, the scent of strong coffee and bacon hits me full-on. I guess it's not too early for the crew to be preparing breakfast, though judging by the fact that it's virtually silent up here, I assume I'll be eating alone. The other guests are probably still sleeping off their hangovers, or maybe they've already left the yacht and headed back to wherever the hell they came from. Well, good riddance.

Following my nose, I pass the lounge area, the galley kitchen, and end up in an airy dining room with its panoramic folding glass doors pulled fully open to admit the sea breeze. But I skid to a stop when the man sitting alone at one of the round bistro tables turns to look at me.

"Armani," I say tersely, prowling over to him like a jungle cat stalking its prey.

The first thing I notice is that he's wearing the same clothes as yesterday. They look a bit rumpled, but not necessarily as wrinkled as they'd be after spending all night crumpled on someone else's floor. Although I guess that proves nothing—Armani is just as likely to fold his clothes neatly over a chair before sex as he is to fling them across a room in a heady moment of passion.

The second thing I notice is that the table is set for two. He's already eating, but the other place setting is waiting with several silver-domed dishes beside an untouched set of silverware and a large plate with a teal, orange, and yellow Moroccan design. How quaint.

I slice a hand toward the breakfast setting. "Which bitch is this for?"

Armani smiles and raises his coffee cup to me. "The one standing in front of me."

"Cute," I say with a glare. I'm not even sure I believe him.

After dropping into the empty chair, I remove the domes and assess the breakfast items on offer. And, wow. Fried eggs with crispy edges, dusted with paprika and herbs; steaming bread of many varieties; flaky pastries I can't identify; yogurt drizzled with honey and pistachios and pomegranate seeds; little dishes of dried apricots and olives and figs as well as sliced fresh fruit; golden pancakes topped with—rose petals?

"Who's going to eat all of this?" I ask incredulously. "This could feed half a dozen people."

Still half expecting the ho squad to show up, I glance over my shoulder, but we're still alone.

"I didn't know what you'd want, so I ordered one of everything," he says.

Admittedly, I thaw just a tiny bit.

"Fine," I say. "Whoever this is really for, I'm taking it."

I help myself to the food, taking a bit of each item because it all looks so delicious. As I'm serving myself, a steward comes over with carafes of sweet mint tea and hot coffee. I take a cup of each and then tuck in to the culinary wonders spread before me.

"These are hands down the best pancakes I've ever had," I admit to Armani between bites.

They've got these delightful little air bubbles in them that are perfect for soaking up the melted butter and honey on top.

"I knew you'd love them. They're called baghrir," Armani tells me with a self-satisfied smirk.

"You don't know anything about me," I say peevishly, just to be contrary.

We eat in silence for a few minutes. I half expect the others to come trickling in, but no one does.

"So. Where's everyone else?" I finally ask.

"Resting below deck, if I had to guess," he says.

"Mm. And...what exactly was your meeting about last night?"

"That's not your concern."

I smile sourly. "Of course it's not. Though, obviously, I didn't expect you to actually give me a straight answer. You never do."

"Says the Brunos' mole," Armani snipes.

"I'm *your* mole now," I remind him. "And I'm not just asking out of curiosity. There was something seriously off about those men. They seemed dangerous and untrustworthy."

Armani laughs. He actually laughs. At me. My fork clanks onto my plate at his response. He shakes his head, gets ahold of himself, and then takes a drink of coffee.

"Something funny?" I ask, my hackles up.

"No. It's just—everyone in attendance is a friend. They go way back with my family."

"I'm sure they do. Birds of a feather," I say, but the insult doesn't faze him.

Stuffing another bite of butter-and-honey drenched baghrir into my mouth, I think back to what Armani said on the plane. About using our time here to decide if I'm still useful to him. What if I'm not? What if that's why these men are here—to take care of me? Maybe that's why they wouldn't look at me. Because I'm their next hit. Maybe that's also why Armani didn't think twice about spending the night with another woman.

Maybe I'm about to be the next tattooed guy.

Panic rises in my chest, and my appetite suddenly vanishes.

"You look flushed, Cassandra," Armani says. "Maybe you should go for a dip and cool off."

I look over and meet his eyes. He gazes back at me coolly, but I know there has to be some ulterior motive here. It wasn't just a friendly suggestion. He's probably chomping at the bit to go join his Italian whore in bed. Or maybe he has more criminal activity to engage in, and I'd be in the way.

Regardless of his plans, it's obvious that I don't have a choice in the matter. He just gave me an order. I know him well enough to understand that, at least. I'm completely powerless.

Throwing my napkin down on my plate, I push away from the table so hard that the silverware and plates rattle. My chair topples to its side as I storm from the room.

Back on the sundeck, I grab the railing and gasp for air. The shoreline is in sight, but it's too far away for me to swim to. Of course. It seems I'm stuck, trapped on this yacht with the man I despise most in the whole world.

I try to breathe slowly and compose myself, but the panic and anger won't go away. I hate how much control Armani has over me. And not just physically, or even sexually, but over my moods as well. On top of that, I'm utterly furious that he used my hated full name back there. He knows how much I can't stand it, but he called me Cassandra on purpose. Just to remind me, per usual, that he's in charge.

Well, screw him. I'm not going swimming after all. I'll go back to my room, lock the door, and pout over my Italian dictionary. If he thinks I'm not going to figure out what he's saying about me to Esme and the rest of those assholes, he's got another thing coming.

And then something else strikes me. Maybe there's a way to make him suffer, too. I may not be able to control Armani's moods, but I certainly have enough experience taunting his body.

I think it's time for him to see how it feels to desperately want something you can't have.

8

ARMANI

"How'd it go with the bosses?" Dante asks.

"Discussions went all night long," I tell him. "I haven't even been to bed yet."

I'm pacing the deck at the bow of the yacht, hand cupped over my ear to block out the wind, my top-of-the-line, $2,000 satellite phone snug in my palm. It's possible that I could get my cell phone to work out here, but unlikely the connection quality would be decent—and this conversation is too important to risk a dropped call. Hence the sat phone. I never travel out of the country without it.

Obviously, I couldn't let Candi see me using it, or else she'd start scheming to "borrow" it from me on the sly. Which is why I sent her away so forcibly. I had a call to make, and not a pleasant one.

"Boo hoo, bro. You can take a nice long nap after we hang up," he says, trying to make light of things, but I can hear the tension in his voice. "What news did they bring us from the other families?"

Wincing, I admit, "Not the good kind."

The meeting I'd called on the yacht was meant to be a debriefing between myself and some of our most trusted mafia allies in Italy, including the islands of Sardinia and Sicily. It was nothing for them to jump on their private planes and fly two or three hours to my location for a rendezvous. Plus, the provision of good alcohol, fine food, and flashy women never fail to secure RSVPs and loosen tongues.

Unfortunately, our friends dropped a bomb. A big one. Not that I'm shocked. But this is the last thing Dante needs to hear right now.

"Spit it out," my brother says impatiently.

"Here's the deal," I say, glancing over my shoulder to confirm that nobody is within earshot. "The Brunos are seeking an alliance with the Russian mob."

"Fucking Christ."

"Indeed. Sergio thinks it'll give him leverage."

"Of course it gives him leverage!" Dante explodes. "The Bratva aren't even *organized* crime. They're bands of free agents with no rules, no hierarchy, no code of honor. They're fucking sociopaths! Not to mention, literally untouchable. There's so much bribery going on with law enforcement in that country, nobody ever gets caught. The Bratva think they're gods. We can't get mixed up in that."

I let out a sigh. "I know all of this, Dante."

And I can see the appeal of such a partnership, too. I've never heard of an Italian family joining forces with the Russians, but the manpower and absolute disregard for human decency make the Bratva powerful allies for deranged men.

He's quiet for a beat, and I give him room to process everything.

"So, what, our friends are getting cold feet now?" he finally says. "They must know that if the Russians get involved, all bets are off. We're talking World War Three."

"They know that. Which is why I've *assured* them that we're going to prevent this nasty little collaboration at all costs," I say. "And we will."

"How the hell do you plan to do that?"

"Just trust me," I say.

"You have no fucking idea," Dante says.

"I have no fucking idea," I admit.

Leaning over the railing, I take a deep breath of sea air and try to come up with something.

"Who do we know that might have an in with the Russians?" I ask.

"That's your area of expertise, brother."

"I'm drawing a blank. Can you touch base with Clayton about it and have him call me?"

"Will do," Dante says.

"Appreciate it. I'd better let you go and work on that."

"Wait. One more thing," he says. "Do you think it's possible Candi knew about this Bratva thing already, and withheld the info from you? Because if so, you need to make it *abundantly* clear that this kind of secrecy poses a danger not just to us, but to her as well. You get me? She should be punished."

A flare of aggression ignites in my chest. But just because I'm instinctively protective of Candi doesn't mean I'm unwilling to consider Dante's words. He's right about one thing—if she purposely fucked us out of vital intel, she does deserve to be punished. This is a matter of life and death. Potentially lots of death.

I work my jaw to the side, considering.

"No," I say after a moment. "The Brunos never would have let her in on something like that. It would have made her a walking liability. She was just a runner for them. Her only job was to spy on us."

"Hm. Guess I'll have to take your word for it."

There's a beat of silence. My brain is still spinning and I'm sure Dante's is, too.

"Give Marco the rundown when you see him next," I say. "Meanwhile I'll work with Clayton on finding us an insider for the Bratva."

"Copy that."

"All right. Take care, man. Talk soon," I say, eager to get off this shitty call.

"Sure thing. Enjoy your honeymoon," he says.

"Ha ha."

I hang up and slip the sat phone in my pocket, running a hand over my mouth. I have a lot to think about. People to call, decisions to make. But first, I need my guests to depart.

It took some doing to peel Esme off of me last night. She's been following me around like a puppy since she arrived, which I guess I should have expected. The only reason I invited her is because Clio Romo, of the Naples Romos, has always had a thing for her, and I knew he'd enjoy the eye candy. But it backfired royally. My ex-fling (if you can even call our random conjugal visits over the last few years a legitimate "fling") stuck to me like velcro. Forcibly removing her from my person only made her worse, unfortunately. She likes a challenge, and she likes it rough.

Luckily, the men and I had a lot to talk about, and the women I invited on board know when they're forbidden from hanging around—girls who don't understand the power dynamic around me and my associates aren't asked to come back. So off they went to their own rooms. As soon as I was alone with my family's mafia allies, we got down to business. A lot of drinks were consumed. A lot of jokes were thrown around. And a lot of concerns were voiced out loud.

The Brunos have been making quite the name for themselves over the last year, and not in a good way. There are a lot of people on the fringes of the mob scene who want to be more involved in the dirty underground, and they've gravitated toward Bruno, pledging their loyalty and increasing his numbers. But those of us who want to keep the playing field clean are united against them. Our numbers are going up, too. We've bested the Brunos before, and Bratva or not, we'll do it again.

For now, I'm tense with pent-up energy. As much as I'm itching to take action, there's really nothing I can do until I hear from Clayton. I've already paced the deck of this yacht so hard, I'm surprised I haven't worn a groove in the boards. I think it's time to go find my wife.

Since I told her to go for a swim, I check the pool on the starboard side of the yacht first. And there she is, swimming a lap, her red hair trailing behind her. She's the only one in the water. I expected to find the other women lounging around as well, but they must be below deck giving my guests one last round of personal entertainment before they depart.

Candi turns and swims back toward me. That's when I realize: she's naked. Completely naked. No straps from a bikini top to interrupt the creaminess of her soft skin, no bottoms down below to obscure the perfection of that ass. When she reaches my side of the pool, she grabs onto the lip and bobs there for a moment. Droplets of water roll down her neck and between her tits, making my mouth water. The pink edges of her areolas are just barely visible below the water line.

My cock jerks. I'm more than ready to give it what it wants.

"Well hello," I say smoothly.

Candi rolls her eyes, turns around, and starts swimming back to the far end of the pool. Gotta love that saucy attitude. A smirk plays at my lips as I watch her go, but my mouth goes dry the second she rolls over into a backstroke, flashing the wet, naked front of her body as she swims.

She's doing this on purpose. Teasing me. Flaunting her assets, just to get a rise out of me.

Consider it mission accomplished.

I whip my clothes off as quickly as I can and lower myself into the water, barely breaking the surface. She's treading water lazily in the deep end now, facing away from me as she stares out at the Atlantic. I've almost reached her when she hears me and spins. Her eyes narrow.

"Why are you here? If you wanted to wash off the stench of your whore, you could have done it in the shower instead."

My whore? At first I'm confused, but then I realize she's referring to Esme. Which almost has me laughing out loud. I can't believe Candi thinks I'd go back to domestic beer now that I've tasted champagne. And although my plan was never to make my wife jealous by inviting Esme on board, it's fun to know I've riled up Candi all the same.

She's clearly ready for a fight, but I don't take the bait. I just smile like the devil and crowd her against the side of the pool, boxing her in with an arm on each side of her.

"You know," I tell her, dropping my voice lower, "there's a good chance a member of the crew might see us now. Which means you have no choice but to let me fuck you in this pool, because that's what a honeymooning couple would do."

"Oh, just like a honeymooning groom would ditch his bride for a bunch of skanks on a yacht?"

"Do I sense some jealousy?" I say, knowing it will rile her up.

She scoffs and tries to duck under my arm, but I grab her by the waist and push her forcefully against the pool's siding again. She struggles for a brief second, then goes still in my arms as my stiff cock nudges against her inner thigh. I lock eyes with her, and she sucks in a shivering breath. The wet glide of our bodies gives me goosebumps.

"Did you forget my no-touching rule?" she says.

"Not at all. Tell me to walk away and I will."

I'm bluffing. There's no way I'm leaving. But she doesn't make a move.

"I'm waiting," I add.

Glaring at me with pure hatred, she wraps her hand around my length and squeezes, making me shudder. Such a good girl. Always hot for me, even when she's fuming mad.

Nuzzling her neck, I nip at her tender skin and murmur, "Nothing like a little hatefuck, I always say."

"You're disgusting," she shoots back, but she's pumping me slowly under the water, her thumb circling the head of my cock after every stroke, just the way I like it.

"Don't pretend it's not turning you on," I growl.

I grab her knees and lift them up, hitching them on either side of my waist, leaving her pussy exposed and open for me. Fully expecting her to sass me more, I'm pleasantly surprised when Candi lines me up against her, tracing the vertical line of her slit with my fat tip. Up and down, up and down, sharp little breaths escaping her. She's soaking wet; I can feel her obvious slickness even in the warm water.

It's easy, so easy, to slide my dick in her. She tilts her head back, taking me in one deep, perfect thrust. I kiss her throat, then bite her neck, drawing a surprised gasp from her throat, a combination of shock and physical pleasure she can't deny.

I whisper, "You were saying?"

"Dis. Gus. Ting," she hisses, but she makes no move to get away from me.

Instead, she repositions herself, wrapping her legs more tightly around me, giving me even deeper access. Groaning at the hot, tight feel of her, I adjust my grip on the side of the pool and begin to fuck her in earnest. The sweet, wet glide has me biting back cuss words and grunts with every thrust. Pumping into her at this angle, both of us weightless in the water, is an experience we've never had together. And knowing one of the staff could walk in on us at any moment only makes it hotter.

"You fucking take that cock, you nasty little exhibitionist," I can't help whispering. "Take it all, you bad girl. Every last fucking inch."

Candi gently bites my shoulder, muffling the sound of her wails. We've found our rhythm, both of us moaning as I pound into her with everything I've got. The warmth and pressure I'm feeling builds higher and higher, my shaft practically vibrating with pleasure. Realizing I'm starting to lose control, I rein myself in, switching to shorter, shallower thrusts. But this only seems to get Candi off even more, judging by the way her nails claw at my back.

"You like that?" I whisper in her ear.

"I hate you," she says, sucking my earlobe into her mouth.

Water laps around us gently, the sloshing sound punctuated by her moans.

"I didn't go to bed with anyone last night," I tell her. "I saved it for you. For this."

"I don't believe y—"

I cut her off with a kiss, driving into her faster again, dropping one hand underwater so I can slip my finger between her cheeks and toy with her asshole. It fills me with power, owning her every hole. Mouth, ass, pussy—all mine.

I break our kiss just long enough to say, "I own you," and then clamp my mouth over hers again, my tongue stroking in time with every thump of my dick.

She moans blissfully, sucking my tongue like she's hungry for it. When her knees tighten at my sides, I know she's about to come. I slow my pace again but stay deep inside her, using my hand on her ass to bounce her up and down on my cock. There's no mistaking the moment of her climax. A choked sound spills out of her as we kiss, as she digs her nails into my scalp, as her pussy contracts around me. It drives me right over the edge.

My body explodes with pleasure, a rush of euphoria washing over me. I ride it out, pumping every last drop of myself into her, until the water begins to still and I can finally catch my breath.

The sound of footsteps has me glancing toward the doorway.

Grinning shamelessly, I expect to see a steward or one of the mafia heads, but instead find Esme standing there frozen. She's in huge designer sunglasses, those six-inch heels, and a string bikini, eyeing me and Candi with a bratty little pout. I give her a slow wink, my cock still buried in my wife's cunt.

Candi turns to see who I'm looking at, and I catch a smile curving her lips when she sees who it is. Her nemesis.

An aftershock gives me a shiver, and Esme huffs, spins on her heel, and stalks off. Candi tenses, her head turning slightly to follow the other woman.

"Bye, bitch," I hear her say under her breath.

Gotta admit—I love this shit.

9

CANDI

MY VICTORY IS SWEET, and I'm enjoying it. Small though it may be.

Yes, I technically broke my own rule about not letting Armani touch me on this trip. But I made him come to me first. I ignored his attempt at flirting, gave him the cold shoulder, and then flaunted my wet, naked body clear as day just to make him want me even more. I left him no choice but to jump in the pool and chase after me. The power was all mine.

Not that I didn't thoroughly appreciate the orgasm he gave me. Or the look on Esme's face when she caught us. I'll treasure that moment of triumph for the rest of my life. Yes, I'm that petty.

I also appreciated Armani's little confession about not sleeping with his ex last night. I acted skeptical in the moment, but my gut says he was telling the truth. After all, he didn't have to come clean to me. Didn't have to bring it up at all. Yet he did. That has to mean something, right? Or maybe I'm just engaging in self-deception.

Christ, we're barely twenty-four hours into this honeymoon and so far it's been nothing but an emotional roller coaster. Not the good kind, either. Which is why the encounter in the pool was such a nice reprieve from my anxiety. I still want to find a way to talk to Juliana and let her know where I am, but the urge is less desperate now. My insides aren't wound so tight and some of my worrying has melted away.

I turn off the water and step out of the shower. I'm in the locker room adjacent to the pool area. The term "locker room" doesn't actually do the space any justice. It's very spa-like. There's wall-to-wall teakwood, not to mention a *sauna*, and everything smells like lavender and mint.

After drying off with a plush Turkish cotton towel that I pluck from a heating rack mounted on the wall—because of course—I slip back into my sundress and head to my room below deck. Armani must have just showered in here, because I can still smell his Burberry body wash emanating from the bathroom on a damp cloud of dissipating steam. He's changed into fresh clothes too (obviously); his leather overnight bag is unzipped. Probably hanging out with his mafia friends again.

Honestly, I'm in no mood to be around them right now. Not to mention the women. I think I'll just stay here in the room and play with my Italian-English dictionary. Maybe see if the TV works.

As it turns out, I'm able to login to Netflix. Which means there's *Wi-Fi* on this boat. It's got to be satellite based. If only I had a way to piggyback on the signal...not that I'd have the password. Or a functioning device with which to use said internet. God, Armani is such an asshole.

Scowling, I put on my favorite baking competition show and lose myself in the lighthearted hijinks. That's why it's called escapism, right? I try to memorize new Italian words during the commercial breaks and then switch to looking up kitchen vocabulary during the episodes. Midway through *The Great British Bake Off*, the boat starts to rock. I sit up with a start. Are we setting sail again?

But no—when I look out the window, I see another yacht approaching us. We're not leaving the dock. More guests arriving, then? Or is it finally time for Armani's man squad to go home? That would be a relief. He and I could go home, too, at least back to the island villa. Who knows, we might even find a way to make the best of our remaining honeymoon.

My stomach gives a little growl and I pause my show, only to find that it's late afternoon. I completely forgot about lunch. Intending to raid the galley, I quietly open the bedroom door and pop my head into the hallway to see if the coast is clear.

It's not silent, but it's nowhere near as raucous as last night when the party was in full swing. And the cigar smell is gone. I do hear music coming from down the narrow hallway where the lounge is, and a low murmur of female voices. Quickly, I dart to the stairs and sneak up to the main deck barefoot, successfully avoiding notice (or invitations to join in) from Armani's cohorts.

But when I get to the kitchen, my plan to grab myself a snack is stymied by the presence of a chef and an assistant, both of whom are hard at work preparing what looks to be a delectable dinner. Mouthwatering smells wash over me, and I freeze in the doorway to just watch for a moment, not sure if I should try to tiptoe over to the refrigerator and grab whatever I can find or ask for help. Glancing over the ingredients scattered across the prep area, I see veal shanks, a few bottles of Bellanti Vineyards white wine, assorted vegetables, zested lemons, garlic, and fresh herbs galore—

"Are you making osso buco?" I ask.

The head chef looks up with a broad grin. "Yes, yes! Your favorite?"

"It's actually my best friend's favorite. Well, one of them," I say, moving closer. My heart sinks a little bit thinking about Juliana, but I push my thoughts of her away as best I can.

"You will love it," the chef promises. "We are close to Italy so everything I make is very, very fresh and very, very good. I am also serving a beautiful risotto Milanese and an arugula salad with grapefruit to, how you say, lighten up the meal."

I'm drooling. "That all sounds amazing. I'm Candi, by the way."

"Mrs. Bellanti, yes, I know," he says. "I am Idris, and this is Luca."

"Pleasure to meet you both," I say, and mean it.

"Here, you must taste the risotto," he says, grabbing a prep bowl and scooping a generous spoonful of risotto out of the skillet for me to try. "Please, tell me how you think."

He watches as I blow the steam off my spoon and take a bite.

"Mmm," I moan, nodding as I chew. This risotto is *magnifico*. It's creamy and savory and buttery. I can taste the shallots, the parmesan, the barest tang of saffron. "It tastes like heaven."

"Right answer!" the chef's assistant teases. "That dish is Chef Idris's pride and joy. He probably would've had a heart attack if you didn't endorse his personal specialty."

In return for his mocking, the assistant gets a playful swat with a dish towel from Chef Idris. Then the chef adds another helping of risotto to my bowl and pulls out a stool for me off to the side of the prep area. When I thank him, he spoils me further by bringing over a steaming chunk of bread with oil and balsamic and a sample of the lemon asparagus that his assistant just finished sautéing at the stove.

An idea strikes me then.

"Chef Idris?"

"Yes, Mrs. Bellanti?" He looks up from the cutting board where he's dicing carrots and celery so fast, I'm a little afraid he's going to lose a fingertip.

"Do you think you might be able to prepare some gnocchi? It's one of Mr. Bellanti's favorites. Especially short rib gnocchi, but really any gnocchi that goes with the meal would be fabulous. It'll put him in a good mood."

All the better to distract him from killing me or renting me out to one of his friends, right? If I have to play the game, I'll play it. Whatever it takes to survive this trip.

"Yes, yes, yes, of course!" Idris says, and it's clear he's swept up in recipe ideas already. Cooking must be like a religious experience for him. "With summer squash, zucchini, sweet corn, some basil…"

As he talks, he zips around the kitchen, pulling out ingredients and tossing them onto the prep counter. Meanwhile, his assistant ducks or catches as necessary. They make a good team.

"Luca, where is the feta?" Idris asks impatiently, waving his hand.

"We don't have any," Luca tells him distractedly as he works on the lamb shanks.

"The goat cheese, then."

"Uh..." Luca frowns and looks over his shoulder. "No goat cheese either."

Idris scowls. "What kind of kitchen is this, then? How can I work without cheese?"

"Mascarpone!" Luca says. "Second drawer down."

Disaster averted.

I get up to pour myself a drink and find another bottle of wine set aside, a Bellanti Elite Reserve cabernet. *Well hello.* It is, hands down, Bellanti Vineyards' most expensive wine.

With a smirk, I start digging around in the utensil drawers until I find a corkscrew.

"Mrs. Bellanti, please!" Idris calls out to me. "Not the Elite Reserve—it's special, for tonight. I have instructions to serve it only to you and Mr. Bellanti alone, to celebrate your honeymoon."

Smiling at Idris, I twist the corkscrew into the cork and proceed to open it anyway. His eyes look like they're going to bug right out of his head. Luca is trying to hide a smile, but I catch his eye and wink.

"My wine. My honeymoon. My choice," I say, wiggling the cork out of the bottle with a satisfying *pop*.

Because honestly, screw Armani. I deserve a little prize after the way I've been treated.

Whipping open the upper cabinets, I start looking around for wineglasses. But then I hear the distinctive *tap-*

tap-tap of Esme's stiletto heels coming down the hall toward the galley. The smile drops right off my face.

Hurriedly, I turn around and hold a finger to my lips. My eyes dart around the room as I search for a hiding spot.

"Mrs.—" Idris starts.

"Shh!" I cut him off, shaking my head.

Esme's heel clicks are getting closer and closer.

There! A pantry door.

I gesture to him and Luca that I'm ducking into the pantry and not to let on that I'm here. The last thing I need is a run-in with that hussy. I barely get the door shut behind me before I hear the unmistakable sound of Esme's Italian-accented English, her voice annoyingly loud over the *chop-chop-chop* of Idris and Luca's knives on their cutting boards.

"Oh good, you're still working on dinner," she says in her Italian-accented English. "I need to request a different dish for Mr. Bellanti. Something more...sophisticated. What is the most expensive thing you have in the kitchen?"

So that bitch is playing the same game I am. Except in her case, it's probably not a matter of preventing her own execution. She's just trying to work her way into Armani's bed again.

I glare at her silhouette, which is visible through the frosted glass of the darkened pantry. It looks like she's wearing a short, dark dress. Her hair is up.

"*Mrs.* Bellanti already left instructions for Mr. Bellanti's menu, *Ms.* Torrio," Chef Idris says.

A little thrill goes through me. Idris is on my side. The last name Torrio vaguely rings a bell, but I don't have time to think on it right now.

"Hmph," Esme grumbles. "'Mrs. Bellanti.' That's a title without a lot of security attached to it, wouldn't you agree?"

"I'm not sure what you mean," Idris replies stiffly.

"Becoming a wife is not exactly like becoming a made man, is it? There are no guarantees of loyalty, or protection, or—"

"If you don't mind me saying so, Ms. Torrio," Idris interrupts dryly, "Mrs. Bellanti has plenty of security. Did you have a nice swim earlier, by the way? I heard the pool was a little...crowded this afternoon."

My face instantly goes hot. Apparently the entire crew knows the gossip about my tryst with Armani in the pool. And also about how Esme caught us *in flagrante*...

God bless this man. I'll have to send him an entire case of Elite Reserve when I get back to Napa.

"I hear things too, you know," Esme hisses nastily. "And I wouldn't say there's much security around here at all."

With that, her heels *clip-cop* away in an angry storm.

Inside the pantry, my stomach drops.

It's already too late for me.

Esme must have heard Armani talking about me at the meeting with his mafia allies. He must have officially decided that he's not keeping me around.

Turns out I won't be leaving this island after all.

CANDI

THE DOOR to the pantry flies open, and I look up to see Chef Idris standing there.

"You may come out, Mrs. Bellanti. The storm has passed," he says with good humor, motioning for me to go back into the kitchen area.

"Thanks."

I smile weakly as I return to the open bottle of wine I abandoned in such a hurry. Trying to act natural, I grab three stemmed glasses from the cupboard and set them up in a row on the counter. But my hands tremble as I pour us each a half glass of the Elite Reserve.

All I can think about is the fact that Armani is a cold-blooded killer. Not just by reputation, either. I've seen it with my own eyes. He's emotionless, skilled, efficient. And now he's plotting my murder.

I've become the embodiment of a true mafia wife. A kept woman who exists solely as arm candy, a trophy to be ordered around by her husband and then killed when she's no longer useful. Replaced, too, I imagine. And quickly.

After I pass around the wine, I recork the bottle and slide it toward Idris.

"See? Still plenty left for Mr. Bellanti tonight," I reassure him. "Drink up."

I sure as hell will.

But before I can bolt down my booze, Idris raises his glass and says, "Let us toast. To health and long life!"

We clink glasses, and I down my wine as fast as I can, hoping it'll take the edge off the dread growing in my belly. When I set the empty glass on the counter, I realize Idris and Luca are staring.

"What is wrong, Mrs. Bellanti?" asks Luca. "You look like you've seen a ghost."

Ha. Maybe my own ghost.

Embarrassingly, my eyes fill with tears. I try to blink them back but there's no use. Idris hands me a clean dish towel to blot at the tears spilling from the corners of my eyes.

"What Ms. Torrio said was not correct, Mrs. Bellanti," he says soothingly. "Mr. Bellanti is very happy with this marriage, I am sure of it. Do not worry yourself over the words of a jealous woman."

I nod, but despite his attempt to reassure me, I'm still in panic mode. The chef has no idea what Armani is really like. Even if my husband's status as a mafioso is well-known, his role as a killer may not be. And nobody knows better than me how cold Armani acted toward me on the flight here, when he straight up told me he was going to use this trip to decide if I was worth keeping around.

There's no way in hell I'm staying here. I can't just sit around waiting for him to bump me off. I have to escape.

"I'm sure you're right," I tell Idris, blotting my eyes one last time. "I think I'd better go to my room and freshen up before dinner."

"Of course. You have a few hours; we are still prepping," he says, nodding. "And we will be sure Mr. Bellanti's food is made perfectly."

"Thank you."

I make a big deal out of walking down the hallway with heavy footsteps, but as soon as I reach the stairway to go below deck, I hang a sharp right around the corner instead. As quickly and silently as I can, I tiptoe along the deck rail until I reach the rear of the yacht where the boat ramp should give me access to the wooden walkway of the dock's pier. But there's no ramp.

Looking over the edge of the boat, I calculate that it's only a few feet across to the pier. Maybe three feet across the water, at most. I can jump that. And it's not like I can't swim, although it won't be a good look if I fall in the ocean. No doubt someone would hear me splashing, and then the crew would come running and my escape attempt would be dead in the water. Ha. Get it? Dead in the —yeah.

Before I can talk myself out of it, I take a deep breath, look both ways, and leap off the yacht.

I hit the pier a little harder than expected, feeling the shock radiate from my feet up to my knees. I start walking, only to realize I have a bad case of vertigo from being at sea the last few days. Stumbling, I go down on one knee with a hiss of pain. Forcing myself back to standing, I rub my knee and look around, but I don't see anyone watching me from the boat. Thank God I'm not wearing shoes, instead of the stupid high-heeled sandals I brought. That fall could have been a lot worse.

There's no time to pat myself on the back, though.

Adrenaline pumping, I run down the pier as fast as I can toward the tree line. The whole time, I brace myself for shouts or gunshots or someone to come after me, but I make it into the dense, humid foliage without being accosted.

I freeze for a moment, my heart hammering in my chest. I have no sense of direction, no idea where exactly on the island we are. All I see is ocean behind me and trees ahead, with those lush green hills rising in the distance. This is a terrible idea. I have no idea where I'm going or what's waiting for me in these woods...but even so, it can't be scarier than what I left behind back on that yacht.

Armani. I know I can't trust him.

Plunging into the forest, I immediately step on a thorny branch and regret my choice to not wear shoes today. I have to stop and pull two thorns out of the sole of my foot before I can take off again, picking my way through the greenery more slowly this time. I don't have a compass, but I use the position of the sun to set off in a roughly eastern direction, and I hike in a straight line as much as I can over the terrain. It's all ferns and moss and bird calls, so repetitive that I worry I'm walking in circles.

As I make my way up and down gently rolling hills which soon turn bigger and more strenuous, I try to brush off the anxiety washing over me. There has to be someone around here who would be willing to help me, a scared woman all alone. If I'm lucky, they'll have a functioning cell phone or even a way off the island. But I need to find one of the other villas first. Which might be difficult, considering that I didn't even realize we'd reached our own villa until our car pulled up to the security gate surrounding it. Still, knocking on the door (or security gate) of one of the other rental properties seems like my best bet.

There are holes in my plan, I'm aware. But it's a start. And if I can find a village, or even just a gas station, I might have even more luck. All I need is a working phone, so I can call Juliana and tell her what's going on. She'll know exactly what to do. She'll take charge. She'll get me out of here. And, worst-case scenario, she'll make sure that Armani comes to justice if I don't make it back home.

Without my phone, or a watch, I can only guess at the time passing. But as my feet begin to ache, and the daylight starts to fade, I realize that I've been on this grueling hike for hours. In a damn sundress, not to mention. And so far, I haven't seen any other rental homes.

The good news, I guess, is that I'm not lost. Every time I crest a hill, I can see the ocean. The island isn't huge. I'm not even sure it's possible to get lost, although there are probably places in the jungle where I could hide out for at least a day or two. But I'm not trying to play *Survivor* here. I have no water, no food, no shoes, and the only thing I want is to find another human who can help me.

Sweaty, exhausted, and demoralized, I sink onto a rock and put my head in my hands. My nerves are shot. Everything feels like it's falling apart. The stress is taking a physical toll. My hope is weakening.

Dammit, I need to find a way off this fucking island.

My life depends on it.

But I've seen no sign of civilization. No homes, no roads, no power lines, even.

Still breathing heavily, I glance around and take stock of my surroundings. Trees, trees, and more trees interspersed with various tropical plants and random spots of leafy open ground. God, what I wouldn't give for a monster size Coke right now, with tons of ice, beads of condensation rolling down the sides of the cup. And a huge carton of salty, hot McDonald's fries to go with it. *Get it together, Candi.*

Okay. Okay. Think. The sun is starting to sink into the ocean, and that means people will be turning on the lights in their houses as it gets dark. That should make it a lot easier for me to find those houses. I just need to get as high up as possible so I can see better. I need a solid vantage point.

Scoping the horizon, I spy a rocky protrusion jutting into the sky that will give me a solid view. Is it the mountain Armani mentioned, where the cell signal reaches sometimes? Mount Verde? Regardless, it's clearly my best option. I don't see any place higher.

With a boost of optimism I forge ahead, taking the long way around a steep ravine, spurred on by the knowledge that I'm burning precious daylight with every passing moment. The incline starts to get more extreme, the terrain more rocky and treacherous, but I persevere. Foot by foot, I manage to climb to the lookout point. Hands on my hips, I catch my breath for a minute until my ears stop ringing and my sweat starts to dry.

I go to the edge of the rock and look out in all directions. There's nothing around me but treetops. I spy the roof of the villa I'm staying in to the south, but otherwise it's just green hills, plant life, and a few rocky peaks. The ocean surrounds the island, much closer than I anticipated. I didn't realize the island was so tiny, and I never imagined there'd only be one house built on the entire place.

It's literally only Armani's villa here.

Clenching my hands into fists, I take a few deep, shuddering breaths and weigh my options...

I have none.

My sore, shaking legs give out and I collapse onto the ground. Hard, unforgiving rock presses into my ass and thighs, but I ignore it. Hanging my head, I sit for a while until the air turns cool and the breeze turns into a strong wind that tangles my hair. My feet feel like bruises, I'm starving, and I'm trapped here in mortal danger on this tiny, godforsaken island. This is hopeless.

There's *one* freaking house on this island. The only people are Armani's friends and employees. No one here will help me if something happens. And it's almost impossible to believe I'm not doomed.

True, I'm currently somewhat valuable to Armani as a spy who can go back and forth between the Bellantis and the Brunos. But once that's over, then what? I know too much, I've seen and heard too much. He can't just set me free into the world with that kind of knowledge.

And it's not as if he needs me around to get his needs met in bed. Esme quite clearly reminded me of that. What else do I have to offer him that would make me worth keeping around?

Sighing with defeat, I steel myself for my return to the yacht. I need to get going before it's too dark to see my way through the trees and back to the dock.

It's much easier to navigate going down, but as soon as I start walking, the dread starts creeping up on me again. Has

Armani noticed my absence? Is he now waiting to punish me for running off? I can only hope he's tied up with his "associates" and won't even know that I left.

I'm almost to the bottom of the mountain when I see a man. I skid to a halt.

The figure is cast darkly against the fading light. He's stocky, muscular, dark haired, and outfitted in dark clothing —and staring directly at me. Alarms sound in my brain. Did my husband send this guy after me to teach me a lesson? Or am I about to go missing in the woods?

"Good evening, Mrs. Bellanti," the man calls out formally. "You're right on time. Mr. Bellanti is expecting you for dinner aboard the yacht. If you'll follow me, please. I have an all-terrain vehicle ready to bring you back."

A sinking feeling hits me. There really is no way out.

"Who are you?" I ask, even though I know I have no recourse but to follow this man.

"Paolo, ma'am. I work for your husband, as we all do."

"I don't recognize you from the boat."

"That's because I'm stationed in the watchtower near the villa, ma'am."

"So...somebody called you? I thought there was no cell service here," I say suspiciously.

"We have two-way radios, Mrs. Bellanti. There are satellite phones for emergency purposes as well. This way, if you please," he says, gesturing for me to come with him.

Satellite phones? Clever. Of course Armani didn't mention that. Where are they kept, is the question. And how can I get one? Maybe I can bribe one of the villa staff to sneak one to me to use in the middle of the night. I have some cash, nice shoes, jewelry. There must be some way.

Swallowing hard, I walk over to the man. As I get closer, I notice the automatic weapon that's casually slung across his back.

Noticing my attention, he smiles and says, "We cannot be too careful. The Bellantis' island sometimes receives uninvited guests."

My footsteps falter. "The *Bellantis'* island?"

His brow furrows. "Yes, of course. You do know that your husband's family owns this land?"

"Oh. Well. I mean, yeah," I say. "I—I guess I thought it was just Armani's. Of course it's his whole family's. That makes sense."

But no, in fact, I did not know the Bellantis owned this entire island. Why would I? My husband conveniently left that part out when he was not-telling me where we were going on our "honeymoon."

I don't say anything more as I climb into the ATV and let Paolo drive.

My husband owns an entire island, and every employee on it is loyal to him. I'll find no resources or help here. He can do whatever he wants to me, and no one will lift a finger to stop him.

There really is no way out.

11

CANDI

"How was your walk, wife?"

"It was more of a hike," I answer dryly.

I barely had time for my second shower of the day when I got back to the yacht, so I just scrubbed the sweat and dirt off myself as best I could and then changed quickly into the only other dress I'd packed—a black silk spaghetti strap nightgown that barely passes for daytime wear. Luckily, it's dark out now, and I don't think anyone will be scrutinizing my outfit all that closely from across the dinner table.

Except...as I look around the dining room, I realize there isn't anyone else here.

Just me and Armani.

"Have your business associates...departed?" I ask.

He smirks as he sets his glass of scotch on the table and stands to pull my chair out for me, like the gentleman I know he truly isn't.

"Clever word choice," he says. "But yes, the men have gone. And all of them alive, I might add. No cement shoes necessary."

Interesting.

"So does this mean we'll be having dinner alone?"

"Yes." Armani raises a brow. "Unless that presents a problem for you."

"No. It's fine."

I sink into my chair and take in the glowing candles, the crisp linen tablecloth, the fragrant tropical flowers at the center of the table. It's all very lovely. And it has me on edge.

Is this my final meal?

My gaze travels to the wide-open panoramic doors, but I see no sign of an assassin lingering out on the deck. Not that Armani doesn't wear a gun at all times. But at least I can relax for a moment.

Reaching for the bottle of Pellegrino on the table, I crack it open and pour myself some of the sparkling water. Then I pour some for Armani, because even though my husband is a criminal, I have manners. As I drink it down thirstily, I realize how dehydrated I am. My hours-long hike/escape attempt this afternoon really took a toll on me.

I know I'll probably pay for my little adventure with full body aches tomorrow, but I regret nothing. Even if I failed to find actual help off the island, I did succeed in acquiring information that I didn't have before. That's worth something. I'm not giving up yet, either. My fight is far from over.

"Beautiful night," Armani comments, nodding his head toward the open doors.

The moon is still low in the sky, making a trail of golden light on the surface of the water.

"It is," I say.

Glancing over, my eyes catch on the flash of bare,

tattooed chest that I can see with the top few buttons of Armani's dress shirt open. I can't tear my gaze away. The artwork stretches sensually over his skin, and my fingers almost ache to touch the designs I know so well now. The Italian words for family, honor, and power; the traditional cornetto to protect him from the evil eye; the crossed Roman daggers. I've seen his tattoos a hundred times, yet I'm still fighting the urge to sit on his lap and rip his shirt off so I can run my hands over the black ink.

Moments ago, all I could think about was the fact that Armani is likely plotting my demise. But in this moment, I'd give anything to forget all that and repeat our scene from the pool earlier. Fearing my husband somehow heightens my desire for him, even as I pray for a way to escape him. It's fucked up.

"Enjoying the view?" he asks.

I'm about to say yes, and something about the moon being incredible, but when I look up at his face I realize that he's been watching me ogle him for the last few minutes.

"Maybe," I say coolly, dragging my eyes away with some effort. "Speaking of views, I made it up to the top of the mountain today and noticed that the rest of the island is deserted. You didn't mention this place was a solitary fortress."

He traces the rim of his glass as he says, "I don't have to explain things to you, Candi."

The bored, nonchalant tone of his voice—combined with the relentless fear and failure and frustration and exhaustion I've been battling—makes something inside me snap.

"Actually, you do. I deserve some basic respect here. I *am* your wife."

"Only in name," he says.

"What the hell is that supposed to mean? We're legally married! There are fucking rights, and...and responsibilities, and other things that come with it."

Much to my consternation, he barks out a laugh. "You're right. I suppose you get a discount on your car insurance now."

Glaring at him, I say, "I also have the legal right to inherit your property upon your death."

"That works both ways," he says, his expression shifting back to its usual serious one.

"Is that a threat? Because I don't have much for you to inherit. Except for my cat."

"Having you out of the picture provides me with other benefits, though," he says, coldly stating the obvious.

"Then perhaps I should take you out of the picture first," I shoot back.

"I don't believe you're capable of that," he says.

"Oh really," I say, and I'm about to follow it up with something nasty when who should come flouncing through the door on her six-inch hooker heels but Esme Torrio. She's in a lime green bandage dress—inexplicably flattering on her, of course—with a bottle of Glenlivet whiskey in her hand.

My heart lurches. What the hell?

"Can I freshen your drinks?" she purrs. "Dinner will be out shortly."

She's looking at Armani of course, not me. I don't even

have a drink besides the sparkling water. But I do have a few questions about why exactly she's here.

Armani slides his glass toward her. She makes a big show out of bending over the table with the whiskey bottle to give him a generous refill, her low neckline just this side of a wardrobe malfunction.

"You know what? I'd love some wine, actually," I tell her, mock sweetly. "Just bring out the whole bottle. A red would be great."

She gives me a half glance and rolls her eyes before sliding Armani's glass back to him.

"I will see what is available. *Solo un attimo.*"

She says this with such confidence and importance, as if we'll be anxiously awaiting her return. Once she's left, I stare daggers at my husband. "You said your guests were gone."

"I said the *men* were gone. Though actually, the other women have also left. Just not Esme."

"And why is that?"

He shrugs. "She needed a place to stay until her ride gets here. I said she had to work for it."

"Oh, I'll bet you did," I say icily.

"Be nice."

His order sours my gut.

When Esme returns, it's with a rolling service cart piled high with food. She begins setting plates and bowls in front of Armani and me, and I recognize everything from my visit to the kitchen earlier: osso buco in a gorgeous red sauce with fresh parsley and lemon zest on top; the risotto Milanese, a buttery golden yellow; the grapefruit salad Chef Idris had mentioned; steaming hot bread with a dish of olive oil and green herbs; and last but not least, the extra special gnocchi I had requested for Armani.

I say nothing, but I'm on high alert. Why is she serving us? Where is Chef Idris; where is Luca? How do I know that Esme didn't tamper with the food after Idris plated it? Especially given her comment earlier about there not being much security around here. For all I know, she and my husband are working together to eliminate me.

Once we've been served our meals, Esme goes back to the cart and then brings a glass of red wine over to me. She goes to set it in front of me, but I wave her away.

"I said to bring the whole bottle. I wanted to open it myself."

She frowns, her eyes briefly darting to Armani. "But the bottle was already open."

She's right. Of course the bottle was already open. I'm the one who opened it.

All the better reason not to trust it, I think to myself. It could be drugged, poisoned...

"Take it back to the kitchen."

"Why?" she asks plaintively. "The chef said this was the wine for tonight. The Elite Reserve?"

"Take it away. I changed my mind," I say dismissively.

She lets out an audible huff of annoyance and storms away with the wineglass and the cart, leaving me with my husband and a table full of heavenly, aromatic, mouthwatering gourmet food.

Food that I have no intention of eating.

Armani digs in, seemingly ignorant of my suspicions. I push my food around my plate a little, sip my water, and watch the moonlight ripple on the waves. I don't take a single bite, not even of the bread. Maybe the end Armani is ripping chunks from is safe, but maybe there's poison inside the loaf. How am I supposed to know? Meanwhile my stomach is growling and my feet are silently screaming from my barefoot hike, but all I can do is sit here and listen to my husband's carefree goddamn chewing.

Tension grows in the space between us. I feel it like an impending storm hanging low over my head, my thoughts a dark cloud.

"I overheard what that man said to you the other night," I finally murmur, as leadingly as I can.

Then I wait to see if he'll react. He doesn't. He just keeps eating.

"What, you don't remember?" I prod. "He offered to 'take care' of me. What exactly did he mean by that?"

Nothing.

"He wanted to *rent me* and then *take care of me*, Armani. Did you make some kind of bargain?"

Instead of answering my question, he says, "You shouldn't have been eavesdropping."

"It was kind of hard not to. When a woman's husband entertains conversation about sharing his wife, especially when it's in the same room, a wife tends to take notice."

He takes a sip of his drink while holding my gaze. A chill races down my spine at the pure impassivity on his face. He doesn't give a shit about me or my concerns.

"Since you were eavesdropping, you should have also heard the part where I said I don't share."

I frown. "I did. But you also said you'd entertain his offer."

"Mm," he grunts.

"So? Did you?"

"I did."

My stomach drops.

"But in the end," he goes on, "I told him I wasn't selling. I said I'd take care of you myself."

A wave of nausea crashes over me. The room tilts, as if I've actually been poisoned or drugged. But it's not because of the food. It's because of this cold, reptilian criminal sitting across from me.

"What are you planning?" I ask angrily, trying to come off formidable and tough even as my knees tremble under the table.

A muscle twitches in his cheek.

"Answer me, dammit. What's going to happen to me?"

Silence beats between us before he pulls a long breath in through his nose.

"Stop assuming I plan to dispose of you."

"You just said as much!" I point out.

"I'm still deciding," he says cruelly.

His tone belies the seriousness of what he's just said. To him, this is normal, everyday conversation. Killing is what he does. Hell, I witnessed it with my own eyes. I thrilled in his revenge. But there's no thrill in knowing that I might be the next person at the receiving end of his violence.

"Eat," he commands, gesturing at my full plate. He must have finally noticed I'm only playing with my food. "Idris is a master chef. This risotto is...*senza paralleli.*"

Without parallel. Thanks, Italian dictionary.

I shake my head. "I'd rather not."

Armani searches my gaze and then starts laughing. *Laughing.* Like this is some kind of joke.

"I get it now," he says.

"Get what?" I say tersely.

"Here."

He cuts a bite of the osso buco and leans over in his chair with his fork outstretched.

"Come on. At least try it," he says. "I've been eating it and I'm fine."

Not taking my eyes off his, heart thudding in my chest, I slowly lean forward and open my mouth. He gently slides the fork between my lips, watching as I deliberately chew and then swallow.

"Well?"

The sauce is incredibly layered; rich with wine, marrow, and garlic; the meat so soft it practically melts in my mouth. There's the slightest hint of cinnamon. And the tang of... something sour. My fear.

"It's good," I admit.

"Better than good," he insists. "Here, now the risotto."

Again, he leans over to feed me from his own plate, off of his own silverware.

"*Senza paralleli*," I say, but there's no joy in it.

Before he can feed me another bite, Esme reappears with the cart, two domed dishes on it.

"Have we finished?" she asks perkily.

Armani looks over at me. My plates are still full. His aren't.

"We have," I answer.

Esme sashays over and sets the domed dishes on an empty chair. Then she takes her time bussing our table, picking up the plates and glasses and silverware and setting them a bit too loudly on the cart for me to think it's an accident. Brat. Once the table is cleared and we have fresh napkins and utensils, she sets the domed dishes in front of us and lifts the domes.

"Dessert. Torta caprese," she says, and then wryly adds, "*Buon appetito.*"

"What is this, exactly?" I ask, my irritation coloring my voice.

"Ehm...flourless chocolate cake," she says, sounding taken aback. "Made with almonds."

With that, she picks up a cloth napkin, shakes it open, and leans over to place it on Armani's lap, giving him yet another front-row view of her plump cleavage.

Nope.

Grabbing her arm, I rise from my chair. "Enough! You're dismissed!"

She jumps back, eyes wide.

"*Puoi andare!*" I add, in case she didn't catch my meaning. *You may go.*

Esme looks at Armani as if he's supposed to intervene, but to my absolute shock, he nods that she should get lost. With a huff, she stomps off, her heels *clickety-clacking* away.

Armani signals Paolo who rushes over, and orders that he personally remove her from the yacht. And the island. So glad I don't have to see this bitch again.

I sit back down and notice my husband looking at me with interest...and a lot of heat.

"You're learning Italian," he says. "*Stai imparando a parlare Italiano.*"

"Working on it."

He inclines his head. "Impressive."

Ha. Like his compliment means anything to me. You know what a good compliment is? Not murdering someone.

I grab my fork and stab a bite of cake onto it, then hold it out to Armani with my brow raised in a challenge. Smirking, he leans forward and wraps his mouth around my fork, then slides back with the bite in his mouth. He didn't hesitate for a second, so I guess my torta isn't poisoned.

What is the game here?

We finish our desserts—mine is technically my dinner, I suppose—and then Armani throws his napkin on the table and rises. He looks at me and then reaches out to trail a finger beneath my jaw, down the side of my neck, so slowly it makes me shiver. My skin lights up, my pulse jackhammering at his touch. He traces a line all the way down to the center of my chest, to the hollow right between my breasts, before he pulls his hand away.

"We'll be returning to the villa shortly," he says. "Nice nightgown, by the way."

Lust drenched, I shift uncomfortably in my seat, squeezing my thighs together against the ache.

"Stop messing with me," I tell him.

"But you make it so easy, Cassandra."

With that, he walks away.

I hate myself for watching him go.

12

ARMANI

I'M in the villa's kitchen with Chef Idris, drinking a Peroni as I thank him for a job well done.

Except this isn't about the excellent dinner he made for me and Candi on the yacht last night.

It's about the report Idris gave me on Esme's impromptu little visit to the boat's galley to try to alter the menu and ingratiate herself to me. As if I'd even give a shit whether my ex-fling knew my favorite dishes or not; as if it would change my mind about the fact that she and I are completely done with each other—a decision I made long before Candi entered the picture.

Esme was never anything more to me than temporary company, arm candy with the option to warm my bed later, and no strings attached. I made those terms abundantly clear the first time we met at an associate's private gathering some years back. But even though she claimed to be like-minded about the arrangement, her behavior on my yacht over the past few days has only proven that her understanding of our prior entanglement is...shall we say, a bit fantastical.

We slept together, sure, but it was never exclusive. Esme becoming Mrs. Armani Bellanti was never on the table. Hell, I doubt we've even spent a combined total of ten days together. In her mind, though, we had some torrid love affair. A romance for the ages. One she has every intention of rekindling.

But even if I wasn't married to Candi, a relationship with Esme is a hard pass from me.

"I've got to hand it to you, man," I tell Idris, raising my beer in a toast, "it was an incredible suggestion to have Esme serve me and my wife."

"Did that help to ease Mrs. Bellanti's mind? She seemed quite concerned," he says, rapidly chopping cucumbers and carrots into matchsticks for the sushi rolls he's preparing.

"Not at all! She actually thought Esme poisoned her food," I chuckle.

Idris suppresses a laugh. "You told her that was not possible, yes?"

"Nah, I let her worry a little."

Idris shakes his knife at me in a scolding manner. "You are lucky to have such a woman. I would not play such games. I would be kinder to her if she were my wife."

"Ah, but she's not. She's mine," I say.

Still, Idris is right about one thing. I'm enjoying these little games with Candi far too much. Instead, I should be focusing as hard as I can on the bigger game at play—the one with the Brunos. Speaking of which, I owe Dante a call.

He left me a mysteriously vague voicemail at 3 a.m., and he's not the type to call me just to check in and say hello.

"Anyway, thanks again," I tell Idris. "I've got to go handle something."

"Of course. Please tell Mrs. Bellanti that lunch will be served in the dining room in an hour."

"Will do," I say, nodding.

But I don't tell Mrs. Bellanti jack shit yet, because this phone call is more important.

In the interest of privacy, I lock myself in one of the villa's unoccupied guest rooms and then go into the en-suite bathroom, turning the shower on to muffle the sound of my conversation. Then I call Dante on the sat phone I've been hiding from Candi.

"It's four in the morning," Dante answers by way of greeting.

"It's almost lunch hour in my time zone," I tell him. "Besides, you sound wide awake."

"Hashtag new parent," he says.

"Oh yeah? Is my sweet little angel of a niece not a good sleeper?"

"She sleeps great. It's the waking up every two to three hours that's the problem."

I laugh. "Can't say I envy you there. So, what'd you call for? Your voicemail was cryptic."

"Check your email," my older brother says, the humor going out of his voice.

"For what?" Pulling my tablet out of my jacket, I add, "Did Clayton find us a solid in with the Russians already? Damn, he's good—"

"No. Not that. It's something else you'll find of interest."

"What's with the cloak and dagger routine? Just tell me what it is."

"Check your email," Dante repeats testily.

"Fine, fine."

Frowning, I tuck the phone between my ear and my shoulder and login to my work email.

"You look at it yet?"

"Give me a damn minute," I snap.

After scrolling past a handful of emails related to Bellanti Vineyards' actual business operations, I find the message from my brother. It's been CC'd to Marco and Clayton as well. Attached are a text-based document and a series of video files. My pulse picks up.

"This is a lot of files you got here," I say.

"Yeah. Read the report first."

Dante sighs, and the line goes silent while I read. Three pages of dense text list all the dates and times that our security system shows signs of irregularity—meaning it's been tampered with—along with long chains of letters and numbers that I can't interpret, maybe some kind of trace for where the commands came from. Fuck.

"Shit," I breathe. "These dates go back at least five years. Who did this?"

"We don't know. Now watch the video."

"Which one?"

"Any one."

I clench my jaw and open the first one. Grainy black-and-white footage shows a dark sedan pulling slowly into the back drive on the Bellanti property in the middle of the night. The next few videos I click on show the same exact thing happening on later dates, around the same time. I can't make out anyone inside the vehicle, and nobody seems to enter or exit the car. It just creeps slowly down the drive, circles, and then goes back the way it came, seemingly without making physical contact with anyone.

"What is this? Someone surveilling us?" I murmur. "Maybe with high-tech audio equipment?"

"I wish that's all it was," Dante says darkly. "Look again, when the car makes the turn."

I tap pause and rewind and replay a few times. Finally, I see it. The car is pulling up to the long-forgotten mailbox that we were required to put on the property because the winery has a separate address from the house. It's never been used. At least, not by us.

"Who's been putting shit in that box? And who the hell is picking up the delivery?" I ask.

"Don't know. I reviewed the footage for each time the car shows up, watched the entire forty-eight hours prior for unscheduled visitors or any other notable activity, but the feed from our cameras has...blips in it. It just goes black. That's why I pulled in a tech person to look at our security system from the back end, see if there was a system glitch. Instead, we found all that evidence of tampering."

I can practically feel my blood pressure rising. "Why didn't anyone catch this sooner? This report goes back five years! You're telling me in all that time, nobody realized we had a problem?"

"Security is your job," Dante reminds me coolly.

"Fuck, I know that. How did I miss this?"

"The entire security team missed it. Probably because there wasn't anything amiss. The only thing the cameras over there ever pick up is a dirt road surrounded by trees. Nobody goes out there, there's no reason to scrutinize it. And since the feeds never blackout for more than a few minutes, there's never been a reason to question the dead spaces. It just looks like a minor, temporary malfunction."

"But presumably, these outages are scheduled to cover up some shady shit," I say.

"Right."

This is bad. Very bad.

"Fuck," I groan again. "We have a mole on the inside. And it's not my wife."

"It's not *only* your wife," Dante corrects.

"It has to be someone on our security team. They're the only ones who could coordinate this. A drop-off, a pickup, a blip on the cameras, all of it perfectly choreographed to escape notice. Even if an outsider is involved, they'd still need someone on the inside to brush those little blackouts under the rug. So it's somebody directly—and regularly—involved with our surveillance tech. I need to call Clayton."

"Clayton is already working on it," Dante says. "He's got a few possibilities, nothing solid though."

Thank God for my Irish add-on. If anyone can flush out a mole, it's him.

"I suggested taking the mailbox out," he adds, "but Clayton wants to keep things as-is so he can have eyes on it. Maybe catch the perp in action."

"Yeah, I agree with that. We could get lucky. Jesus, fuck. When's this shit going to end?"

Dante laughs humorlessly. "With the Bratva on our heels? Never."

"I guess this at least clears my wife's name, then, doesn't it?"

"Not in my mind," Dante says. "She's still a mole, and she's still leaked intel about us to the Brunos, regardless of her level of involvement in our current security issue."

"Still. Maybe she's not as bad as we thought," I insist. "Maybe we judged too soon what she was responsible for.

"Maybe. Or maybe you're just making excuses for her."

This is the problem with having brothers. They always call you out.

"Regardless, we have bigger fish to fry at the moment," I tell him. "We need to find this other mole. I personally vetted everyone on the security team, every last soldier. It has to be someone new."

"Negative. We've employed the same guys for years. There are no obvious weak links."

"Then it's someone with the capability to trump up false credentials so good that even I didn't see through them, which is an even scarier prospect," I admit. "Someone had to bankroll that kind of thing. Falsifying documentation ain't cheap."

We talk it through and toss a few ideas around, but by the time we get off the call, I'm no closer to narrowing down a suspect. Our long-term employees are devoted and loyal. None of them strike me as a double-crosser. Then again, I hadn't pegged Candi as a spy initially, either. Maybe I'm losing my touch.

Running a hand through my hair, I walk out to the guest room's balcony and look out at the greenery surrounding the villa. It's beautiful, but it does nothing to ease my nerves.

I'll never give up on my family's safety. Never. It's my job to protect them.

But sometimes I wonder what it would be like to delegate more of the tasks I'm constantly juggling. Give myself a little more breathing room, a little less stress. God, what would it be like to take a break from the intense state of alert I'm constantly in? I can't imagine. All I know is, the human body isn't meant to run on pure adrenaline all the time. Yet for my entire adult life, it's been my daily fuel.

Until my wife.

Something about her gives me a rush, a spark. The kind of energy that's not based on fight-or-flight, but experiencing more of what life has to offer. Sex, beauty, pleasure, heightened emotions. I'm not saying I was numb to the world before, but Candi gives me a kind of energy I've never known.

Realizing it's nearly lunchtime, I go searching for my wife and find her asleep in our bedroom. The sunlight pouring through the windows casts her body in a golden glow. Her auburn hair is spread out over the pillow, strands of coppery red glinting in the light. I'd give anything to hike up her dress and wake her with my dick inside her, but I know she'd be pissed at me for breaking her little "no touching" rule. The one she was more than happy to break herself in the pool, but still. I'm more than happy to let her fuck me on her terms.

And that's when it hits me.

As much as the constant conflict with Candi amuses me, as much as I love riling her up, as hot as it makes me when I see that combination of rage and lust flashing in her eyes...

I think I'm softening toward my wife.

Realizing that makes me almost as uneasy as facing the reality that my family isn't safe right now, and that I have no idea when we will be.

13

CANDI

I'M HALFWAY THROUGH LUNCH—A delicious array of sushi prepared by my new favorite chef, Idris—when, out of nowhere, Armani says, "Let's go to the beach after we eat."

He suggests this causally, as if we're accustomed to making plans on a Sunday afternoon.

Lowering my chopsticks, I scrutinize his face for signs of furtiveness or deceit.

"To do what, exactly?" I ask, suspicion pumping in my veins.

"To feel the sand between our toes, to watch the waves, to...I don't know. Take advantage of the fact that we're the only guests here?"

"Yeah. That's the part I'm worried about," I tell him pointedly. "There will be no one around to hear me scream."

I push my plate away. As good as the spicy tuna rolls are, I've suddenly lost my appetite. A sense of impending doom will do that to you.

Armani spreads his hands in a gesture of openness that I

really don't buy, saying, "Look, I promise that nothing is going to happen to you. Let's just...try to enjoy the day."

As I study his gaze, I see something spark in his eyes. I wish I knew what it was.

"Swear you won't lay a hand on me," I say.

As if it matters. As if he can't just lie to my face right now and erase me later anyway.

"I swear I won't lay a hand on you," he says, and then adds, "at least, not in any way that you don't want me to."

He sounds sincere, but at the same time, our conversation over dinner last night was hardly reassuring. Nothing he said made me feel any better about my position in this marriage, or my dispensability. And now he suddenly wants to go for a romantic walk on the beach? How can I trust it?

"I don't really have a choice, do I?" I say. "So fine. We'll go."

His brows knit together. "I'm not trying to force you, but we're heading home in a few more days. I thought it would be nice to get some vacation out of this vacation, that's all."

"I said fine. I'll go change."

The suit I brought is a tomato-red bikini with cute bows on the shoulders. Not super flashy or anything, but the color still makes me feel like a walking target. I pull on a tie-dyed coverup dress and grab my sandals and a floppy hat.

Minutes later, we're walking on the path that leads through the rear of the villa property all the way to the beach. The sun-warmed tropical flowers are sweetly fragrant, the cool shade of the trees making the short hike a pleasant one, unlike my marathon trek up to Mount Verde. It's beautiful, serene. Armani seems to be enjoying the walk as well. In his board shorts and tight T-shirt, there's nowhere for him to hide a weapon. I start to let my guard down a little.

We crest a hill and my breath catches in my throat. I'm utterly dazzled.

Pristine white sand spreads out before us, endless blue-green water glimmering beyond, not a single boat on the horizon to mar the perfect view. The island's coastline curves away in both directions, leaving us in a perfect little half-moon shaped bay.

Puffy white clouds drift overhead, the breeze tossing my hair. It's all so soothing. I can't help sighing out a long, contented breath. Armani passes me his water bottle, and I take a few sips from it. He's been drinking the same water this whole time and he's fine, so I'm not worried.

After I hand it back, Armani gently takes my hand in his, shocking the hell out of me.

When I glance over, I see him gazing pensively out at the waves.

"What's going on?" I ask.

"Nothing."

He's lying. Something is weighing heavily on his mind. I don't think it's me, though. I have a feeling this has to do with whatever is waiting for us when we get back home to Napa.

"Did you find out something new about the Brunos? Do they have a plan to move against your family soon?" I prod.

"This is the last thing I want to discuss on my honeymoon," he says dryly.

"Right. Because we're having such a romantic time," I say, pulling my hand away.

It's not as if I'm expecting him to spill his guts about all the Bellanti family secrets, but I'd at least like to be prepared for the impending shitstorm ahead. Especially considering the fact that I'm supposed to be playing spy games with the Brunos until Armani says otherwise. But no. My husband would rather keep me ignorant of the larger picture, even if it means I walk right into a trap.

Armani stays a few steps behind me as we make our way down four flights of narrow but sturdy wooden stairs to the beach.

We walk along the shoreline for a while, in no kind of hurry, shoes dangling from our hands. Neither of us speaks as the seafoam laps gently at our ankles, the waves crashing and rolling and tossing flecks of spray at us. The silence between us isn't exactly unusual, but there's an undercurrent of tension prickling at me. Clearly something is bothering him, but he won't talk about it. How typically male.

"I'm going in," I say.

Screw it. Armani can pout and brood all he wants, but I'm going to enjoy the water.

I drop my hat and sandals next to a big rock and then pull my coverup over my head, tossing it next to my shoes. When I turn around, I see Armani watching me, his eyes traveling the length of my body. Guess he likes the bikini.

"Care to join me?" I ask, adjusting the cups of my top so my breasts jiggle enticingly.

"No," he says, glancing away.

"Suit yourself then," I say, walking into the surf.

Too bad. I wouldn't have minded seeing his half-naked body slicing through the water, cool droplets running over his tattooed chest and tight abs as he surfaced. But no matter. I'll enjoy my swim alone. And I do. The water is refreshingly cool and unbelievably clear, and I waste no time diving in. I see waving aquatic plants, coral formations, tons of colorful fish. I had no idea Morocco had water like this.

I don't swim back to shore until my skin begins to chill. Even then, I wade in the surf for a while, letting the waves rush past my thighs, hips, waist, before they pull back into the ocean. Armani sits on the rock by my things, his forearms resting on his knees, hands clasped together. His expression is actually relaxed, which is a rarity. If I didn't know any better, I'd say he's enjoying watching me.

"Sure you don't want to come in?" I shout to him, slogging across the soft, dense sand of the seafloor as I emerge from the surf.

"I'm sure," he says, gathering up my shoes and hat and draping my coverup over his arm.

"Not even for a quick dip? The water's actually pretty —sss!" I hiss as I lose my balance and feel something slice the underside of my left foot, leaving a trail of bright pain in its wake. "Shit."

Clenching my jaw, I hobble the rest of the way onto dry sand, putting my weight on my left heel instead of the sole. My foot is throbbing, and I can feel hot liquid leaking from it, which I know must be blood. Armani is on me in an instant, dropping my stuff and kneeling before me with a frown.

"You're bleeding," he says. "Here, sit."

He spreads my coverup on the sand, helps me lower myself onto it, and then rinses off my foot with the water that's left in his bottle, me hissing in pain the whole time. Then he looks at my foot and lets out a low whistle.

"Wow, you really did a number on yourself," he says.

My good mood deflates. "I must have stepped on a piece of coral or something. It stings. Do you think I need stitches?"

"Hard to tell. You're still bleeding quite a bit. It's not a long cut, but it looks pretty deep."

Oh, shit. "Is there a doctor on this island?"

"If you need one, I'll figure it out. Let's just focus on getting you back to the villa first."

Armani pulls off his shirt, which I can't even appreciate as he winds the shirt tightly around my foot. He sets my hat on my head, hands me my sandals, and then he's lifting me into his arms.

"I can walk," I insist. "Really."

"The hell you will."

I don't argue. From the way my foot is pulsing, I could swear I'm bleeding out.

By the time he gets us up the first flight of steps, I'm feeling slightly woozy. To Armani's credit, he's barely breathing hard when he finishes the second. But I don't feel any less guilty when he slows down a bit on the third and has to pause for a minute before tackling the last incline. Keeping my face buried in his shoulder, I clamp my jaw against the pain and ride it out.

Once we're back to the villa, he carries me straight into the kitchen, where he deposits me on the center island. Finding a stack of dishtowels, he props up my injured foot.

"Stay there. Keep that foot elevated. I'll be right back."

It feels like I've bled through his shirt. The cotton is

clingy and wet. While I wait for Armani to return, I measure my breathing to keep myself calm.

"Here we go," he says.

Looking over, my heart flutters when I see the medical kit in his hand. It's a big kit, a lot bigger than a normal household first aid box. There's obviously more than Band-Aids and Neosporin in there.

"Are—are you sure I don't need a doctor?" I ask, panicked.

"I am the doctor." He meets my gaze. "The closest medical help is the mainland, and it'll take us hours to get you there. You're going to have to trust me, Candi. Okay?"

Cracking open the kit, he takes out supplies and lines them up on the island. Then he finds a basin and a pitcher. He fills the pitcher with bottled water and squirts some brown liquid into it.

"What is that?" I ask.

"An antiseptic."

After that, he places my foot inside the basin and then fills a big syringe with the mixture. Luckily, there isn't a needle on the syringe, or I might have passed out.

"I need to flush the wound now," he tells me. "It's going to sting. I'm sorry."

He removes the shirt from my foot.

"Armani, wait—"

The warm water offends the laceration. Yelping in pain, I shove my fist into my mouth and squeeze my eyes shut. It takes all my effort not to kick Armani in the face.

Ignoring my twitching and my groans, he works confidently, deftly, calmly...as if he's done this a million times before. After a few rounds of flushing, my foot doesn't sting as much.

"How's it feeling?" he asks.

"Surprisingly better already," I admit.

"That's because I gave you a lidocaine injection."

"Seriously? I never even felt it."

Maybe all I need now is some gauze and a bit of medical tape, and I'll be good to go? I start to relax. Until Armani grabs a suture needle and thread.

"What the hell is that for? Are you giving me stitches?"

"Yes. That's why I gave you the local anesthetic. But believe me, you'll barely feel it."

My stomach drops. "I don't want to. I don't like this."

"Hey," he says, his voice going soft. "It's just a few stitches. Little ones. I promise you're going to be fine. You can do this. Okay?"

I nod and then cover my eyes. The first suture feels more like a tug than anything else. I feel a quick stab of pain on the next stitch, then nothing, then more tugging. He does this a few more times, and once I realize that it's actually not that bad, I move my hand away from my eyes and look at him.

His dark head is bent low, his concentration unwavering, his hands deftly working.

"You're really good at this," I whisper. "How come?"

"I was a really advanced Boy Scout."

"Is that a thing?"

He makes a sound something like a laugh right before he stabs my foot again. For a moment, he goes still and I think he might be done, but then he resumes the slow pull of the thread, the odd tugging.

"The truth is," he says quietly, "I learned how to do this from my father. Upper level first aid is a good skill to have when your family is involved in criminal activity. You never know when someone's going to get shot or stabbed. So. I stitched up my first bullet wound when I was fifteen."

My eyes are wide. "Your dad?"

"One of his associates. The hospital wasn't an option. He healed up fine. You will, too."

"Jesus. That's a lot to put on a teenage kid," I murmur. "What a life."

He snorts and then picks up a roll of cotton gauze, which he starts wrapping around my foot and securing with medical tape.

"It's not like I had a choice," he says. "I mean...you're born into what you're born into. I might've run away if it weren't for my brothers, but we had to stick together. Especially after we lost our mom and Liliana. There was no love lost between us and our dad, but at least we had each other."

For a moment, I say nothing. This is the most open and vulnerable Armani has ever been around me, and I can only hope he says more, keeps showing me this tender, hidden side of himself.

Despite the fact that I was convinced he was going to kill me on this trip, he honestly doesn't seem to be in a hurry about it. Maybe there's time for me yet. And maybe...maybe the tiny sliver of him that feels something for me can be made to grow. There was no mistaking the look on his face when he scooped me up of the beach and carried me here. He was concerned. He was gentle. He *cares*.

Even if he won't admit it.

Finally, I gently say, "I'm sorry. There wasn't a lot of love in my house growing up, either. But that doesn't decide your fate. It's okay to want more than what you've been given."

I reach over and cup his face, but he immediately pulls back and clears his throat.

"All done," he says gruffly, his eyes barely meeting mine.

With that, he sets down the gauze and walks out.

But now I'm certain of it. He does care about me. More deeply than I ever realized.

And it scares the hell out of him.

14

CANDI

Since I can't get my stitches wet, I have to skip the shower and take a long, luxurious bath instead. Hardly a punishment, especially once I've got the tub loaded with lavender bath salts and mountains of bubbles.

As I ease myself down into the hot water, I let out a content little sigh. Now *this* is what I call honeymoon-worthy. My injured foot is firmly propped on a towel draped over the edge of the tub, the rest of my body relaxing amidst the suds. I wash my hair quickly, put in a leave-in conditioner, and then scrub myself from head to toe. Well, with the exception of the sole of my foot. Then I close my eyes and allow my thoughts to drift. But all I can I think about is the way Armani acted at dinner.

Over the course of the meal, he played the part of his cold, distant, stoic self, but for the first time in our relationship, his attitude didn't make me feel discouraged. In fact, it was the exact opposite.

Because I knew his behavior had nothing to do with me.

Instead, it was apparent that he was still deeply uncomfortable about what had happened in the kitchen earlier—when he'd revealed more about himself and his troubled childhood than he'd intended. That vulnerability had wounded him. He was in uncharted waters, having exposed himself like that to me. The weak spot in his armor had been revealed.

Now that I've seen the hurt little boy inside Armani, I understand him so much better. Unlike the rest of the world, I've finally gotten a glimpse of the man behind the intimidation, the cruelty, the guns, the tattoos. Beneath all that is a son who longs for so much more from his father than a legacy of tyranny and violence. How can I not feel tender toward him?

I'm not saying the Big Bad Wolf has been tamed, but this definitely shifts my perceptions.

It reminds me of a conversation I had with Frankie, back when we were still friends, when she tried to tell me that the Bellanti brothers were the kind of men who'd put you through hell before they let their walls down. She said it was because of their rough childhood that they had so many defenses. Which, yes, makes total sense. She also said...that sticking it out with a Bellanti was worth the effort.

Maybe she was right all along.

I doubted her words at the time, but now I'm not so sure.

The water is starting to cool, so I carefully get out of the tub and dry off. Then I wrap up in the fluffy spa robe I've been using and limp back to the bedroom to find some pajamas.

I've just tossed the robe over a chair and slipped into a silky green chemise when the door opens and Armani walks in. Before I can say a word, he's crossed the room in a few strides and stopped in front of me. His expression is so intense that I just stand there, expecting some kind of bad news.

But what comes out of his mouth is, "I need you."

He doesn't even have to explain. Because I immediately realize that this is his way of asking for more—just like I told him it was okay to do when we were in the kitchen earlier. And I meant it.

"Yes," I whisper, my voice husky.

I don't even care that it's my own rule I'm breaking as I throw my arms around his neck and press myself tight against him. I catch a flicker of emotion in his eyes and then he lowers his lips to mine. He kisses me in no hurry at all, like we've got all the time in the world. He's never kissed me like this before. Deep, soft, slow. Heat spreads through me from head to toe, my insides turning to liquid.

This is *something*.

I think this is the first time in my life I actually understand the meaning of the word *swoon*.

I'd expected his usual method of attack—the kind of hungry, fiery, aggressive kiss that feels like being eaten alive, that makes my adrenaline rush and my pussy ache—but this...this is a sweetness I feel all the way to my soul. I revel in it, returning his kiss in kind, moaning softly into his mouth, encouraging him. Armani holds me close, robbing my breath, making my heart beat faster. I know I shouldn't be doing this. Letting him draw me back into his orbit, my defenses down. But I can't help it.

This is exactly what I want, exactly where I want to be.

Maybe I need him, too.

My hands roam over his shoulders, down his chest, and then I start unbuttoning his shirt. Once I finish with the last button, Armani shrugs out of the shirt and drops it to the floor. Then he gently pushes me down onto the bed and climbs over me, never breaking the kiss.

I moan happily as I trace the lines of muscle along his back and waist. When I reach for the bulge in the front of his pants, he rolls onto his side to unbuckle his belt and unzip his fly, managing to kick off his pants without leaving the bed. Then he resumes kissing me as if it's the very air he needs to breathe.

My lips are swollen and I'm kiss-drunk by the time he breaks away to trail his hot mouth along my body. Pulling my chemise down as he goes, he kisses his way from my neck to my chest, down my torso, teasing over my hip bones. But still, he moves slowly and patiently, with purpose but no urgency. It's intoxicating. I'm writhing on the bed, my fingers lacing through his hair.

"Armani," I groan.

He bites my hip softly and then looks up at me.

"More?" he asks.

I nod, and he tugs my nightdress all the way off. Then he positions himself between my legs, pushing my thighs apart. I let out a gasp as his warm breath tickles my slick lower lips. Desire thumps through me, my thighs tremble, and I can hardly stay still as anticipation thrums in my veins.

The first brush of his tongue against my slit has me moaning, toes curling, hands fisting the blankets beneath me. It only gets more intense from there. Our eyes meet again and he doesn't break our gaze as he uses his mouth to please me like only he knows how. It's magic, the way he draws every delicious spark of pleasure out of me. Taking his time, feasting on me, teasing me in cycles and waves like the tide rolling toward release.

I feel the pressure build and recede, build and recede, all the while chasing the high, rocking my hips along with the sensations. It's so good that I know I can't hold out, so I don't even try. Within minutes, my orgasm crests and then pulses in gentle ripples, deep inside me.

"Oh God, Armani," I whisper, riding his face. "Oh my God, *yes*."

Shivering, I pull away a little and draw his face up to mine for another kiss. I can taste myself on his tongue, and it somehow makes me feel even more tender toward him. My climax endures, the contractions soft but lasting, lasting, lasting. It's amazing and new, something I've never experienced. A soothing kind of release, relaxing me even as it shatters me and puts me back together all at once.

"I can't stop coming," I tell him.

He laughs. "You're beautiful."

"No, you are," I say.

We kiss again and he adjusts his hips, the tip of his cock pressing against my wet opening. All I want is for him to pound into me, but he holds back, focusing on our kiss. It's maddening.

Unable to wait any longer, and practically squirming, I lift my hips to encourage him. He seems to get the message, drawing my left leg up and around his waist so my foot rests against his lower back. Finally he enters me in one smooth thrust, dragging a fresh moan out of both of us.

"Yes," I groan as he takes my lips in another kiss. "Mmm."

He pumps in a rhythm that's gentle and regular, all the motion in his hips, allowing me to feel every inch of him as he grinds against me. This isn't how he usually fucks me, but it's incredible. A key aligning perfectly with its lock. No one will ever fit me the way he does.

Still, I'm not sure what to do with this softer version of my husband. I feel good, better than good, but I want—I crave—the other side of him. The one that takes no shit, that seeks revenge, that won't hesitate to make things right with his own two hands. The dominant man who people know better than to cross. I want my alpha male in the bedroom. I *have* to have it.

"Armani," I gasp. "I need—"

He thrusts a little harder and I moan around what I was going to say. His fingers slide into my hair and I wait for the blessed sting of him taking a fistful. He doesn't.

"Armani," I try again. "I need...more."

A growl works from deep in his throat. "More what?"

He pushes into me a little faster, a little harder, lightly fisting my hair.

"*That*. More that."

Another hard thrust, deeper this time, hitting that spot inside me that makes lights explode behind my eyelids.

"Tell me how you like it," he demands.

I gasp for air, losing myself in the feel of him inside me.

"Hard. Faster. Rough. I love it when you're rough with me."

He pulls my hair, hard enough to bring tears to my eyes. Yes. It's exactly what I want.

"*Yes*," I encourage him.

Grabbing my left ankle and setting it up on his shoulder so I'm stretched even wider for him, Armani rams into me, fucking me so hard that the bedframe knocks the wall. Once he unleashes, he doesn't stop. Biting my neck, tugging my hair, holding me in place as he fucks me. When he pinches my clit, my moans pitch even higher. Pleasure and pain mix together, a heady and potent combination. I love this. And he knows it.

"So good," I pant. "Fuck, you're so good."

"You're perfect for me," he grunts.

"I know," I say. Because it's true—I know I am. And I also know that he likes it rough, too.

"Perfect," he repeats, chanting as he thrusts. "Perfect, perfect, perfect."

He might as well be talking dirty, because the admission sends me right over the edge. Throwing my head back, I cry his name as I come, wrapping both of my legs tight around his waist and pulling him as deep inside me as possible. As my pussy pulses around him, he spills into me with a groan, thrusting hard a few more times until we both sink heavily into the mattress.

He rolls onto his side to face me, still breathing hard. I stroke his jaw with my thumb, feeling possessive as I admire him from head to toe.

This is my man. All mine. Powerful, dangerous, and hot as fuck.

"How's the foot?" he asks.

I sit up and check my stitches. They're perfectly intact, though the wound is a little sore.

"All good," I say, crawling over to him and dropping a kiss onto his lips.

He turns so he's on his back and then pulls the blankets up and over us.

In typical male fashion, he's asleep in minutes, the post-coital comedown knocking him out. But my brain won't quiet down. And the dang lights are still on.

Carefully easing out of bed, I gingerly make my way toward the light switch by the door. But a few steps in, I almost trip over Armani's pants, sending something skittering across the floor.

"What the—"

I kneel down and pick up the object. It's heavy, black, made of hard plastic. At first I think it's a walkie-talkie, since it has a short, stubby antenna sticking up from the top of it. But upon further inspection, I see the keypad with numbers on it, the small screen, the little USB port...and I realize it's a phone. A fucking satellite phone. My heart starts to pound. He's had this thing all along, hasn't he?

Which means he lied to me about being able to make calls from here on the island.

And yet.

The anger I'm expecting to rise up in me like a blazing inferno just doesn't make an appearance. I'm a bit annoyed at Armani, but am I mad? *Really* mad? I don't know.

I look over my shoulder at Armani. He's still asleep, but I watch him for a moment to be sure. And, yeah. He's out. I could easily sneak away with this phone and call Juliana right now.

Except I don't think I need rescuing anymore. At this point in the game, I no longer believe that Armani wants to get rid of me. I no longer believe I was ever truly in danger from him. So the fact that I haven't been able to call Juliana up until now...it doesn't bother me that much. I'm not even sure I still feel the need to talk to her. There's no urgency.

A few more seconds of staring at the phone in my hand is enough to make me realize that I'd much rather be warm and safe in bed with Armani's arms around me than hiding out in a linen closet down the hall trying to make contact with my former best friend. So I put the phone back in the pants pocket where it came from, turn off the lights, and then climb back under the covers next to my husband.

He stirs in his sleep, reaching for me and pulling me close. I snuggle my back against his chest, but I don't feel tired. My mind is whirling.

How would Armani's life be different if his mother and sister had lived? Would he be a completely different person? It's obvious that his childhood affected him deeply, viscerally—and the loss of his mom and sister seemed to set things in motion. They were the buffer between him, his brothers, and their father. Everything he's been through, for better or worse, has shaped the man he is today.

At the same time, am I supposed to ignore his dark side simply because he had a shitty childhood? Armani takes revenge as if it were nothing. He doesn't think twice about offing someone who has done his family wrong. He's deadly and dangerous and he knows nothing of humility.

But who am I to judge? I watched him kill a man and it thrilled me that he got his revenge. I screw him every chance I get because I can't get enough of him, body and soul. And honestly? His dark past is something I'm honored he shared with me, whether he did so intentionally or not.

There's no sugarcoating it. Armani Bellanti is a murderer. A criminal. A mobster.

And he's the man I've fallen completely in love with.

15

ARMANI

It's time to check in with Clayton, because so far I haven't heard a peep from him—and that's not like my brother-in-law. The radio silence has me uneasy. When it comes to the mafia, no news is rarely good news.

Usually, it's an indication that your enemy has the upper hand.

I rose with the sun today, like usual, and once I'm dressed and showered, I take a few minutes to check on Candi's stitches. Her wound looks like it's healing well, which is a relief. Not that I doubted my skills, but being this far from the mainland presents certain logistical challenges, so it's good to know my patient is in top form. I change out her gauze and tell her to relax when she mumbles drowsily at me.

"It isn't even seven yet," I add. "And you're on vacation. You can sleep in."

Not that I don't have an ulterior motive for keeping her in bed—because I have to make that call, and the less effort I have to put into hiding the sat phone from Candi, the better.

"Where are you going?" she asks, propping herself up on her elbows to look at me.

"Hush now," I tell her, cupping her chin and rubbing my thumb over her plush lips. "Just lie back and close your eyes and I'll reward you."

She smirks but does as she's asked.

Whipping the blankets off her feet, I go around to the bottom of the bed, grab her by the ankles, and tug her toward me until her ass is right at the edge of the mattress. I gently position her legs so they're wide apart and dangling almost to the floor and then I kneel, burying my face between her thighs. My tongue quickly finds her clit, and I give it a few strong, hard licks before sucking it into my mouth and slowly circling it with my tongue.

"Ahh," she sighs.

I pull back just long enough to mock-scold her. "Those eyes better be closed."

"Mm-hmm."

Satisfied, I dive back in, dipping a finger inside her hole. I pump into her wetness with my finger, keeping time with the lapping of my tongue on her swollen nub.

"Armani," she moans, the sound of her pleasure making my cock go stiff against my fly. "*Yes.* Just like that."

When she grabs the back of my head and starts thrusting against my mouth, I know she's getting close, so I add a second finger. It only takes a few minutes before she's panting out her orgasm, groaning softly as she clenches around me, frantically digging her nails into my hair.

Gasping for an entirely different reason, I finally come

up for air and start kissing and nibbling my way down her inner thigh, over her knee, down her calf. Then I get her tucked back in with the pillows freshly fluffed behind her head, the blankets tucked tightly around her.

"I'm taking a walk," I say, which isn't a total lie. "Get some rest."

"You'll come get me when breakfast is ready?" she murmurs, pulling the covers up to her chin.

"Of course."

I leave then, without saying goodbye. As if to prove to myself that I'm less invested in her than I am. Ha. I've been feeling edgy overall the past few days, but something between Candi and me has felt subtly off-balance lately as well. Our dynamic has shifted. Not necessarily in a negative way, but...I haven't quite wrapped my head around it. And if I'm honest, I have to admit that I'm not entirely sure what I'm doing anymore. What *we're* doing. Things have gotten complicated.

Shaking my head, I try to banish the turmoil. I don't have time to think about Candi right now.

My brother-in-law picks up on the first ring, even though it's after 10 p.m. in California.

"Clayton. Talk to me. What's with the lack of updates?"

I'm downstairs now, in the first floor office. The door and windows are closed, but I turn on the radio for an extra layer of privacy. You never know who might be eavesdropping, intentionally or not.

"I was waiting to hear back from a contact," Clayton says, "but he's been MIA for a few days."

"Shit. That's not a good sign," I say gravely, feeling the hair on the back of my neck rise.

"Nope. Not good at all."

Pacing in front of the window, I ask, "Who was the guy?"

He hesitates, and then says, "Our Bratva go-between. Or at least, he was supposed to be."

"Fuck." I huff out a breath. "Why the hell wasn't I informed when you got him on our side?"

"Because he wasn't on our side yet. That's why."

"Money talks, man. We could've paid him plenty enough rubles to turn on the Bratva."

"The offer I made him was more than generous. But it's not about money, nor loyalty," Clayton says. "The Bratva has no code. They're feral. So if our guy did walk away, it's likely for reasons of self-preservation."

"Right. Or more likely they just killed him," I point out pragmatically.

"Could be. Or could be he got paranoid, or something he heard or saw spooked him. Could be the Russians got wind he'd been cozying up to an outsider and they roughed him up or relocated him."

"I highly doubt they 'relocated' him," I scoff. "Unless it was to a shallow grave."

Clayton lets out a dark chuckle and then gets serious again. "Either way, the odds are that we've lost our inside man. Meanwhile, the unholy union between the Brunos and the Bratva seems to be moving forward. Last thing I heard from my missing contact, the parties involved were discussing a possible meeting in NYC. Nothing firmed up yet, but obviously my intel's out of date now."

Pinching the bridge of my nose, I sink into the chair

behind the desk and take a deep breath. My adrenaline is pumping, the blood rushing in my ears.

"We need to find someone else then, and fast," I say.

"I'm working on it."

"Work faster," I snap. "That meeting might've already happened by now."

"Aye, it might have," he says dryly. "But it's not like we were going to stop it from happening, were we? If we're fucked, we're fucked. How've things been going on your end, by the way?"

"I met with our Sicilian allies and the Marzellos from Trieste. None of them want to see the Brunos form this union. But with the Bratva at play, they're reluctant to get involved."

Clayton makes a sound of disgust, but I can understand where the other families are coming from. The combination of the Brunos and the Russian mob isn't something to be taken lightly. Even so, I know full well that without the protection of other families, Bruno will have the upper hand on us. My brothers and I can't stand alone against such a force. There's simply no way. We don't have a big enough arsenal, and we don't have the manpower.

My gut clenches to think about being at the Brunos' mercy.

Never.

"Regardless of their hesitation," I go on, "I won't stop until they see it my way. And I already told them that if the Bellantis go down, any of them are just as likely to be next—except that each toppled family leaves fewer reinforcements with which to fight back against our mutual enemies."

"They'd better come around real soon," Clayton says.

"Who knows how long it'll be before the shit hits the proverbial fan? You sure you don't want to fly me out to go calling on them? I can be very persuasive, as you know."

"It won't do us any good," I tell him. "All the Italian families are well protected, so they're not going to feel threatened by us. Plus, we don't want to make things ugly. As for bribes, they're wealthy enough on their own. There's nothing we can offer them that'd sway them over to our side."

"I don't understand. These are your family's allies," he points out. "Isn't this the time for them to step up? Sure, the Russians are scary, but Italians are supposed to be honorable."

"They are. Which is why I'm confident they'll come around," I say. "Well. Mostly confident."

"Let's hope that confidence isn't misplaced, then."

I switch gears then, asking Clayton how the hunt for the newly discovered mole is going.

"My money is on one of the bodyguards," I add. "They've got higher security clearance and more mobility. But anyway, Dante said you had a few suspects in mind, said you had the mailbox under surveillance. Anybody step out of line yet, or you still waiting for them to make contact with the enemy?"

Clayton takes a breath. "Yeah. Bit of news there. You're not gonna like it, though."

"Just spit it out."

"It's Donno."

My chest goes tight. "The fuck? Donno Romero? You're sure?"

"Caught him red-handed at the box, I'm sorry to say it."

"Give me a minute," I say quietly. "This is a hard fucking pill to swallow."

"It is. Threw me for a loop, that's for sure, and I know it's not what you wanted to hear."

I drop my forehead onto the cool surface of the desk, the room tilting around me. This is unbelievable. Donno has worked for our family since way before my father's death. The man was my father's personal bodyguard and then mine when I was younger, before I could take care of myself. He's watched over all of us in turn, and has taken the security of our household as his personal mission. What the hell did the Brunos offer him—or threaten him with—to compromise his loyalty after all these years?

Not that it matters. In my line of work, there's no love for traitors.

"Is he in custody?" I finally ask.

"He's in...our custody. Below ground."

"Good. Do whatever it takes to get him talking. We need to know everything he gave the Brunos, everything they have on us now. Show no mercy."

There's a pause. "You sure?"

"I don't need you questioning me," I bark.

"Copy that."

Resisting the urge to throw my phone, I stand up and pace the office again.

"Look, Armani. I know you don't need me telling you so," Clayton says, "but this alliance needs to be crushed ASAP, at all costs. Especially given the Brunos have been working with Donno for God knows how long. They likely know our weaknesses. We can't play a long game here."

"You're preaching to the fucking choir," I tell him. "The

faster we launch an offensive, the better chance we have at destroying them before they're fully organized."

"So we're in agreement then."

"One hundred percent. I'm going to plan a strike. We're going to hit them hard, where it hurts. If we take all their top guys out of the game, they won't be able to recover before we clean up the rest. In the meantime, you work on Donno. We need every last bit of intel we can get from him before he dies."

"I'll go visit our friend now."

"Good. And keep me posted. The second you hear anything worth mentioning, I need you to call. I don't want to hear about it after the fact, like with your Bratva contact."

"Like I said, he and I were only talking," he says. "I wouldn't tell you we had someone on the hook who wasn't. That's the only reason I didn't—"

"Yeah, yeah. I got it," I interrupt. "I just...this Donno thing has me in a shit mood."

"I get it. Just let me handle him and see what I can find out. I'll be in touch."

We hang up, and I stare out the window trying to ground myself, my mind fully blown.

I never would have suspected Donno. Never would have even thought to suspect him. After decades of service, he's practically a member of the family, and I'm not talking about the mob kind of family. Who knows how much longer this would have gone on without Clayton.

There's something else nagging at me, too.

Candi's involvement is nowhere near as far reaching as any of us thought. How much is Donno responsible for, compared to her? Considering the length of time he's been with my family, it's got to be a lot. His history with us means he has a metric fuck ton of information to feed to our enemies.

Why did it have to be him? My gut clenches. I can't believe he's a spy. A traitor.

He deserves to die for his sins. He will die for his sins. Even if the Brunos are blackmailing him in some way, he should have come to me first so I could have helped. His betrayal is inexcusable.

Candi, on the other hand, could still be useful. She's much more low level than I realized, but it doesn't make her less of a playing card.

My wife, it turns out, might be good for me after all.

Maybe it's time to bring her into the fold.

16

CANDI

As we're finishing a leisurely late morning breakfast (complete with baghrir, of course) that the staff set up for us in the villa's bird- and greenery-filled courtyard, Armani sets his coffee cup aside and gives me an appraising glance. Catching his eye, I drag a finger across the honey on my plate and then lick it off slowly, just to see the lust flare in his eyes.

"Good breakfast?" he murmurs.

"So good. I'm thinking we should bring the chef home with us."

"I'll certainly offer him the option," Armani says.

"Make sure it's an offer he can't refuse," I joke.

My husband stops short of laughing, but he can't keep the smile off his face.

Smiling back, I toast him with my teacup and drain the last of the cooling mint tea.

"How's the foot?"

I shrug. "As good as can be expected. You checked it earlier, didn't you?"

"No pain?" he presses.

"Why? You planning to take me on an adventure today?" I tease. "Because if so, I'm sure I can hobble along, I just can't put too much pressure on it. So maybe no hiking. Well, or swimming."

He smirks. "You'll be off your feet, for the most part."

"Oh really?" My cheeks flush as memories of him eating me out this morning flit through my mind. I could certainly handle another few rounds of *that*.

"Really," he says, his eyes trailing lazily down my body and back up again.

My pulse is pounding, liquid desire already pooling at my core. "Then I'm in."

I start to push my chair back to stand, but Armani grabs my wrist.

"Not in that nightgown, you're not. Go get dressed. I'll be waiting for you."

So commanding. So confident. So caveman. Guess the old Armani is back.

Not that I mind, not even one tiny bit.

In the closet, I find a flirty pink sundress and pair it with some comfy black slip-on sneakers, because foot injury. Still, the outfit looks cute enough. Then I put on sunscreen, a few swipes of waterproof mascara, and run a brush through my hair. A lightweight backpack gets slung over one shoulder with my sunglasses and water bottle inside. The only thing I can't find is my floppy hat.

When I get downstairs, however, I find Armani in the entryway with my hat in his hands.

"Ah. There's my hat."

He puts it in my backpack, zips me back up, and then

pulls me in for a kiss. A long one. By the time he pulls away, I'm out of breath and tingling all the way down to my toes.

"Are you sure you don't want to just...go back to bed?" I ask.

"Not yet." He leans in for another kiss and then adds, "We'll have plenty of time for that later."

I can hardly be disappointed as he wraps an arm around my waist and leads me toward the front door. Leaning into him, I let out a happy sigh. This is the most focused Armani has been on me since we arrived on the island, barring the minor foot surgery in the kitchen yesterday. And if he seriously planned this whole day around taking me out for fun? I'd call that the honeymoon of my dreams. Especially considering the fact that my morning orgasm was apparently only the first of many.

As we step outside, curiosity washes over me. What on earth does he have in store?

There's hardly time to speculate, because the first thing I see in the driveway is a classic-looking, red-and-white motorcycle waiting for us. It's similar to bikes I've seen in old movies or foreign films. The keys dangle from the ignition. I look up at Armani suspiciously and then slowly shake my head.

"Please tell me that is not for us."

He goes over to the motorcycle and takes a helmet off the back, then hands it to me.

"Well, you can't walk the distance for what I've got planned today. And although I'd be happy to piggyback you, I'm not sure it'd be comfortable after the first mile. So... motorcycle it is."

"That thing is a million years old. Does it even run?"

"*Does it even run?* You kidding me?" he sputters. "This is a 1955 Royal Enfield Continental GT! It's a classic! And *yes*, it was one of the last to roll off the production line before manufacturing was moved to India. And *yes*, it is both incredibly awesome and incredibly hard to find in this condition, so *yes*, Marco is going to have a shit fit of supreme jealousy when he finds out that you got to ride on it."

"If making your baby brother insanely jealous isn't enough of an endorsement for me to ride this thing, I guess I don't know what is," I concede, slipping the helmet on.

Armani fastens the strap under my chin and instructs me to get on the bike behind him and wrap my arms around his waist. As I get myself situated, I notice what looks like a woven picnic basket strapped to the back. I grin to myself, but I don't ask. I'll let whatever he has planned unfold naturally.

He starts the engine, revs it a few times, and then pushes back the kickstand.

"Hang on tight," he says.

Nodding, I squeeze him in a death grip and rest my head against his back. With a heart-stopping jolt, we take off down the driveway. I let out a little yelp that has Armani laughing, the low rumble vibrating against my chest. Bright green tropical plants fly by, the fresh air cool against my face, and I have to admit, this is exhilarating. And fun.

After slowing down to pass through the perimeter gate and wave at the security guard, we zip along a bumpy dirt trail that serves as a road down the mountainside. It feels like we ride forever, even though I know we're on a small island. I start to wonder if he's taking us in circles just to prolong the experience, but if he is, I don't mind. He's an expert driver, I quickly realize. The sea breeze smells fresh and salty, and I relax enough to close my eyes and just breathe in the scent of ocean mixed with Armani's cologne. I hope I never forget how I feel in this moment.

Eventually, we make our way up a hill, on a narrow path that leads to the top of an incline. He parks the bike, helps me remove my helmet, and grabs the picnic basket. Then he takes my hand.

"You okay to walk a short distance?"

"I'm fine. You can stop fussing."

Armani lets me set the pace, which I appreciate. I'm definitely more than a little slow since I have to walk on my left heel so the sutures on the sole of my foot don't rub inside my shoe. But he doesn't say a word, just strolls casually at my side, his fingers interlaced with mine. I am loving the comfortable silence. It's not something we've ever had much of an opportunity to share.

We reach a stand of young trees, and I can hear water rushing before we see it. A few more paces through the forest and the landscape suddenly opens wide to reveal a breathtaking cascade, tumbling down a series of rock steps before pouring into a pool below us. Rainbows shimmer in the misty spray, the droplets glittering as sunlight bounces off them.

"Wow," I breathe. "This is incredible. Our own private waterfall."

Armani sets the basket down and leads me closer.

The mist dances across our faces from this proximity, cool and refreshing after our hike through the dense trees. Laughing, I push the hair out of my face and step back. If we stand this close for much longer, we'll get soaked.

"If we hike a little farther down the trail, we can get into the pool at the base of the waterfall. I know you said no swimming, but—"

"No. I want to go. Maybe I can just keep one leg out of the water."

He hitches a brow. "Actually, I brought something for that."

Out of the basket comes a plastic bag and a roll of duct tape.

"Seriously?"

"It should keep you dry enough," he says.

And I laugh, because it's perfect, and because I'm completely stunned that Armani planned our trip to the waterfall right down to waterproofing my injured foot. I can't believe it was only days ago that I feared for my life. My husband has surprised me yet again with this thoughtful, gentler side of himself.

We carefully make our way down to the base of the waterfall, where a pool of crystal-clear blue water spreads out before us. At the far end of the pool, the water spills over the edge and pounds onto more rocks below. It then creates a river which runs out into the ocean.

Armani sets the basket on the ground, pulls out a woven blanket to spread over the damp earth, and then goes over to the water to test the temperature with a swipe of his hand.

"How is it?" I ask.

"Warm, like bath water."

"You think it's deep?"

He grins. "Only one way to find out."

With that, he stands and pulls his shirt off. I get instant butterflies at the sight of his bare torso, his tattoos, his tight abs. My mouth is watering. He notices my ogling and saunters over to me.

"Why don't you take a seat on that rock," he says, "and I'll take care of your foot first."

He makes quick work of wrapping the plastic around my foot and ankle and then securing it with duct tape to make it watertight. I slip out of my sundress, glad I wore one of my new matching bra and panty sets today, which Armani seems to appreciate.

"I like you in blue," he says.

"I like you in nothing," I shoot back.

Instead of smart-assing me in response, he unceremoniously drops his shorts and steps out of them. He's not wearing underwear, either. He's completely naked. My pulse instantly picks up.

Turning his back to me, he walks over to the pool and steps right in. It's shallow initially, but quickly deepens, the water climbing to his mid-thigh. I find myself licking my lips at the sight of his firm ass, daydreaming about gripping him tight as he pumps into me, urging him on, faster, harder—

"Look at all the fish," he says, interrupting my reverie.

"Fish?"

He looks over his shoulder and motions for me to join him.

I enter the warm water and gingerly make my way over to Armani. When I reach him, he positions me so I'm standing in front of him and then wraps his arms around my waist.

"Look," he whispers.

Peering down into the crystalline depths, I can't miss them. Small fish, hundreds of them, not more than a few inches long. They're beautiful, swimming in tightly packed schools, their scales flashing bright colors. Some are a silvery blue, some are turquoise, some are a bright, almost fluorescent green. All of them have patterns of bright red stripes or speckles along their flanks.

The water is so clear, I can see all the way to the rocky bottom of the pool, which is made up of smooth rocks, each carpeted in delicate green moss and leafy, undulating plants. Some of the fish swim around our legs, brushing against us without a care.

"This is amazing!" I whisper excitedly. "They're fearless."

Armani leads me closer to the waterfall until we're standing right next to it. The gentle force of the spray drenches us in no time. He laughs as I shake the water out of my hair, right into his face. I look up at him and have a sudden rush of breath. He looks like a fantasy come to life, standing here naked beside this magical tropical waterfall. We're truly in paradise. I don't want it to end.

He grows serious as he pulls me close, cupping my face and leaning in for a kiss. It's so perfect that I can almost forget that this whole thing—the honeymoon, the marriage, the relationship—is all a ruse. But either way, I see no reason not to enjoy myself.

Feeling him stiffen against my thigh, I reach down and give him a squeeze.

"Is it later yet?" I tease, stroking him gently in the warm water.

Instead of answering, he lifts me in his arms and carries me out of the water and over to the picnic blanket. After gently laying me on my back, he slowly peels off my soaked underwear and unclasps my bra, leaving me all but trembling for him. I reach to put my arms around his neck, but he crawls over to the basket and digs around until he finds what he's looking for.

"A plum?" I ask.

He nods, then straddles me and holds the fruit in front of my mouth.

"Not just any plum. The best plum you will ever taste," he says.

When he lowers it, I take a tentative bite. The second my teeth break the deep purple skin, sweetness explodes in my mouth. It's rich, honey-sweet, decadent. The juice leaks down my chin, the flesh firm and slick, the perfect mix of sweet and tart. I let out a little sigh and Armani takes his own bite.

Our eyes lock as we take turns eating the fruit and kissing in between bites. I can't explain it, but it's one of the most erotic experiences of my life. When we finish, we take turns sucking the juice off each other's fingers and lips and tongues, groaning softly, our movements growing more and more urgent, more feral, more hungry, until suddenly Armani is inside me, his thrusts hot and urgent and perfectly timed with the rolling of my hips. I want this. I need it. I have to have it. Have to have *him*.

We're in the middle of the forest, the waterfall thundering nearby. There's not a soul on this island that will be able to hear my cries. Knowing it sets me free, and I let myself moan as loudly as I want, my voice deep and throaty and sensual, nothing holding me back. I lock my ankles around his waist and grab his ass, feeling the muscles there flexing as he strokes hard into me. It's so good. So perfect. So fucking perfect.

The orgasm hits me in waves, each deeper and more toe-curling than the last. My eyes flutter, my mouth falling open as I gasp for breath, and then Armani covers my lips with his own as he comes inside me with a shudder. I can feel his entire body go tense and then relax, and when he tries to roll off of me I wrap my arms tighter around him to keep him exactly where he is.

"Stay," I whisper. "Right there. Don't move."

After a while, once we've caught our breath and our bodies have cooled, Armani takes the plastic off my foot and we get our clothes back on. Then he unpacks the picnic. It's simple but perfect: more fruit, bread and cheeses, olives and hummus, peppers and carrots and radishes and tomato salad. There's water and wine and slices of Moroccan citrus cake, which Armani says is called meskouta.

Smiling at him, I tease, "You know...if you're not careful, you just might make a girl fall."

"Maybe I'm trying to make her fall," he says.

That takes me completely by surprise.

"You already put a ring on it," I remind him. "A little forcibly, but still. You don't really have to try."

"But I want to," he says.

He leans over to tuck a lock of hair behind my ear and then brushes his thumb over my bottom lip before giving me a quick kiss. And as we eat, I realize that everything about this day has been perfect. Perfect for me, anyway.

I couldn't have imagined a better honeymoon if I'd tried.

17

ARMANI

I DON'T LIE to women. Usually.

Not because I'm a paragon of integrity, but because I have no need. Generally speaking—and yes, maybe this is my father's influence casting its shadow—the less that's said, the better. This method of operation applies to anyone I deal with. The reason is simple: control. Hold your cards close to the vest and you'll always have the upper hand.

Furthermore, what does come out of my mouth when I talk is as direct, purposeful, and as to the point as possible. Ergo, I'm a man whose words are taken at face value. Taciturn, laconic, reserved, take your pick of adjective. It's a trait that historically has served me well. Very well.

When it comes to women specifically, I find that more often than not, this translates to me getting what I want with minimal effort. I never offer platitudes or promises; it's simply not how I operate. Instead, a woman knows within seconds of meeting me if she's amenable to what I have to offer. Namely, unapologetic straightforwardness, dominance in and out of the bedroom, and zero emotional involvement.

I don't play games. I know exactly who I am and what I'm about, and I don't try to hide those things. I've found it's the most convenient arrangement for all parties. A woman I've set my sights on can either come along for the ride or walk away. Her choice. It's no skin off my back either way.

But over the course of this trip, I've come to realize that during my time with Candi Gallagher, my entire foundation for interacting with women has crumbled to dust.

Despite the fact that I know better. Despite the fact that showing weakness or emotion in front of her is a death sentence. She's already proven that she can see straight through me, that she can somehow coax things out of me that I thought I'd buried too deep to ever be retrieved. That makes her unspeakably dangerous. Not just to me, but to the entire Bellanti family.

Unfortunately, I can't kill her. I couldn't order it, either. In fact, in all honesty, I wouldn't hesitate to destroy anyone who even tried to lay a finger on her. That much is certain.

Being protective of her doesn't undermine me, of course. Giving her pleasure and taking my own doesn't compromise me, either. I have plenty of experience with these things. Getting attached, though?

Big fucking red flag.

The emotion my brothers show their wives has always been foreign to me. As far as I'm concerned, it's a weakness. Though of course, everyone has them. Soft spots, vulnerabilities, an Achilles' heel. All I can do is keep extra vigilant and uphold my commitment to protect the Bellanti clan. I can't afford to acquire the same weaknesses that my brothers have.

And yet. I can't deny the fact that Frankie and Karina have brought something back to Dante and Marco. Something intangible. Something that my brothers and I all lost when our mom and our sister Lili died. I can't pinpoint what it is exactly. A softness, maybe. An openness. The kind of thing we had to let go of in the face of our father's tyranny and rage. We built up our defenses, and we lost our innocence.

We also lost the childhood joy we'd experienced when our mother was alive, but now it's almost as if I can see glimmers of it in my brothers again. They smile more. Laugh. Tell jokes. The way Dante looks at his baby girl, the serenity he radiates when she's asleep on his chest. As for Marco, he's mellowed out, too. He and Karina don't have any kids yet, but it seems like he's stopped trying to burn all the bad memories out of his mind with rash decisions and dangerous rivalries and reckless racing.

An uncomfortable part of me envies them, but I can't let myself fall into the same trap that they have. Not with so many threats weighing on me every day. Our lives are once again uncertain and unsafe. It's hard to believe my brothers and I ever thought we could walk away from the mob.

So no, I won't indulge Candi's fantasy version of our marriage. That's not what we have. We keep each other company. We fuck. She does what I tell her to do, including delivering false intel to the Brunos. She's useful to me for the moment, which is why I'm keeping her around. That's it.

The problem is, I can't stop thinking about our day at

the waterfall, and I don't know why. It's like...seeing her smile and laugh and marvel at nature, the way her pupils dilated as we shared that plum, the loud, lusty cries I drew out of her while we were having sex, the feel of her warm, welcoming body beneath me, all of it just...it *moved me*.

It wasn't just yesterday, either. If I'm honest, something shifted for me when she cut her foot open at the beach and I saw all that blood...even knowing logically that it was a minor injury, I felt anxiety and adrenaline pump through me the instant I realized she was hurt. I couldn't take care of her fast enough. I was compelled. I had to make it better.

Aside from my brothers, I've never experienced that kind of urgent, primal protectiveness toward anyone before.

What is happening to me?

"Car's all packed," Candi says from the bedroom doorway. "You ready?"

"Yes. Let's go."

We head downstairs, climb into the car, and make our way to the island's tiny airstrip.

Once we're aboard the private jet, Candi settles into her seat across from me and requests plain soda water with lemon from the flight attendant. I wave the woman away when she asks if I'd like a drink, turning to stare out the window instead. I'm trying to avoid interacting with my wife.

My thoughts are a dark tangle. I'd convinced myself that I'd be able to work Candi out of my system on this trip —through relentless fucking, or various other means—but my feelings are as conflicted as ever. Maybe even worse now. Compounding my foul mood is the fact that we're taking off in just a few minutes. I couldn't be less thrilled about the prospect. I'm in no hurry to leave.

For her part, Candi's made it abundantly clear that she can't stand being here with me. But it's different for me. Here, we're safe. Hidden. Untouchable. Back home, a mountain of problems is waiting for us.

After our day at the waterfall, I finally realized just how much I'd missed out on the peace and quiet around us. I'd spent most of my time on the island conducting business instead of taking advantage of the fact that I was supposed to be on vacation. Not that my work or my calls or my meetings weren't necessary, what with the Brunos entertaining the Bratva and making moves behind my back. But still, I was robbed of the chance to relax.

I have no idea when the last time I relaxed was.

———

THE ENGINES ARE REVVING, the captain's voice coming over the PA to tell us about our flight time and how the weather is looking in Northern California. When the flight attendant takes over with her safety information spiel, I lean back in my seat, shut my eyes, and clench my jaw. I'm not afraid of flying, I just don't particularly enjoy takeoff and landing. Statistically speaking, they're the most likely times for a fatal accident to occur.

My entire body tenses as the plane begins to taxi. As we pick up speed, I take a deep breath. That's when I feel Candi's hand slide over mine. I keep my eyes closed as I wrestle with my inconvenient emotions. I've been terse and distant with her all morning, yet here she is comforting me.

The warmth of her touch seeps through my body and soothes my frayed nerves. She really is a good person.

But I'm not, and that's where the line will always be drawn.

The pilot lets us know when we've reached cruising altitude, and that's when I sit up and pat Candi's hand to let her know I'm fine.

"I think I've changed my mind, actually," I tell the flight attendant. "Scotch and water please, when you get a moment."

Candi reclines in her seat, pulling a sleep mask over her eyes. Good. I can brood in peace.

Drink in hand, I look out the window again. The sky is dark and threatening rain, one of the reasons we're leaving slightly earlier than planned. The other is that Donno hasn't been cooperating.

"He's basically given up already," Clayton had told me when he called earlier.

"Meaning what?"

"Meaning he knows he's going to die, and he's not interested in talking. He'll probably have a heart attack before we get anything out of him."

"Fair point," I had said, "but that doesn't mean we stop trying. We have no idea how long he's been double-crossing us. We need to know what our enemies have on us because of him."

"He seems determined not to crack."

"Then stop trying to crack him. See if you can soften him up a little. Tell him we'll let him live out his remaining years quietly, under mob surveillance, if he cooperates."

Clayton had paused, and then asked, "Will we? Let him live?"

I'd let out a cruel laugh at that.

It was after 1 a.m. in Napa, and Donno had been in the Deep Cellar for over twenty-four hours without divulging a single thing of use to Clayton. Our prisoner refused to say who he was working with, what information he'd given them so far, how much he was being paid. He hadn't given up a damn thing.

Which means I'll have to go to work on him myself. There's no time to waste.

I take a long pull of the scotch and allow myself three seconds of despair over what's going to happen to the bodyguard who used to take me and my brothers to school, and then I tell myself to get the hell over it. What Donno has done to my family is unforgivable. He has to pay.

"Hey, Armani?" Candi says.

Glancing over at her, I see she's pushed her mask up like a headband. She looks wide awake. So much for napping and leaving me in peace.

"What?" I snap.

She lifts a brow, studying me with that penetrating gaze. "May I have my phone back?"

"Sure."

I get my bag out of the overhead and rifle through it until I find her cell. When I power it back on, it's still got a good charge on it.

"Here," I say, handing it to her. "Enjoy the Wi-Fi."

But she just shoves it into her bag and then pulls out a dog-eared Italian-English dictionary.

Slyly but haltingly, she tells me, *"Sto inizianda...ad apprezzare...di più la lingua Italiana."*

"You're starting to appreciate Italian more?" I repeat back to her. "It's *iniziando*, actually."

"Iniziando! You knew what I meant, though," she gloats.

"You're doing well."

Visibly pleased with herself, she takes out a legal pad covered in vocabulary words and verb conjugations and starts writing more notes. When the flight attendant comes over to check on us, Candi proudly orders another club soda in Italian. I might think it was cute if I wasn't so stressed out right now.

Looking over at me, she says, *"Voglio ringra...ziarti...per ieri."*

"You want to thank me for yesterday?" I ask, making sure she said what she meant to say.

She nods, visibly blushing, and then drops her eyes to the notebook, where she's written something out for herself. *"So che questo viaggio..."*

In my head, I translate into English instantly: *I know that this trip...*

"non e stato davvero uno luna di miele..." she goes on.

Wasn't really a honeymoon...

"In Italian, they call it *viaggio di nozze*," I interrupt. "Wedding trip."

Candi smiles. "I think *luna di miele* is prettier, even if it's more literal."

"Suit yourself," I tell her. "But a real Italian won't—"

"Let me finish!" she says teasingly. *"Ma vedendo quella cascata con voi—"*

But seeing that waterfall with you...

"*Con tu,*" I correct.

"*Con tu...sarà sempre una delle...esperienze più magiche...della mia vita.*"

I put it all together and replay her words in my mind: *I know this trip wasn't a real honeymoon, but seeing that waterfall with you will always be one of the most magical experiences of my life.*

My throat goes tight. I take a gulp of scotch and then say, "You're welcome."

God, I want off this plane. I have no intention of continuing this conversation.

Some of my father's classic words of wisdom suddenly come to me unbidden: *Women are for men to enjoy, and discard once we're done with them. They're disposable goods. Don't forget that, boys.*

The man may have been an asshole, but he had a point. Keeping emotions out of the equation makes everything easier. I can have a wife and not love her. It's not what my brothers have, but that doesn't mean it won't work for me.

My father wasn't someone I'd ever wish to emulate, but maybe it's too late for me to pretend I'm not just like him. Cold and unforgiving. Calculating. Mercenary. Not the type to nurture someone else. Obviously, the last thing I should be doing right now is giving Candi false hope that there can ever be more between us than the marriage of convenience I tricked her into.

Getting out of my seat abruptly, I say, "I'm moving to the back of the plane to do some work."

"Want some company?" she asks, already gathering up her notebook and dictionary.

Without a moment's hesitation, I say, "No."

I can see the effect of my rejection register on her face like a slap.

Tempted to explain myself or at least apologize, I decide against it and simply walk away.

Let her pout until we land, for all I care.

18

ARMANI

My skin creeps with a chill as I descend the stairway to the Deep Cellar.

Pausing outside the arched wooden door at the bottom, I hesitate before knocking. I can hear the sound of my heavy, thudding pulse rushing in my ears. Whatever comes next is going to change things. I'm fully aware of that. Regardless, I'm prepared to do what needs to be done.

Which is why I came straight here the second Donovan dropped me and Candi off at home after he picked us up from the airport. I didn't even go upstairs, I just sent Candi away with our luggage and instructions to get some food and take a nap, and then I drove one of the UTVs to the cellar compound. The staff at the Bellanti estate will see to her needs. As for me, I have my own priorities.

It's not like I have a choice. I've got to remember who I am: Armani Alessandro Bellanti, the dangerous brother, the violent enforcer, the family protector. Hell, my middle name means "defender of men." It's up to me to take care of business, just like I always do. And then handle whatever comes next.

Clayton nods at me when he opens the door. He steps aside and I stroll into the huge concrete chamber. A familiar form sits with his back to me on a folding chair in the center of the dimly lit room. I don't need a clear visual to know that it's Donno. Bound tightly, head lolling, shoulders sagging.

I also take note of how snowy white and thin his hair has gotten. It's shaved, showing pink scalp through the stubs. It hits me suddenly, how old he is.

Movement from the corner catches my attention. In the shadows, I make out Marco and Dante, slouching against the wall. My brothers step forward, their mouths set hard and expressions grim.

"The fuck are you two doing here?" I ask.

"Nice to see you, too. Welcome home," Dante says.

I don't like this. Not one bit.

"Get out of here, both of you," I practically growl. "This isn't a show."

Marco pulls his bottom lip between his teeth. It's something he used to do as a kid when he was anxious, to the point of chewing it bloody and raw. I haven't seen him resort to that in, hell, forever.

"I mean it, Marco," I say as authoritatively as I can, hoping that if I sway my youngest brother, Dante will go along with him. "You don't belong here."

"I'm staying," he says, shaking his head. "I want to hear for myself what he has to say. The man who used to drive my ass to school and taught me how to shoot a no-fail three pointer."

A low cough. A gurgle. "Ah, Marco, you...made it every time," Donno wheezes.

His jagged voice makes my gut clench.

"You're damn right. Every time," Marco echoes, unable to keep the emotion from his voice.

Looking over at Clayton, I ask, "How far did you get?"

He shrugs. "I didn't. I've been goin' easy on him, like you asked. Says he'll only talk to you."

It had occurred to me on the plane that Donno might pull that card, so I've tried to mentally prepare myself for this moment. The fact is, I know I can't show mercy. Even though it's Donno.

Even when he starts pleading for his life.

Giving my brothers a warning scowl, I walk in front of the chair and crouch before the old man. He attempts to smile with bloodied, cracked lips.

"Welcome...home, Armani."

"Donno. This isn't how I expected to see you when I got back."

"I'm sure...it's not."

Clayton was true to his word. Donno doesn't look all that bad, considering. His face is swollen and his lip is split and bloody, but he still has one good eye.

"You know what I'm going to ask," I tell him.

He grunts in agreement followed by a coughing fit. Standing again, I shrug out of my jacket. My double shoulder holsters are visible, as are the pistols they hold. Crouching again, I rest my forearms on my knees and level him with a blank stare.

"Talk. Please. Don't make this any harder on yourself."

A rueful smile curves his lips. "You know this game, Armani. You...know I can't do...that."

"You've always been like family," I remind him. "So why don't we try this the easy way? Name your price."

He seems to wilt a little with relief. His body goes slack against his bonds as if he'd been waiting to hear those exact words. There are many ways to get information from someone; pain doesn't always have to be the accelerator. Especially not when it comes to family.

"I only got one grandson," Donno says. "His mother won't talk to me no more, you know, me being in the life and all. A cousin told me my grandkid got accepted to Harvard medical..."

"Tuition? Done."

Donno shakes his head. "No, dammit. No." He goes silent and when he speaks again, his voice is thick. "Just put a copy of his Harvard diploma on my grave. That's all I ask."

Fuck.

"Is that really how you want to play this?" I say.

"Both of us know you can't let me walk out of here alive," Donno says. "I'll talk, but I need your word that you'll bring me that diploma after I'm gone."

"You have my word," I say.

"Jesus Christ," Marco says under his breath.

He storms past us to pull the heavy cellar door open, then walks out without looking back. The harsh slam of the door shutting behind him reverberates through the room. I can feel it in my chest.

Centering myself, I eye my prey. "Tell me, Donno. What exactly did you give the Brunos?"

"Documents, mostly. Financials. Contracts you've made

with other families. Outstanding debts owed to you. Things too in-depth to take photos of. Copies were better."

I take a deep breath, bile burning my throat. "Money is one thing. But there's more to it, isn't there? You fed them all the intel they needed to hurt us. For years."

In the corner, Dante moves out of the shadows and into the light.

"How could you?" he says, his voice full of disgust.

"I never thought you'd get shot, Dante," Donno says. "At the raid. You wasn't supposed to get hurt."

"Whatever that bullet did, it's nothing compared to the damage you've done to me," Dante says. "Me and my entire family."

It takes some time, but Donno divulges his full list of misdeeds and the outcomes, in excruciating detail. It's clear that he's been carrying the guilt of his betrayal for some time. And he should be.

He's had a hand in everything. From Dante's wife and her sister's brutal assault to their sister Livvie's kidnapping, from Marco's wife Karina's abduction to the appearance of the armed thugs who crashed my wedding reception, not to mention the Bellanti warehouse fire my brothers and I had assumed was Candi's fault and countless other aggressions. The raid setup that nearly killed Dante. The tampering to Marco's race car that made him crash during a race. The death of our employee Monica.

Pretty much every catastrophe that has hurt or compromised my family and our livelihood over the last few years came from intel that Donno fed to the Brunos.

"I never meant it to go this far," he says. "It started out small. Jobs your father was lining up, horse races he planned to fix. Once he died, it...it turned into something else. I got in over my head."

Anger heats my face. "I'm shocked we're not all *dead* because of you. What the fuck did you think Bruno was going to do with the information you were spoon-feeding him?"

"I fucked up."

"You did. Fatally."

He closes his eyes. "After Enzo died, I panicked. I had debts to pay and you and your brothers wanted out. I thought, how was I going to keep getting my cut? Your dad always gave me a share for taking care of things, you know. But I gambled a little. Made some enemies. Couldn't afford to pay back any of that if my cut wasn't coming no more. Bruno knew I was in a bad way. He—he said he'd make it all go away if I agreed to work a little harder. Dig a little deeper for him. So. That's what I did."

"You sold us out."

"I didn't want to," he says.

"But you did all the same."

The worst part is, my brothers and I *were* out. We had stepped back from our father's illegal activities after his death—no, murder—and had agreed to go legit and transition our family business to wine and wine alone. We had every intention of parting ways with the mob once and for good.

And then, suddenly, shit started hitting the fan. We found out our father's car accident was no accident at all. Then Marco's car got rigged, Dante's wife was threatened, and shady characters started popping up. When Dante found out Frankie was pregnant, and realized that the future of the entire Bellanti legacy was on the line, he pulled rank as the head of the family and formally exchanged our loyalty for the continued protection and support of our mafia allies. It was the only way to keep us safe.

It's only now that I'm realizing the full extent of the forces that had been at play. It was no coincidence that the threats started piling up at almost the exact same time my brothers and I decided to get out of the life. Because that was exactly when Donno began feeding the Bruno beast, giving those fucks all the ammunition they needed to make a strike. Which means this man, who I've known my entire life, who I've trusted for decades, is responsible for bringing us back into the fold.

"You forced us back into the mob."

He shakes his head. "I didn't mean to."

"YOU forced us back in. Fuck!"

Standing, I snake a hand through my hair and pace in front of him, trying to calm down.

"What ever happened to loyalty, Donno? Huh? What about that?"

"I fucked up, Armani. I said I did."

"You helped start a *war*. Now tell me about the fucking Bratva."

His brow knits. "The...Bratva? What've they got to do with this?"

Pissed, I draw my Walther and aim it at his head. "Don't act like you don't know! The Brunos are forming an alliance with the Russians. I want to know when that contract is being signed."

I flick off the safety, my finger firm on the trigger.

"Armani," Dante calls. "Wait."

Without taking my eyes off Donno, I say, "Fuck waiting. Talk, Donno. The contract."

His wrists are bound to the arms of the chair, but he manages to put his hands up slightly in surrender. "I swear I don't know. Bruno don't tell me nothing. He takes what I give him and pays me."

Dante pulls me aside. Tucking the gun away, I dip my head as he speaks in my ear.

"If all the shit that's happened is on him, what about Candi?" he says. "None of this was her."

"Which is what I've been trying to tell you," I say. "No matter. I'll sort it out later. Let me clean this up first." I'm about to turn back to Donno but pause. Is Dante actually trying to defend my wife? "Why do you care? You hate Candi."

"I never said that. I just...don't trust her. But maybe we need to rethink her position."

With that, he claps me on the shoulder and leaves. Clayton is the only one left to bear witness now. He's leaning against a table on the far side of the cellar, arms crossed.

"Leave us," I tell him.

He does, and the room goes still. Donno's breath is shallow and silent, to the point that I watch his chest for movement to make sure he's still alive.

Finally, he lifts his head. "I'd have you tell those boys I'm sorry, but I know it won't do no good."

"It won't. You broke Marco's heart."

His voice is almost imperceptible. "I know."

"Once Dante and I got older, we weren't there for him

much anymore. But you were. You picked him up every day from school. Played some ball. You even watched a few of his games. He'd look for you in the stands, you know. You showed up more than our dad ever did."

"I'm not a good man."

"You can be a bad man and still make good choices." Shaking my head, I add, "I wish you'd come to me about your financials. We would have helped you."

"Nah. My debts were in Bruno hands."

"I would have paid them off."

"Could never ask that of you."

"It was the least I could have done to repay you for being good to us."

He looks away, eyes glistening. I expect him to beg now, to apologize, to ask for another chance.

But he doesn't. And a part of me withers, because I can't give him another chance if he doesn't ask. And even if he does ask, I have to deny him.

"I'll put the diploma on your grave myself," I say.

He nods. "I'm ready."

Pulling the Walther from my holster again, I take aim. I watch. I always watch. If I'm going to take a life, I'm damn well going to see it through, so I never forget who I am and what I'm capable of.

But this one I don't need to see to know that I'll feel it in my heart until the day I die.

I close my eyes.

And pull the trigger.

19

CANDI

THE FIRST THING I did when I got back to Casa Bellanti was collect my cat from the chef's assistant, take a hot shower, and crawl into bed for a nap. I was jet-lagging hard, and Armani had abandoned me to attend to some "business" pretty much the second Donovan dropped us off in the driveway. But after alternating between dozing and tossing and turning for a few hours, I finally give up on sleep and set myself to the task I'd been dreading ever since Armani gave me my phone back: dealing with the Brunos.

Or, more specifically, dealing with Juliana.

I'm sitting in the cushy armchair by the window in my and Armani's bedroom, Mr. Sprinkles curled up in my lap, my stomach churning as I read (and listen to) all of my (former?) best friend's messages. Her tone goes from casual to annoyed to concerned and then wavers between worried and pissed off. Typical Juliana.

Not that I blame her. With no warning, I dropped off the face of the planet for a week, and with my phone turned off, all her calls were going straight to voicemail. I guess it's a good thing I was only gone for a week, because I'm sure she's about to call the police or show up on the Bellantis' doorstep demanding to see me. Jules isn't the type to just sit around and wait for a body to show up.

It's almost funny. On the island, I couldn't wait to hear her voice, but now that I'm back in Napa, I feel sick just thinking about dialing her number. I have no idea what I should say. She knows that Armani and I got married in a quickie Vegas ceremony, but all I had said about our elopement was that it was my idea, that I had him wrapped around my finger...which might be the most egregious lie I've ever told. Jules has no idea I've been compromised, that Armani's plan is to have me playing both sides.

Now, I'm terrified to face Juliana. What happens if I slip up and give myself away? Or if she sniffs out my lies? If the truth comes out about me, the Brunos won't want to use me as a mole anymore. They'll tell me nothing. They might even kill me. And even if they don't, I'll still be useless to the Bellantis as a double agent. I know Armani cares about me—at least, I think he does—but ultimately, Dante is in charge of their family. If he tells Armani to divorce me, where will I go? What will I do? How will I ever feel safe from the mob after getting cast out by not one, but *two* notorious mafia clans?

My entire future seems dangerously uncertain.

Taking a deep breath, I go to Juliana's contact and hover my finger over the call button. *One, two, three, call.* My finger doesn't move. *Come on. Just tap the damn button.* Still, I don't budge. *You can do this, Candi. You've called her a million times, it's no big deal. Let's get this over with. Aaaaand GO.*

But even with all the silent pep talking, I still can't force myself to call her. My pulse is pounding in my ears, and my hands are shaking. I need to work up to it a little more, I guess.

First things first, I go downstairs to the kitchen to make myself another cup of tea. Something calming, soothing, stress relieving...and then I find it. A tin of lavender honey chamomile. Perfect. Steaming cup in hand, I'm about to head back to the bedroom when I pass the Bellantis' home office. Oddly, the door is cracked open. Someone is pacing inside the room.

I hesitate outside for what must be a moment too long, because suddenly the door flies open and I'm face to face with Armani. Shit. This is not a good look.

"I wasn't eavesdrop—" I start to say, lifting my tea as if in explanation.

Armani shakes his head at me, gesturing to the phone pressed to his ear. I didn't even realize he was talking to someone.

"*Non buono abbastanza,*" he says coolly into the phone, and even with my limited Italian, I can translate it: Not good enough.

Sorry, I mouth to him, about to tiptoe away and leave him to his call. But he rests his hand on my shoulder and steers me into the room, gently closing the door behind us.

I'm led to the couch, where I sit down and proceed to slowly sip my tea. Armani goes back to his pacing, something I've noticed all the Bellantis do when they're angry or upset or otherwise in some kind of turmoil. Clearly, this isn't a productive call he's having.

The person on the phone must be done talking, because Armani starts barking at them in rapid Italian again. The words roll off his tongue so quickly, I barely recognize anything aside from *no*. Which must be why he's letting me sit here—because he knows I won't understand the conversation anyway.

Still, the tone of his voice is enough for me to put together that things are heated. This must be a mob thing, right? Or am I reading too far into it? Maybe the reason I'm allowed to listen in right now is because he's talking to an Italian vendor of Bellanti wines, and nothing of import is being said. For all I know, they could be arguing about discounting the price of the Elite Reserve.

Armani's voice rises again. He's been tense since we left the island, even more so than usual. I don't know if it has to do with the Brunos specifically or just the Bruno-Bellanti war in general...or if there's more to it than that. It's probably wishful thinking to hope that he's reevaluating the terms of our marriage, but I can't stop replaying our day at the waterfall, remembering how tenderly he'd looked into my eyes while we were sharing that plum, and then everything that happened afterward. I felt so connected to him. It wasn't just the sex, either. It was like nothing I've ever experienced before.

What if it's all in my head, though? Is it completely idiotic to believe he's starting to feel something real for me?

He ends the call and stares out the window for a while, his jaw clenched.

Clearing my throat, I ask, "Everything okay? That call sounded a little...intense."

I try to sound as casual as possible, so he doesn't feel pressured or even more stressed out. My voice seems to pull him from his thoughts and he slips his phone into his pocket.

"You mean you weren't following? I thought you were getting pretty fluent in Italian," he teases.

"Yeah, no. I'm still just working on basic vocabulary. You were talking way too fast."

Turning to face me, he seems to consider, and then says, "Our allies are still hesitant to back us if we end up going to war with the Bratva. Aka Sergio Bruno's new best friends in Russia."

For a moment, I sit in stunned silence, trying to process my husband's words. I'm shocked. Because that wasn't some frivolous sales call about wine. It was a call regarding serious mafia business.

And Armani just made an admission of his family's vulnerability that could hurt the Bellantis very, very badly if I ran back to the Brunos with it.

Which means that...if he's sharing that intel with me, Armani must actually *trust* me.

It doesn't escape me how much this means.

"Wow," is all I can say. "No wonder you're so stressed out. Maybe you're the one who should be drinking this lavender tea."

A laugh escapes him, though it's not the humorous kind of laugh. More of a, "we are well and truly fucked" kind of laugh.

"I'm sure your allies will come around," I tell him, though I don't know if that's true. I hope it is.

"Honestly, I'm not so sure they will," he says. "But if they do, they'd better do it fast."

Pensively looking out the window again, Armani exhales as if he's deeply exhausted.

I hesitate and then plow forward with the burning question on my mind: "Why did you just tell me that? Why did you even let me into the office in the first place?"

He shrugs. "Because I needed to talk to you."

Stomach turning, I say, "About?"

"About the fact that you're off the hook," he says nonchalantly.

"Excuse me?" I sputter. That is not at all what I was expecting to hear.

"New information has come to light that clears you of any involvement in some of the more...aggressive actions taken against my family recently. Doesn't clear your name completely. I'll still be keeping tabs on you. But we got someone in custody who confessed to a number of misdeeds, going back years. So. Here we are. Even Dante suggested that we reevaluate your position."

My heart feels so, so light all of a sudden. My name has been...well, at least partially cleared. There's no denying that I *did* betray Armani—and his whole family—when I initially started spying on them for Juliana and the Brunos, but finally, finally, I feel a massive lifting of the guilt I've been carrying.

"That's some kind of news," I say quietly.

He just grunts in response, as if he isn't even sure how to feel about my semi-exoneration.

Grabbing my tea, I get up to leave. If Armani wants to continue playing the tough guy, let him. He'll come around eventually. Meanwhile, I've got my own messes to sort out. Like what I'm going to say to Juliana. If I'm too much of a wimp to call her, I at least need to respond to her texts.

Crossing the room to Armani, I go up onto my tiptoes and place a gentle kiss on his unmoving lips. I let the kiss linger until the tension in his muscles softens and his chest deflates. And then I pull back and touch his face. The need to comfort him pulses through me like a second heart.

He searches my eyes, like he still isn't sure about me, like he's trying to figure out my angle.

"It's going to be okay," I tell him firmly, with a conviction that comes out of nowhere. I'm not even sure who needs to hear it more, me or Armani, but saying it somehow makes it seem possible.

Then I leave him standing there.

But my good mood doesn't last long. Back in the bedroom, Armani's words come back to haunt me. *The Russians.* Juliana's uncle, Sergio, has made some kind of deal with them. Is it a deal to take down the Bellantis specifically, or more of a long-term, general alliance? Either way, it doesn't bode well. And then I realize the obvious benefit to me playing the Brunos' mole: I might be able to get more information from Juliana about the situation. She's close with her uncle, so maybe she knows what's going on with the Bratva.

A thrill goes through me. I might just be able to help out the Bellantis after all.

Phone in my hand, I lock myself in the bathroom and

lean against the door. My heart is racing, my emotions all over the place.

SORRY, I JUST got home, I text Juliana. *Armani whisked me off on a surprise honeymoon to some island in the middle of nowhere. I had no idea we were going and cell service was crap because Middle Of Nowhere. Home now. Talk soon?*

She responds immediately. *OMG you have to tell me everything. How about tomorrow? Brunch at 11 at the Plaza.*

Taking a breath, I close my eyes and try to steady my nerves. I need to mentally prepare for the game I'm reentering, and decide what, if any, hands I'm going to play when I meet with Juliana.

She'll be expecting intel from me. How could she not? I married my mark.

Just then, I hear the bedroom door open. Heart in my throat, I delete the chain of texts and put my phone in my pocket. Armani locks eyes with me as I exit the bathroom patting my hair, as if I just went in there to freshen myself up.

"Hey—" I start to say, but he's on me in an instant, pushing me into the wall and feasting on my mouth like he's a dying man.

I'm immediately drunk on the taste of him. It happens so fast. He strips my pants off, lifts me in his arms, and pushes his cock into me. A sharp gasp escapes me as he starts to pound me against the wall. Instantly turned on, I wrap my arms around his neck and give myself up to him.

He came to me to take what he needed to feel better. To use me. So why does this make me feel like I've won, somehow?

It doesn't matter.

We come at the same time, quickly, in a hot rush, and I cling to him like I'll never let go.

His head is on my shoulder, his arms braced around my body, gripping my shirt so hard that his fingers feel like they're bruising my ribs.

That's when I realize...Armani is clinging to me, too.

20

CANDI

I FIND out that Juliana has a private table reserved in the courtyard for us when I arrive at the Plaza. The hostess leads me outside to a table that's tucked away in a corner, surrounded by potted palms, with a thatched umbrella shading it. The ambient sounds of a string quartet and the other diners chatting lend a classy but relaxed vibe to the space.

My BFF is sipping a mimosa and scrolling on her phone as I approach, huge designer sunglasses adding extra glam to her sleek black outfit. She looks great. Also intimidating.

As for me, I picked out a maxi-length sundress and a linen blazer to wear, but seeing Juliana makes me somehow feel both underdressed and overdressed all at the same time. My stomach flips, my nerves spiking. Though I'd lain awake long into the night trying to figure out what to tell her, I hadn't come to any clear decisions.

But the second I see her look up at me and wave, I realize exactly what I need to do. I need to take advantage of the tidbit Armani gave me about the Russians, about how the Bellantis are struggling to secure the protection of their allies when it comes to the Bratva-Bruno union. It's the only actual "secret" I have that I can spin—and giving it up seems like my only possibility of staying in the Brunos' good graces. If I'm lucky, I might even be able to gather *more* info about the alliance from Juliana.

"Oh my God, Candi! Look at you! And they say redheads don't tan!"

She bursts from her chair to hug me. I hug her back, surprised at how happy I am to see her.

"I thought you'd been abducted by aliens or something!" she adds. "I was about to call the FBI."

I laugh and then get myself settled across from her. "Abducted yes, aliens no. Ha. Like I said, Armani planned the whole trip behind my back...we went shopping in Nob Hill and then all of a sudden, instead of going home, we were getting dropped off at the airport. It was a total surprise."

Her head tilts, her eyeline shifting to the huge diamond ring on my finger that's greedily gobbling up all the sunlight. Whipping off her sunglasses, her face shines with excitement.

"There it is. You brilliant little slut!" she crows. "Let me see it! How big is the stone?"

"Um, I have no idea," I say.

I really don't. Furthermore, I had no part in selecting it. Armani had given me the "engagement" ring in the most unromantic way possible. Since we had never actually been engaged, and since Armani had never actually proposed to me before we were married, he had waited until the night of our wedding reception at the Bellanti estate to unceremoniously drop the ring into my palm and tell me that I had to wear it "for the optics." I hadn't worn it since. Well, at least not until I was getting ready for my brunch with Jules this morning. I knew she'd want to fawn all over it. She loves jewelry.

Taking my hand, she turns my ring this way and that, cooing at the diamond's sparkle.

"It's three carats, easy. Maybe three and a half, even. And an oval cut stone, look how nicely it elongates your finger. Gorgeous." She glances up at me and grins. "See? Told you there'd be perks to shacking up with the guy. How the hell did you get him to the altar so fast?"

This is the part where I don't mention *at all* that I was drugged by Armani, nor that I woke up in a hotel room in Vegas with a gold band on my finger and a marriage certificate that I had zero recollection of signing. As far as Juliana knows, I plotted the whole thing myself, in an attempt to get even closer to the Bellantis—so I could be an even better Bruno mole.

"Oh, you know...just took advantage of the whole Vegas vibe," I say. "Plus, the combination of alcohol, adrenaline, and hot tub sex."

She throws her head back and laughs, delighted at my ingenuity. Of course, it's all lies.

"Sorry I couldn't invite you to the reception," I say. "I know we couldn't risk blowing my cover to the Bellantis and everything, but I really wish you could have been there."

"Psh, it's fine," she says. "You got our message at the cake cutting, so that's all that matters."

"Right." I nod vigorously, even though I had no idea Juliana was involved. "The cake cutting."

"We just wanted you to know that we're always looking out for you—protecting you," she adds. "But don't worry. It'll all be over soon enough."

My heart skips a beat. Over? Meaning...the Bruno-Bellanti feud will be over? Meaning...the Bellantis will be dead, or run out of town for good? Over how? But before I can fish for more information, the waiter comes up to our table to pour me a glass of water and refill Juliana's mimosa.

"Can I get you something else to drink?" he asks.

"Coffee, please. And can we get a couple menus?"

"Oh, I took care of ordering for us already," Juliana cuts in. "It gets so freaking busy here for brunch, I figured I'd just get one of everything so we could eat right away. All their food is amazing, I promise. I hope you don't mind."

"Not at all."

The waiter disappears, but he's back right away, carrying a huge tray loaded up with plates. One by one, he sets the dishes before us. Crisp bacon, smoked salmon, steaming croissants, pancakes topped with caramelized bananas, yogurt and granola, eggs, the works. There's no way we'll eat all this.

"You weren't kidding," I say, shaking my head. "Dibs on the pancakes."

"Nice choice," Juliana says.

She smiles, watching me as she saws a bite out of her avocado eggs benedict. Maybe I'm being paranoid, but I think she's giving me a suspicious once-over.

"What?" I say.

"I just—is it...okay? You're safe, right? He's not hurting you or anything?"

Her brows knit together as she searches my gaze.

"No, no. Not at all. He's been great," I tell her.

Which isn't exactly true. Armani *has* hurt me, but mostly on an emotional level. Still, I'm touched that Juliana is worried about me, and that she's been looking out for me. Even if I didn't realize that's what was going on when those Bruno gangsters crashed my reception.

But the thing is…I'm not so sure I want to be saved from this fake marriage after all.

"Sooo? Where the hell have you been?" she asks. "Tell me more about the surprise honeymoon."

Sipping my coffee, I consider what to say, because the Bellantis' island is clearly a secret.

"Honestly, I have no idea where the island was," I tell her. "Somewhere. In the ocean."

She pouts. "Seriously? What language were the people speaking? French, Spanish, Dutch, some kind of accented English? Surely you at least found a postcard at one of the gift shops."

Shaking my head, I tell her, "Actually, it was a private island, so there weren't any gift shops. There weren't many people there, either. Just a bunch of armed guards who didn't talk much."

"Wow," she says. "Talk about James Bond level shit. Okay."

"I know. Crazy, right? It was beautiful, of course, but other than that, all I can say is that it was beachy and tropical. What about you, though? What have you been up to while I was gone?"

"We'll get to that in a minute." She takes another bite of her eggs. "I have to say, I'm just…really proud of you for trapping Armani into marriage like that. Well played."

The way she worded that turns my stomach, but I nod and smile. "Thank you. And, um, when you said it'd all be over soon, did you mean there was some kind of plan in motion?"

Juliana looks at me intently. "You know I can't tell you that, babe. Wish I could, but it's way over your clearance level. But listen, if at any point you don't feel safe, or if something happens with him, I'll get you out of there right away. Okay?"

"Right. Yeah. Of course."

"Honestly, I can't imagine what it's like being married to one of *them*, but you seem to be handling it well."

"It's not so bad. He takes care of me," I tell her, thinking about my still-healing foot injury.

She snickers. "I'll bet he does."

"Not just in bed!"

Juliana starts cackling. I force myself to laugh along with her, but I have to bite back the defense of my husband that's trying to burst from my lips.

Because Jules only knows what she *thinks* she knows about the Bellantis. It's all hearsay, based on things her uncle has told her. She doesn't know the family the way I do. She has no clue about Armani's tender side. Or how much it kills him to show it. There's something good inside him, and inside Dante and Marco, too. If there wasn't, their wives never would have stayed.

Yes, these men have been trained since childhood to be criminals, to live their lives by a code of violence and intimidation. But each of them has made a concerted effort to separate themselves from that legacy—their father's legacy. They might still be in the thick of it all, but they're not trying to stay there. I know for a fact that the Bellantis would love nothing more than to leave the world of the mafia and become heritage winemakers. But Juliana would never believe me if I told her that.

And she sure as hell wouldn't believe me if I told her that I feel like I'm finally making some headway in my relationship with Armani...like maybe somewhere, underneath all the stoic coldness and the holstered guns and the icy gaze, there's someone I might actually, really, possibly even...love.

Suddenly, I have perfect clarity. There's no way I can tell Juliana what I know about the Russians. I can't do that to the Bellantis. I can't let the Brunos find out that Armani's family is at a disadvantage right now. It would only prompt the Brunos to strike sooner, harder, and more terribly.

Jules chatters away, mostly just innocuous small talk, but I can't get into it. I barely follow what she's saying, but I must nod and respond at the right times because she keeps going.

Meanwhile, I can't stop puzzling over how Armani has been acting since we got home. That initial disappearance, the way he'd pulled me into the office to tell me I was off the hook and that new information had been revealed. He'd gone to the Deep Cellar, hadn't he? But who had been down there?

"So, that brings me to *my* big news," Juliana says, puffing out her chest proudly.

"Oh?" I say, doing my best to act like I've been listening to her this whole time.

Folding her hands on the table, she leans toward me and

grins, looking like the cat who ate the canary. Little alarm bells start to go off in my head.

"You see, I've been involved in some...international business dealings. Which have been great for me because, frankly, the money is insane."

"Excellent..." I say slowly. "And so your big news is...?"

"That I'm getting married, too!" she crows.

"Oh my God! That's incredible!"

I squeeze both of her hands in mine, genuinely excited for her.

"Okay but let me show you the ring and then you'll really be over the moon for me!" she says, digging in her purse for her phone. "It's getting sized right now. It's a four-carat Asscher cut with a halo of Muzo emeralds. You think yours sparkles? Just wait until you see mine. I designed it, of course."

She passes me the phone and I scroll through the photos, agreeing with her about how gorgeous the ring is, but something about all of this is bothering me. Something just isn't right. My soul screams it. Juliana barely ever keeps a guy around for longer than a week or two, and her official boyfriends have been few and far between because she basically eats them alive. Marriage? Juliana? No way.

"Wait, so...who exactly is this guy?" I ask, handing her phone back.

"Well, that part doesn't really matter since it's a green card thing," she says, waving her hand nonchalantly. "But I'm still going to throw a huge, extravagant wedding for myself and you *must* help!"

My mouth goes dry. "Wow, this is all just...wow. Have you at least met this person?"

Her expression falls. I've squashed her excitement, and much like Armani, if I say the wrong thing or react the wrong way, Juliana shuts right down.

"I'm not judging, I swear, I just want you to be happy," I tell her quickly. "Okay? Seriously. Whether it's a green card thing or not, it doesn't matter, as long as it's what you want. I'd love to help."

Her smile returns.

"It *is* what I want. He's been working with me on some of the international deals, but his visa is expiring soon. So we decided getting married was a good move for our partnership. Sure, he's a little rough around the edges, and he doesn't have a business degree like me, but he's smart. And he really knows how to handle people. We'll be quite the power couple.

"Plus, we can get divorced in a few years and it won't affect his application for citizenship." She keeps rambling and I realize she's trying to justify her actions to me. "And I mean yes, this *is* for the business. I won't lie about that. It's not a love match or anything, obviously, but what's good for the business is good for me, right?"

Ah, so she's nothing more than a pawn. Sounds familiar. I wouldn't be surprised if this entire idea came from Uncle Sergio, or even one of the elder Bruno dons over in Italy.

Plastering a reassuring smile on my face, I take her hand. "I'm happy if you are. So, congratulations?"

"Yes! Yes, congratulations are in order! Waiter, more mimosas!"

Leaning over the table, we hug.

"So where is he from, anyway? Is this another Italian stallion?" I ask.

"Don't freak out and no, he's not Italian."

Grabbing her phone off the table, she pulls up a photo of man with dark, tousled hair, an admittedly panty-melting jawline, and heavy brows. He's not as refined as Armani, and he looks more like a bareknuckle boxer than a business-man, but he's certainly attractive.

"Okay, I don't feel bad for you anymore. He's definitely hot," I tell her teasingly.

"He's *super-hot*. And loaded. Oh, and he has the best accent, seriously."

"Does he?"

"Oh, yeah," she says, nodding. "He's Russian."

21

CANDI

"What's wrong? Candi? Hey. Say something."

Juliana's sharp tone forces me from my shocked stupor.

My best friend just told me that she's entering an arranged marriage and her fiancé is Russian.

What are the odds? And what better way to seal an alliance between powerful mob families than a wedding that binds two clans? No matter which way I turn, it seems like Russians are popping up everywhere. And once the Brunos officially join forces with the Bratva, there will be no stopping them.

"Sorry. You just caught me by surprise, is all," I say, lifting my coffee cup to my lips to hide the grimace I can't erase.

"I know, right? Here I was, thinking I'd never get married at all, and then an eligible bachelor just falls into my lap. Not that we have to treat it like an actual relationship or anything. It'll just be on paper."

"Yeah. Totally." As if I don't know *exactly* what that's like.

I feel sick at the thought of her getting married like this, though, especially to a man who is—in all likelihood, though she hasn't confirmed it—a gangster.

Which must seem ridiculously hypocritical of me.

But my experience being fake-married to a made man is *exactly* why I have room to judge such an arrangement. I know I'm no better than Juliana. I just don't want her to end up in a relationship that's anything like mine. What I wish I could tell her right now is this: Just because you're involved in an ostensibly loveless marriage, it doesn't mean you can't get hurt. Pragmatism and logic have no power against the lunacy of emotional attachment. It can creep up when you least expect it.

Unfortunately, I can't dole out that kind of advice. It would be akin to admitting that my marriage to Armani isn't at all what I've made it out to be. At which point, Jules would realize that my husband is the one playing *me*, not the other way around. My cover would be blown to smithereens. She'd know I'm a Bellanti stooge, that I'm double-crossing her and the Brunos.

So all I can do right now is pretend to be thrilled for her.

And hope to God that she doesn't catch feelings for this guy and start to think that she loves him. It won't end well. Just look at me.

I think back to when I was first considering Armani's offer for me to move in with him at the Bellanti estate for six months. He wanted to skip the casual dating and just jump right into cohabitating. The whole thing had thrown me for a loop, but Juliana had been all for it right from the get-go. She'd even told me to make my own list of demands in exchange for agreeing. In her eyes, moving in with Armani for a trial-by-fire relationship was a smart move, something I could leverage to my own benefit.

She's always been so cold and calculating. No wonder she doesn't seem at all upset about being a pawn. Unlike me. When I woke up in that hotel room with a wedding ring on my finger, I thought my marriage to Armani was the worst thing that ever happened to me. Now, I'm not so sure.

Clearing my throat, I ask, "So do you two have something in writing already, or..."

A smile breaks the concern on her face. "We're working on the contract. It's all planned out, Candi. Don't worry a minute about me. He knows what's expected of him. And so do I."

"Okay. As long as you're sure about this."

"I am."

Juliana takes my hand. Her eyes grow warm. Little lines crease beside them and the tension eases from her face as she grins. It's easy to think that she really might be happy about this.

"Candi, I...I want you to be my matron of honor. The wedding is next month. Super short notice, I know, but I can't do this without you."

Next month? It seems fast, but that's not as confounding as the fact that Juliana knows full well that she and I are not supposed to be seen together. Because obviously, we can't risk tipping off the Bellantis (or anyone in their network) about my link to the Bruno family.

In reality, of course, Armani and his family already know about me being a mole for the Brunos. But Juliana doesn't know that *they* know. And the Bellantis certainly don't know who my Bruno contact is. Being a member of

Juliana's Big Fat Bruno Wedding party? It screams suspicious.

Still, I'm over the moon that she asked. I'd be devastated if she hadn't. But…I don't know how to navigate this. Is she testing me? Testing my allegiance? What will happen if I say no? Although, honestly, how can I say anything but yes? My back is up against a wall. There's only one way out.

"Are you *sure* you want it to be me?" I say. "I mean I'd love to, but—are you sure it's safe? The Bellantis—"

"Of course I'm sure! The Bellantis don't know anything about me, and you can just tell your hubs that I'm an old college friend from UCSF. That part is completely true anyway. Besides, my last name isn't Bruno. There's no reason for him to suddenly want to go digging into my genealogy."

"Then yes! A thousand times yes!"

"Yay! And here's the waiter with our mimsies!"

She's referring to the mimosas she yelled across the courtyard for. Once we've clinked glasses and sipped, she scoots her chair over to my side of the table to sneak bites of my pancakes in between showing me all the potential wedding dresses she's added to her Pinterest.

I try to ooh and ahh the best I can, but my anxiety about Juliana's nuptials is through the roof. Not to mention, I'm worried that Armani might be getting suspicious. All he knows about my plans today is that I needed Donovan to drive me to a catch-up brunch with my college roommate, but this meeting with Jules has lasted far longer than I'd expected. I need to get back home soon.

"I still have so much wedding planning to do," Juliana groans. "My fiancé doesn't care about the details, so that helps, but it also makes it almost impossible to nail down anything when I know I can do whatever I want. Luckily, I was able to reserve Aurelia Manor for the venue. Can you believe I'm getting married in an olive grove? Talk about the future Mrs. Orloff winning at life."

"Wait, how did you manage that for *next month*?" I ask. "Don't they get booked out like two years in advance?"

She sips her mimosa, a pleased expression crossing her face. "Bruno money talks, Candi. Someone else probably had to rearrange their wedding plans, but tough titties. Obviously my situation is more urgent."

The way she says it makes my stomach turn, because my brain immediately conjures up images of Sergio Bruno's men hunting down some poor bride and groom and roughing them up until they agree to move to a different venue. Maybe Jules is right, though. Maybe the other couple just got paid off, and handsomely. Maybe they'll even be able to have an even nicer wedding now.

Or maybe I'm lying to myself.

"I'm sure it'll be perfect." My voice is overly cheerful. "Did you get the trellis on the water?"

"Oh, of course."

Aurelia Manor has three venues, one of which is right next to the river and includes an ornate trellis made from woven olive branches that sits waterside. The trellis is stunning when decorated with flowers and greenery and has made the cover of many a bridal magazine. I believe I read one time that it costs over forty grand to have a wedding at the manor, and that's before catering and florists and entertainment and God knows what else. Bruno money talks, is right. Maybe Bratva money, too.

At this point, she's all but confirmed that her fiancé is tied to the Russian mob. I don't think Uncle Sergio would be willing to fork over this kind of money for her wedding if the groom wasn't directly benefiting the Bruno clan, would he? Which means Juliana's intended is probably also a high roller. Someone the Brunos respect.

Someone dangerous.

"What business did you say your fiancé works in?" I ask casually. "You mentioned international deals...I know you're an account manager, is that what he does, too?"

Her entire expression changes. "Geez, Candi. If I didn't know any better, I'd think you were trying to get intel out of me."

Chills race down the back of my neck. "No. Of course not. I was just curious."

"It's not important what he does. This is about me and *my* wedding. The important thing is making sure it goes off beautifully."

I nod. "And it will. I'll help you make sure of it. Just tell me what I can do."

The waiter returns with the check. Juliana takes it and gives me a scandalous look.

"Should we get a dessert? You're not too full, are you? You barely touched your food."

"Dessert sounds good. Let's do it," I agree, trying to act like my stomach isn't in knots.

"We'll share a slice of the strawberry cheesecake," she tells the waiter. "Thank you."

There's nothing I'd rather *not* do than eat dessert right now, but I'll choke down the cheesecake if it means my friend will trust me again. It was stupid of me to ask anything personal about her fiancé, but it had come out naturally. I *am* truly curious...and also curious on the Bellantis' behalf.

Dammit. I can't have Juliana questioning my loyalty. I clearly pushed a wrong button, and she's not the kind to forget a misstep easily.

When the dessert arrives, she digs in with gusto. I force myself to follow suit, even though each bite makes my stomach lurch. Sipping water in between each small bite, I'm thankful when she doesn't resume the conversation right away, because I need a minute to think.

My heart is so conflicted right now. I'm being pulled in completely opposite directions. Whose side am I really on? Bellanti or Bruno? Where do my loyalties lie? Which mob family is the lesser evil?

This shouldn't be hard. Juliana has been my best friend for years and I promised to help her by gathering information about her family's enemies. But that was before I knew so many terrible things about the Brunos and what they've done to Armani's family. And before I fell for Armani himself.

Have I officially switched sides?

It's hard to admit it, but pleasing him makes me feel good. What makes me feel even better? The fact that he's starting to trust me. That's huge. I love knowing that he's opening up to me and letting me in a little bit. I love when he's vulnerable. I love that we're connecting on an undeniably deeper level lately. That's something I never even imagined when I first entered into this game. And the more time I spend with him, and the more details he shares about his family and his childhood, the more I long to see him happy. Maybe even...happy with me.

It's twisted; I'm aware. As the days go on, I do feel myself becoming more entwined with the Bellantis, even though most of them have shunned me because of my spying. Would that change if I pledged my loyalty to them? Or is it too late for that?

I just don't know.

On one hand, there's Juliana. My longest and best friend. The woman who saved me from my past and taught me to be confident and strong. There's no denying that she's always been there for me.

On the other hand, there's Armani. Just thinking about him sends a little thrill through me.

With a contented sigh, Juliana pushes the dessert plate away and smiles. "That was delightful."

"It was," I agree, even though I barely ate two bites of it.

Drumming her fingers on the table, she cocks her head and looks at me. "You know, there actually *is* something I need you to do for me right away."

Pulling out my phone, I open up the notes app so I can start a list.

"Sure. What is it? You want me to look into caterers, florists...?"

"No, no. Not that." She leans closer. "I want you to find out who exactly was on that yacht with you and Armani. The heavy hitters. Uncle Sergio needs to know who's loyal and who's lying."

The phone slips from my hand and hits the table, my stomach dropping.

I didn't mention the yacht. I didn't mention anything about my time on the island at all.

She draws back and laughs. "Oh, come on. Did you really think we didn't know about Armani's little rendezvous with his family's mob besties? We had tabs on you two ever since the Bellanti plane took off from SFO."

My mouth opens but nothing comes out. I can feel my pulse blip with a beat of fear.

For the first time, I'm truly afraid of my best friend.

"Find out who was on that yacht, Candi," she repeats. "The sooner, the better."

ARMANI

It is a rare occasion, indeed.

The Bellanti brothers are gathered for an official Bellanti Vineyards wine tasting.

I don't usually attend these things, but this is no routine tasting. We're sampling variations on a brand-new blend that our winery is soon to be introducing to our product line.

The reason for the new wine? For the last four years, we've been selling a rosé that we pressed using Mourvèdre grapes purchased from Spain. It had brighter, fruiter, more acidic characteristics than it should have, but we just assumed it was a natural variation of the grapes. It certainly sold enough cases that we saw no cause for concern.

Enter Dante's wife Frankie, who studied viticulture in Italy.

"These aren't Mourvèdre grapes," she'd informed us last season. "They're Graciano."

"Impossible," Dante had said.

"Look at those bronze tips," she'd insisted. "Graciano, all the way. I'd bet my life on it."

And so they'd gone back and forth about it for months—an argument that was only settled after a sample of the cuttings had been sent to UC San Francisco for genetic testing. Turns out, Frankie was right. Graciano all the way.

We're still not sure how the mix-up happened. But what we do know is that we can use this new varietal of grape to make a Tempranillo-Graciano blend. We've unanimously agreed to call it Lili Grace, after Dante's daughter. And today, we get to taste the literal fruits of our labor, all thanks to Frankie.

Marco is running late, which surprises none of us. Prior to his marriage to Karina, I'd probably assume that he was up until sunrise with his flavor of the week and had only just put his pants on when he realized the meeting was starting at that exact moment. Now that Marco is married...well, I'm guessing his tardiness is due to similar reasons, with one very specific personnel change.

Dante is still updating me on how things are going with the baby when our little brother bursts into the Little Cellar —the exclusive, private space located beneath the large pavilion where the public samples Bellanti wines—and collapses into an empty chair like he's sliding into home base for a run.

"I'm here," he says breathlessly.

"We noticed," I say.

"So. What are we going to do?" he asks.

"Drink," Dante says, filling our glasses with a few splashes of the first Lili Grace blend.

"I mean *what are we going to do about the Brunos*," Marco says impatiently.

"I know what you meant," Dante says. "But first, *la prima bottiglia*." *The first bottle*.

He raises his glass and Marco gives a little huff of impatience but then raises his as well. Without much fanfare, we each go through our own tasting steps, more or less similar versions of sniff, swirl, sniff again, sip, swallow. The only real difference seems to be in speed and thoughtfulness. Marco drinks the fastest, Dante ponders the scent and flavor of the wine for the longest amount of time, and as for me, I'm somewhere in the middle.

"It's a good blend. Really good," I say. "No question."

"Yeah, it's great. So about the Bratva," Marco says, pushing his empty glass away.

As Dante opens the second bottle, he says, "Armani, why don't you recap the meeting you had in Morocco with our allies? Marco's a little short on the details."

He fills clean glasses for us, a bit heavier on the pour this time.

"There's not much to add, honestly," I start, and then I succinctly give them the rundown.

By the time I'm done, Dante has another full glass of Lili Grace number two in front of him.

"You sure you should be drinking like that when your daughter's christening is in a few hours?" Marco says rudely.

"I'm celebrating," Dante says dryly, followed by a healthy swallow of wine.

I've got the christening on my mind, too. It's the first time since my wedding that we'll all be together again as a family, and there's no telling if the Brunos have something planned like they did with the bloody cake. Dante has arranged for plenty of security, of course, but I can't help worrying that my niece's christening might present itself as the perfect time for our enemies to strike.

"So. Lili Grace one or two?" Dante asks us, all seriousness.

"They're both good. Maybe we should try the third before we pass judgment," I say.

Marco lets out what sounds like a growl. "Why are we still talking about goddamn wine? Can we get back to the real problem? This shit with the Brunos isn't a game."

His tone irks me. My youngest brother has been extremely belligerent lately, which is out of character for him. Granted, he's always been a little moody, but this is different.

Any time family business comes up nowadays, this petulant, bad-tempered version of him appears. As if Marco has any right to insert himself in the most critical Bellanti affairs after spending the last decade and a half as the black sheep; a notoriously hard-partying playboy-slash-race car driver who didn't give a shit about our legacy. He's settled down since marrying Karina, but that doesn't mean he can sit here and talk to Dante like he doesn't know what he's doing.

"No. It's not a game," Dante says coolly. "But we can't move against the Brunos or even begin to pull a plan together until we have more information about this alliance with the Bratva. The second we strike, they'll counter. And if we strike too soon, or in the wrong place, or with the wrong kind of firepower, they'll fucking take us out. For good. So do forgive me if I'm not in a hurry to show my ass."

Marco slumps in his chair.

"I know it feels shitty to be sitting around twiddling your thumbs," I tell him quietly. "But we're not doing nothing. Even if that's what it looks like to you."

He looks away. I'm pretty sure he rolled his eyes in the process. "Guess we might as well try the third wine, then. Since that's all we're going to get done today."

Dante nods. I don't appreciate Marco's passive-aggression, but I say nothing.

This time, Marco does the honors. Once we all have our wine, I take a sip and roll it around in my mouth. It's easily the best of the three. But I don't comment on it. My hackles are still up.

Here's the thing about my little brother. He talks a big game, but he's not really here to help me and Dante come up with solutions. He'd rather act like a brat because Dante dragged him into our family drama once again, meaning that Marco can't keep his head in the sand right where he likes it. Honestly, I don't know why Dante forced Marco to join us in the first place. But I do know this: we'll end up talking in circles if I don't pull rank and take charge.

Leaning back in my chair, I say, "I want to send someone inside. We can't get the intel we need from where we're at. And we don't have time to keep trying to woo Bratva loyalists. Even Clayton is getting nowhere. The lead he had fell right off the map."

Dante frowns. "So you want to plant another mole? Haven't we had enough of that?"

"Think about it. If we can figure out what this alliance

is based on, maybe we can eliminate whatever leverage or blackmail or bribe Sergio Bruno has offered the Russians," I reason. "And if we act fast, it might not be too late to prevent the Bratva from joining the Brunos."

Marco scoffs and I shoot him a withering look.

"Which is why we need someone who can play all sides seamlessly," I go on. "Someone unassuming, who won't draw suspicion."

Dante nods. Finishing off my wine, I set the glass away from me and smooth my tie. The room grows quiet. I let my brothers think over what I've just said.

We're all sick of dealing with the Brunos. But the addition of the Bratva makes our enemies practically invincible, and it guts me that I didn't see it coming. I should have suspected that Sergio Bruno would stop at nothing in his attempt to keep control of Napa, and if word on the street is true, parts of Italy, too. He's never been a man of honor. This kind of underhanded move was right in front of me all along. I guess the only real surprise is that he didn't try to join forces with the Russians sooner.

"If we do go ahead with this plan, do you have someone in mind?" Dante finally asks.

I nod. "I do."

"Fuck this." Marco stands, clattering his chair as if trying to make the most noise possible.

"Is there a reason you're being even more of an asshole than usual, Marco?" I ask.

"Yeah, there is." He doesn't miss a beat. "I'm tired of this shit. I have better things to do with my life than constantly look over my shoulder. Now you're telling me we got Russians up our asses, and you know what that says to me? That this shit is never gonna end. Whatever happened to *getting out*?"

Dante gestures to Marco to sit back down. "Marco, listen—"

"No. I don't want to listen. I hate this." He slams back into his chair.

"Hey," I say, raising my voice in anger like I rarely do. "You need to stop disrespecting Dante. He might be your brother, but he's also the boss of this family, and that attitude ain't gonna fly. Like it or not, you're a Bellanti. We live by a code."

"Sorry," he says to Dante, but not very sincerely.

"No big," Dante says.

I'm not done talking to Marco. "Do you think *any* of us want this kind of life? We want out, too. That's still our end game. But we can't get there without violence, whether we like it or not."

"I know someone who likes it," Marco says under his breath, crossing his arms. "So, what? Is that supposed to make me feel better?"

"It's not my job to make you feel better," I remind him. "It's my job to keep you safe."

"Which you've done a great job of so far," he retorts sarcastically.

I jerk out of my chair, but Dante puts a hand on my chest and tells me to sit back down. I do.

"So you're sending Candi in, then?" Marco says.

Glaring daggers at him, I say, "No."

"We're not doing that," Dante agrees.

"Why not?" Marco presses. "She's an experienced mole. She knows how to play both sides. The Brunos trust her.

There's no one better."

"I said no."

He smirks. "Seriously? She won you over that easily? A little spread of the legs and you're a goner, huh?"

Slowly moving back my chair this time, so as not to aggravate Dante again, I stand up and place my hands on the edge of the table to keep from throttling my brother.

"Look who's talking, Mr. *Pussywhipped*," I growl.

"That's rich coming from you, Mr. Sprinkles," Marco says.

"Boys," Dante says warningly, sounding eerily like our late father.

"You've got no room to talk," I tell Marco. "You married the *enemy*."

It's true. Karina is—was—a Bruno. Sergio Bruno's niece, in fact.

Marco's upper body goes tight, his biceps bulging and relaxing as if he's holding himself back. But instead of launching himself at me, he grins humorlessly and narrows his eyes.

"And you married *their mole*, so I guess we're even! You know what would make us even more even? If you turn Candi over to me so I can interrogate her in the Deep Cellar, just like you did with my wife. Then we'll see how you like it," Marco says. "Or are you the only person in the family who gets to torture people for fun?"

I'm moving before he gets the last few words out, my fist connecting with his lips even as they're still moving. Marco's head snaps back, but he's quick—he's always been quick—and he's on me in a blink. Gripping my collar in both hands, he drives me backward into the wall. As he pulls a fist, Dante jumps between us, his eyes wild with fury.

"Knock it off!" he commands. "There will be no further punches thrown. Not on my watch. Jesus. Now sit the fuck down, both of you."

As the oldest, Dante has broken up plenty a fight between Marco and me over the years, so he knows what he's doing. Still, my blood is boiling. Marco likes to conveniently forget that his wife came from the enemy's side, but the simple truth of the matter is that the reason I interrogated her was because I needed information to ensure the safety of our family. I had to do it. No question.

But I didn't lay a finger on her. I employed...other methods. Was I nice about it? Hell no. A little mental warfare didn't hurt her any, though. And at the end of the day, I got what I wanted.

Would I let the same thing happen to *my* wife?

Fuck no.

"My daughter is getting christened later today and you two are trying to kill each other," Dante lectures. "Marco's going to look fucking wonderful in the photos with that fat lip!"

All I can do is spread my hands as Marco gingerly touches his split lip. Dante remains standing before us, shaking his head like we're two ill-behaved children who have disappointed him. Which I guess we kind of are.

"Armani, who did you want to send in?" Dante asks, getting us back on track.

"Clayton. He'll know who to talk to. He has connections everywhere and he's our best resource for getting information from multiple families. He may have even reestablished contact with his Bratva guy already, or maybe linked up with someone else."

I don't mention my suspicions about Clayton having worked for the Bratva in the past. It's just a hunch, but I can't have my brothers questioning his loyalty to us right now. Logically, though, it's the only thing that explains how he was able to get that last Russian contact at all. It's not something I'd hold against him, either. The Irishman worked for mob families for years, not pledging to anybody, just following the money. At least, not until he met Frankie's sister Charlie. Now that he works with us, his past experiences are a boon. He's well-connected. People like him. Better than that—they *trust* him.

Marco nods at me grudgingly. "Clayton's got a light touch, and he's good with people. Plus, he's the one who brought the tattooed man to our door." His eyes drop to his lap then, and his voice gets quiet as he adds, "And he sussed out Donno."

Dante winces. "I don't like it. He's good for the job, but I'm the one who's going to have to answer to my wife if her sister's husband gets killed."

Here we go again with the wives. I can't fathom how my brothers allow their women to have so much control and influence over them.

"That's between you and your wife. Clayton's a big boy. He'll decide if he wants in or not."

Dante sighs. "Fine. For now, you two do not speak again until I've talked to Clayton."

He turns to go, but before he reaches the door, I call after him, "By the way, it's three."

"Three what?" he asks, checking his watch with a frown and then looking over his shoulder.

"Lili Grace number three," I say. "For our Tempranillo-Graciano. It's the winner. No contest."

Lifting a brow, he glances at Marco. "What do you say?"

"*Tre*," he agrees. "It's the most memorable. They're all a good balance of sweet and spicy, that mix of cinnamon and plum and sage and cocoa powder, right, but the last one reminds me of..."

He picks up the bottle and sniffs it, then sets it back down.

"Raspberry licorice," he says. "And it's medium-bodied, so it's versatile with food pairings, but also good enough to drink by itself. Think about it. Sweetness, structure, balance. And yeah, it'll get ya drunk. People will go crazy for it. Trust me."

For a moment, Dante and I just stare at our little brother with our mouths hanging open.

"What?" Marco says. "I'm a Bellanti. You think I don't know wine? It's in the blood."

"Lili Grace number three it is," Dante says, recovering. "And you better watch out, kid, or you just might find yourself with a job in the marketing department."

He picks up the winning bottle and walks out. Marco and I watch him go. Once the door slams at the end of the hall, I glance over at Marco.

"I think fatherhood is making him soft," I murmur.

"Agreed."

Marco meets my gaze, his mouth quirked up at the edges. It's as close to a smile as I'm going to get from him.

I'll take it.

23

ARMANI

The church is secured with bodyguards at every possible entry point, a guard patrol circling the building, and a photo ID checkpoint at the entrance to the parking lot.

It's a sanctuary. It should feel safe. But I can't stop imagining armed Brunos bursting inside during the christening and doing something unforgivable on my niece's special day.

The threat of violence looms like a dark cloud overhead, even as golden sunlight pours through the church's stained-glass windows. Clayton is posted at the front of the church, off to one side, so he can keep his eyes on the entry doors at the back, but it isn't enough to assuage my anxiety. I suddenly have a lot more empathy for Marco's recent edginess.

Candi has been unusually quiet since she returned from her brunch this afternoon. Probably just nerves about coming to this event. I can't blame her. While I received plenty of warm greetings, hugs, and handshakes when we arrived here, no one in my family acknowledged Candi beyond a few polite nods. Well, except for Frankie's mother, Miriam Abbott, who knows nothing about Candi's former role as a Bruno spy. Mrs. Abbott is always kind to everybody, so I was glad to see her chatting up Candi.

The worst thing about my family's behavior toward my wife is that I know I can't force them to forgive her. Not only that, but I understand why they feel the way they do. Candi might be working for me now, but she'll have to prove herself in order to regain their trust. There's nothing for it but time.

We're in a second-row pew, facing the front of the church where the priest chats quietly with my brother and his wife. Baby Liliana is dozing in Dante's arms, her small form draped in an heirloom lace christening gown that traveled across the ocean with my ancestors from Italy over a century ago. My brothers and I each wore it in our own time, just as our father had before us. The delicate bonnet hides most of Lili's cherubic face, but a downy tuft of dark hair peeks out of the front.

The priest greets us all and begins the ceremony. Frankie sniffles a little, then looks up at Dante. They lock eyes over their baby, sharing an intimate smile, and my chest swells with a strange emotion. There's no denying how connected they are, the three of them. A family unit all on their own. An island.

How easily they could take their baby and leave Napa to start fresh somewhere else, far away from the threats and violence here. But if Dante did flee with his family, would Bruno send his men after them? Even if Dante stepped down as the Bellanti clan's leader? My gut says yes. Sergio

Bruno would never stop until he snuffed out every last flame. He wouldn't want to risk Dante returning to Napa.

The good feeling inside me turns sour.

I can't even fantasize about a future where the Brunos decide it's in their best interest to leave us alone. That future, that peace, it only exists if we destroy our enemies completely. We have no other choice. It kills me to admit it, but it's true.

As the priest goes on with his Bible readings and prayers, Liliana suddenly yawns hugely, her little face scrunching, her fist popping up as she stretches in Dante's arms. A ripple of coos and soft laughter goes through the guests. Across the aisle, I see Mrs. Abbott sitting with Frankie's sisters, Charlie and Livvie, all of them snapping photos of Lili's sleepy antics. But I notice that Livvie isn't smiling.

Though she's attentive, her face is pale and drawn, her lips pressed into a line. She hasn't been the same happy-go-lucky, horse-loving teenager I used to know ever since we rescued her from her Bruno kidnappers. She came back a changed woman. Scarred emotionally and mentally by her ordeal.

Candi shifts slightly beside me, leaning forward to watch as Frankie takes Liliana from Dante and he removes the baby's bonnet. Then Frankie holds Lili over the baptismal font, and the priest prepares to baptize her. Candi's hands turn to fists in her lap. She's tense, every muscle in her body taut. It can't just be my family that has her on edge. There's something else on her mind.

Has Bruno contacted her since we got back from our vacation? Is he demanding fresh intel? Did he give her a job to do? If so, she hasn't breathed a word about it to me. I do want to trust her, but I'm not entirely confident that she'd tell me right away if Bruno was up to something. Still, there are ways I can remind her which side of this war she's on—ours—and I'm not above using them.

Sliding my hand to her thigh, I reach for her fist and squeeze it gently until she relaxes her hand and laces her fingers through mine. She looks over at me and I give her the slightest nod while watching the priest. After a second, she slides over in the pew until we're thigh to thigh, then rests her head against my shoulder. My pulse picks up just enough that I notice.

The thin silk of her skirt does nothing to hold in the heat of her body. It seeps comfortably against my leg but gives me a new awareness of her proximity. My skin tingles in response, desire spiking in my blood. It takes all my willpower to focus on what's happening in front of me instead of on the woman at my side. A few minutes pass before I glance at her again, and when I do, I see her wearing an expression of pure longing as she watches the baby in Frankie's arms.

Does she want children one day? The topic has never come up between us. Not that it ever will, since I'm sure we'll be divorcing as soon as this business with the Brunos is concluded...

"Let us pray."

The priest's voice draws me back to the christening and I dip my head just in time as he begins a closing prayer. Soon enough, the ceremony is complete. Dante tells everyone that refreshments are being served in the gated courtyard outside, including catered food and some Bellanti

Vineyards selections handpicked by Frankie. Candi meets my eyes and my stomach drops. The only snack I want is my wife.

We all rise and I join my family near the altar for some photos. Candi hangs back, uncertain, shaking her head as I motion for her to join me. I don't force the matter. Neither does anyone else.

Suddenly Dante turns and deposits baby Lili in my arms. I wasn't fully expecting it, and I hold my breath and look down at her in awe as she stirs.

"She's waking up," I whisper to Dante in warning. "You should take her back."

Her face turns red, mouth puckered and ready to release a cry that seems lodged somewhere. She can't quite get it out, but she's sure as hell trying.

Dante smiles. "The only reason she slept through the christening is because she was up all night, so I've already pulled my fair share of baby duty in the last twenty-four hours. She's all yours, brother."

"Ah, no."

"You're the one holding her," he points out.

I'm man enough to admit that the thought of Liliana going ballistic gives me a beat or two of panic. What the hell does a man do with a screaming infant?

"Then take her back," I insist, inching toward Dante.

Grinning, he slips his hands in his pockets and takes a leisurely step backward. "I think she wants her uncle Armani."

"No, she wants her da—"

Just then, a wail sharp enough to make my ears bleed spills out of the baby's toothless little mouth. And then another, and another. Dante quickly takes the baby, laughing as he soothes her with a series of rocking motions, baby talk, and butt-pats. I guess he's gotten pretty good at the daddy stuff.

Frankie quickly takes over, scooping Lili out of Dante's arms, and moves toward the side exit doors with her mother and sister Charlie. Livvie checks something on her phone, sighs, and then follows after them. Marco's eyes track her, his lips pulled into a frown.

After giving his wife a kiss and suggesting that she join the others in the courtyard, he turns to me and says, "When are you going to tell her what happened to her boyfriend?"

He's referring to Livvie, of course. He's been overly protective of Frankie's youngest sister ever since he met her. To be fair, Dante and I have, too. Maybe some part of us is looking to fill the hole that our sister left in our lives when she died.

That said, Marco's bond with Livvie is something special. They're both the youngest of three siblings, the sibling most likely to get banished from the room during "grown-up talk," the sibling who constantly struggles to be taken seriously by their elders. So when Livvie got kidnapped by the Brunos, Marco took it personally. He made it his duty to save her. And he did. We all did, but Marco...his actions were beyond heroic. I'd never seen him go out on a limb like that before, risking everything for someone else. The whole experience matured him in a big way, seemingly overnight.

"When the time is right," I answer. Although I'm not sure the time will ever be right to tell my sister-in-law that I was forced to kill her boyfriend.

Marco motions me into a side chapel that glows softly with the light of dozens of flickering prayer votives lined up in rows on an iron stand. He digs in his pocket, pulls out a few crumpled dollars, and drops them in the collection box, then grabs a fresh white candle and motions for me to do the same.

"You know I'm not religious," I tell him.

"You should still be respectful," he says. "Do it for Lili, at least."

"Fine."

I donate a crisp fifty to the box, pick up a candle, and light it alongside my brother. Once we've fitted our burning candles into holders, he nudges me.

"Now pray."

I grimace. "I'd rather not. I doubt the supreme creator would care to listen to me anyway."

"Come on. It can't hurt," he says. "And what if it helps?"

With a huff, I close my eyes. I have every intention of saying a prayer for my niece, asking the powers that be to guide and protect her, to help her have a life that's good and joyful and peaceful. Instead, my thoughts veer to Candi. And how she, too, deserves a life that's good and joyful and peaceful. I'm still trying to figure out exactly how to word my prayer when Marco gives me another nudge.

"You need to tell Livvie," he whispers. "It's cruel to keep it a secret from her. You don't have to admit it was you, but at least tell her you found out her boyfriend died. Otherwise she'll just keep waiting for him to come back. I mean, haven't you noticed how miserable she is? She's suffering."

"It's not my problem if her broken heart is keeping her up at night because she thinks she got ghosted," I snap.

"Armani—"

"Don't 'Armani' me. She should have known better than to get involved with her bodyguard."

"She didn't know he was working for the Brunos," Marco hisses. "Besides, she's *young*. She's innocent. Dude was her first boyfriend. You can't blame her for being a little naïve—"

"I'm not blaming her, but I can tell you one thing: she's better off learning how shitty men can be now, so she can learn to build some walls," I say. "Trust me, she'll get over it. Eventually. And it's not like she'll never have to go through a breakup again. This experience will toughen her up."

"Right," Marco says sourly. "So basically, you did her a favor by killing the guy."

I scoff. "Can you imagine if we'd let him live? He would have turned her against us eventually and we'd have another disloyal woman to contend with. You will say *nothing* to her. Understand?"

"Whatever. I just hate seeing her like this." Marco shakes his head. "I need a drink."

With that, he storms off to join the rest of the guests who are slowly filtering out of the church and into the courtyard. The doors are propped open, so I can hear the low chatter of everyone enjoying the reception, the punctuations of laughter, the random, happy shrieks of the baby. I head toward the noise, but then I see Candi still standing off to the side of the altar. Her hands clasped in front of her, and her eyes wander the interior of the church. It's obvious that she's pretending not to notice that the entire Bellanti family has left without so much as a backward glance at her.

Everyone but me.

She turns her head as I approach. When I snag her hand in mine, she visibly relaxes.

"There you are," I say as I walk her toward the door. "Did you enjoy the ceremony?"

"Yes. I've never seen one before. It was really beautiful."

"It was," I agree, acting like this event is the only thing on my mind—and like I don't know that Candi is doing the same exact thing.

In reality, we're both carrying the burden of our own secrets and tensions, not to mention the constant stress of this looming mafia war. It's fucking exhausting. And the only thing that would make me feel even marginally better isn't logistically possible at the moment. Unless I snuck away from this reception to pull my wife into a closet.

Or a confessional.

Like the one across the church, to the right of the sanctuary.

Pausing outside the exit doors, I listen for sounds coming from anywhere inside the church. The priest has left to join the family, and all the guests are gone as well. We're alone. *Well now.*

Spinning Candi around, away from the doors, I lead her past the pews and toward the ornately carved, dark wood confessional booth.

"Where are we—"

"Shh."

I open the door and push her inside. Then I follow, closing the door behind us.

She turns to face me in the close, dim space, but I don't give her a chance to speak.

Taking her face in my hands, I press my lips to hers and shove her back against the wall. Her chest stalls with a hitched breath, and then she's devouring me in kind. Hot need races through me with a demanding pulse. I want to consume her inch by inch.

"Do you have something to confess, Candi? Something that's weighing on your mind?" I whisper in between kisses.

"I—I don't know."

Moving my lips over her throat, down her neck, I nibble the soft skin there while grabbing handfuls of her skirt and bunching it up around her waist. She's wearing a thong, barely a scrap of fabric between me and what I want most. Working my zipper, I hitch her leg around my hip, pull her panties to the side, and slide straight up into her. God, she feels good. Slick and tight, like a hot, hungry mouth.

I start pumping, shallow and fast, my toes curling inside my polished leather shoes.

A harsh little gasp escapes her. "We're in a church!"

Fucking right we are. But despite her scolding, she's meeting me thrust for thrust, her eyes rolling back in her head with pure lust. She's going to clean away my sins right now. She's going to take them all. I move faster, plunging deeper, ramming her into the wall. Her arm tightens around my neck, her free hand reaching down to cup my balls. It's a struggle to keep myself from groaning.

"Have you sinned?" I growl against her ear. "Have you been a bad girl?"

She murmurs something that might be an affirmative, but I can't tell. The liquid velvet feel of her clasped around me is robbing me of my ability to think clearly. Supporting her with one arm around her waist, I bring her other leg around me, too, so I can thrust even deeper. Her knees dig into my sides as she gives herself up to the pure, sweet fucking.

"Oh my God," she whispers, her tongue flicking over the soft skin behind my earlobe. "God yes."

"You're taking the Lord's name in vain," I scold, slamming into her so hard that the confessional wall trembles.

"Fuck yes," she corrects herself.

"You're still a bad girl," I pant.

"Mmm. I sinned the moment I agreed to our first date. Look what you've done to me."

"We're all sinners," I tell her. "Now it's time for you to atone."

"How? I want to be absolved."

Leaning so close that my lips brush her ear, I say, "Come for me. Come for me, Candi. Come for me, wife."

I say it over and over until I send her over the edge. She whispers my name as she comes, wetness gushing out of her, spurring me on. But I don't last much longer. The feel of her pussy contracting on my cock pulls me right into the orgasm along with her.

Covering her mouth with mine, I muffle both of our groans as I explode inside of her, spilling my seed with abandon.

Being bad has never felt so good.

24

CANDI

JULIANA'S WEDDING has been heavy on my mind since yesterday. I haven't been able to bring myself to mention it to Armani yet. I'm dreading the conversation.

It's one thing for me to be vague about meeting up with my college roommate for brunch, but I can't be as evasive about my role as said roommate's *matron of honor* next month, especially since Armani won't be invited to the wedding. Even if her name is Juliana Guerra, her guests will all be Brunos and random Russians. Which means I'll have to come clean about the fact that Juliana is a Bruno, in order to explain why Armani can't be my date. Which is going to make me look shady as hell at a time when my husband is only just starting to trust me. It'll have him questioning my loyalty all over again.

Because of course I should have mentioned my Bruno best friend to him already.

And of course I haven't. Not that he ever asked about my friends.

The alternative, however, is me lying about the entire

thing (either fibbing about who exactly my engaged friend is, or not telling him I'm going to a wedding at all) and waiting for my husband to find out the truth himself later—which, believe me, he will—after which he'll immediately put two and two together. He's too smart to ignore the obvious: that my Bruno best friend is also my Bruno handler.

Again: his trust in me, obliterated.

It seems like the right move is to just tell him that my BFF is a Bruno, impress upon him how important it is for me to be at her side on her wedding day, and not divulge any further details. He'll know the truth without me stating it explicitly, but...maybe it won't matter if he knows who my handler is.

Surely Armani will reason that it would be very poor strategy to hurt Jules—because that would instantly tell the Brunos that I've A) been compromised and B) leaked intel to the Bellantis. Because I'm the only one who could lead Armani to Juliana. So in order to keep the Brunos in the dark about me switching sides, and to ensure that I'm still useful to the Bellantis as a double agent, Armani will have to act like he doesn't know Juliana is my contact.

Maybe I can even frame it as a strategic move on my part...attending a Bruno wedding will further cement my alleged loyalty to the Brunos. Right? Ergo, Armani should be *encouraging* me to go.

Except it's not that cut and dried.

The logic is there, but I don't trust it. I'm no expert in spy games, and there's no denying that my husband is. He's also a stone-cold killer. He's dangerous. Calculating. Cruel, at times. Revealing Juliana's role in this war with the Brunos doesn't seem like a remotely smart move. Neither does lying about it. And it's too late for me to back out as her matron of honor. I have to keep my word to her.

But if I tell Armani—

"Something wrong?" Armani asks from across the table.

Startled from my thoughts, I jerk back just enough to spill my coffee onto my breakfast, soaking my poached eggs on brioche.

Throwing my napkin over my plate, I shake my head. "No. Sorry. I was just...thinking."

He starts to stand. "Should I have the kitchen staff remake your breakfast?"

"Um, no. It's okay. I wasn't that hungry anyway."

I can feel his eyes tracking me as I purposely avoid his gaze and focus on sopping up the mess I just made. My adrenaline is spiking. He's obviously on to me. At minimum, he knows I'm hiding *something*. He's a professional interrogator, for fuck's sake. How long can I keep this secret from him? It's stupid to even try.

But I can't tell him about Juliana. I can't. Maybe I should just sit on the big wedding news for a bit. Ease into it instead. Maybe I can reveal it to him in stages, rather than one big truth bomb.

"You need to eat," he scolds mildly. "You barely touched your food. Here."

He slides half of his own eggs and toast onto a plate of sliced avocado and then pushes the whole thing toward me. I take it and nod.

"Thanks."

He tilts his head. "What were you so deep in thought about?"

Taking a big bite of eggs to stall for time, I try my best to act natural when I answer, "The christening, I guess. I can't stop thinking about how happy Frankie and Dante looked yesterday. The ceremony was really special. And Lili looked like a perfect angel."

He lifts a brow. Does he not believe me? Or is he nervous that I might be getting baby fever? Or is he merely remembering our little tryst in the church confessional booth?

"The christening was nice," he finally says neutrally.

"It was."

We return to our food, but there's no ignoring the current of tension in the room. When I look over at him, I find him studying me still. As if he's waiting for me to slip up. Waiting to pounce.

"How did your brunch date go?" he asks. "You never said a word about it."

I smile over my coffee cup, praying he can't see the flash of panic in my eyes.

"It was great. I haven't seen my friend in a long time. It was good to catch up."

"She was your sorority sister, you said?" he presses.

I had told him she was my roommate. Is he trying to catch me in a lie? Or does he really not remember what I said?

"My roommate," I remind him. "When we were business majors together at UC San Francisco."

"Mm."

I rapidly think back to my conversation with Jules, sorting through tidbits and pieces of information that I can string together for Armani without giving too much away or revealing who Juliana's family is. He needs enough to feel satisfied, but not so much that he gets suspicious.

"She actually asked me to help her with something that I'm...kind of on the fence about," I tell him. "I've been feeling conflicted ever since. Maybe I could get your advice?"

"Maybe I could give it," he says. "If you tell me more."

Nodding, I take a deep breath. "So the thing is, she's planning to...go into business with someone she barely knows. They've worked on a few projects together and she's convinced it'll be really lucrative, but I think she's taking a huge risk. Which I told her, but she wants to do it anyway."

He considers this. "What kind of business is this?"

"Consulting," I answer right away, relaxing into the facts that I can easily share. "She works in the international division at her company. Basically, she builds strategies for setting up global communications networks. They have a lot of clients in Japan, China, Germany, India, but that's all I really know. She's always acted like the nuts and bolts of her job are too boring to talk about. But anyway, this new business wouldn't interfere with any of that. It's more of a...side hustle."

"And you don't approve of this business partner. Have you met this person before?"

"No. I mean, this new venture could be totally fine. But personally, I think it's smarter to proceed with caution when it comes to new partnerships. Instead of just, you know, rushing into things."

My cheeks go warm as I realize how hypocritical I sound. Armani smirks, but kindly doesn't say anything about our own rushed "partnership."

"So you want advice on whether you should push the issue with her or not?" he asks.

"No. Something else. She, um, she asked me to do her a favor...related to her new business deal...that I'm not really comfortable with."

I drink more coffee, suddenly second-guessing my decision to talk to Armani about this at all.

"Something illegal?" he asks, sounding intrigued.

A nervous laugh escapes me. "Not illegal, no. There's nothing technically 'wrong' with what she's asking. She just wants me to get her some information. Related to the new business partner."

It's a bit of a stretch, but Juliana *does* want me to hand over the names of the mafia allies Armani met with on the yacht—the ones who presumably will be standing with him against the Bruno-Bratva coalition. That's definitely information relevant to her "partnership" with the Russian, since it will tell her family who exactly they and the Russians will be up against when they move against the Bellantis.

But I know full well that relaying information about the identity of my husband's colleagues will get people killed. And I don't want to be a party to that. This spy stuff is about much more than right and wrong, legal or illegal. I didn't realize that when I initially signed on, but I sure as hell know it now.

"Makes sense," he says, warming to the topic. "It'd look bad for her to get caught digging into this person's history after she's already agreed to strike a deal. Especially if something untoward does get uncovered, and she needs to back out at the last minute. Much better for her to have plausible deniability. It's almost impossible to cover your tracks these days when it comes to electronic trails."

"So you're saying I should do the favor?" I ask.

His response has taken me off guard. I was expecting him to get all alpha-male and tell me walk away, to stay out of anything that might put me in a compromising position. Instead, he actually seems interested in considering all the angles of the situation and helping me figure out what to do.

"Maybe. Depends on how involved she wants you to get. Did she say what she's looking for specifically, or is it more of a treasure hunt with no map and no guarantee that there's actually treasure?"

"It's not that complicated," I tell him. "She just wants me to contact someone...a former colleague he worked closely with...and see if I can find anything she should be concerned about."

Another stretch.

"Why you? Wouldn't it be better to ask someone within that organization? Maybe someone who no longer works for that company, or else someone who's less closely involved with the partner?"

"This colleague she wants me to talk to is a...mutual acquaintance of ours," I say haltingly. "So it would be totally not-suspicious for me to chat this person up over coffee. But if she reaches out to anyone else in the other organization directly, it'll be a flashing neon sign that she's poking around about the new partner. And if it gets back to the new partner, I guess it'd show a lack of trust that might make them skittish about moving forward."

Armani silently mulls it over while he refills his coffee

from the carafe on the table. I finish the last of my breakfast, waiting for him to speak.

"Would this fact-finding mission put you at risk in any way?" he finally asks.

I pause. "It...could. If people found out I did this for her, it wouldn't reflect well on me. It's not like I'm a key player in the consulting world like she is, but my reputation is something I'd like to protect. And I don't want our mutual acquaintance to feel like I betrayed them by digging for this information."

"Got it," he says. "Is there anything else that makes you uncomfortable about her request?"

Glancing down, I admit, "I think just the fact that I'm supposed to be sneakily asking these questions of a mutual acquaintance." I look back up and add, "Honestly, I would do anything for my best friend. I want to do the right thing and make sure nothing bad happens to her. But this doesn't feel good."

I'm embarrassed by the tears stinging my eyes, but that last bit came from the deepest part of my soul. The part that's been struggling all this time with the Bruno-Bellanti war and how I'm processing my feelings for Armani differently than I did before I knew him. *Really* knew him, and the rest of his family.

The truth is, I've come to realize that the things Juliana has told me about the Bellantis don't always align with what I see with my own eyes, or the information I've gathered myself or through Armani. My role has blurred so much. I can't see the way forward anymore.

"This is your best friend, you said?" Armani asks gently.

I nod. "We met at UCSF. I was kind of a lost cause, but

she took me under her wing. She made me...*better*. We've been like sisters ever since. She helped me through some really dark times."

"Did you express to her that you're not comfortable doing what she's asking you to do?"

"Not directly. I hinted at it."

"Okay. I see two problems." He leans over his forearms on the table and holds my gaze. "First, if she were as devoted a friend to you as you seem to be to her—and I can hear in your voice how much you care for her—she would have recognized your hesitation for what it was and withdrawn her request. She would have respected your feelings on the matter and put you first. But she didn't."

I take a sip of coffee, blown away by the soft, considerate way he spoke just now.

He's also not wrong. Juliana knows I'm hesitant to continue spying on the Bellantis and I made it pretty clear that I think her rushed marriage is a mistake. What would she say if I told her I was done helping her altogether? Would she disown me if I dropped out completely? I really don't know.

"You're right," I finally respond. "You said there were two problems. What's the other one?"

"That you only *hinted* at not wanting to help her, instead of asserting yourself and saying no."

"I'm not good at saying no. Especially to her."

Armani seems to weigh his words, tapping his fingers on the tabletop, and then says, "After meeting your family and hearing about how you grew up, I can understand that. Your father and brothers didn't give you many opportunities for asserting your wants and needs. And when you did, they were brushed aside. Experiences like that, especially at a young age, teach you that speaking up is worthless. That what you want is worthless, particularly compared to the wants of others."

Slightly stunned at the corner this conversation has turned, I give myself a moment to shore up my feelings before responding. "You'd make a pretty good therapist, Mr. Bellanti."

"Maybe. I think I'd hate it. But my point is, all that stuff you internalized—it's all lies. What you want *matters*. That little kid inside you who thinks they don't count? That's not who you are anymore. Even if you sometimes feel like it is. You've had to overcome a lot of shit, a lot of obstacles, a lot of long fucking odds to get where you're at, and that makes you stronger than you realize. You have power.

"From what you're telling me, though, it seems like this friend may also be happy to take that power away from you. Not necessarily on purpose. Maybe she doesn't even realize she's doing it. But either way, it's not serving you. I think if you were accustomed to telling her how you really feel all the time, she'd be able to read you better. Instead, she's free to take advantage of your need to please her."

Fuck, he's good. Juliana did teach me to be more assertive, but not where she's concerned. Between her and me, I've always been the pleaser. The codependent one. Displeasing her makes me unhappy and anxious and I never realized until right this second just how unbalanced our dynamic is.

Armani could have twisted this a different way. He could have encouraged me to go through with something I'm not comfortable with to make my friend happy, just to make the point that it's okay to sacrifice my feelings to please someone else—someone like him. But he didn't. In fact...looking back, it dawns on me that for all the uncomfortable things he's put me though, he's always given me the opportunity to change my mind or say no or back out. Except for our wedding, of course.

And knowing him like I do now, I truly believe that his motivation for marrying me was to protect his family. They always come first. He did what he thought was necessary.

Now, it's time for me to do the same.

"Thank you," I say softly. "You've given me a lot to think about. I really appreciate it."

"Hey." The tenderness in his voice draws my full attention. "Don't let her or anyone else make you feel powerless. Trust your intuition, go with your gut, and do what you know is right. If you decide to talk to the coworker and want me to tag along, I will."

He checks his watch and stands, and with one last look at me, nods and walks out of the room.

For a few minutes, I sit in stunned silence, sipping my cold coffee. I can't believe Armani just gave me such lovely and genuine advice.

He's a better man than I ever guessed.

25

CANDI

DARKNESS HAS FALLEN by the time I work up the courage to call Juliana.

The wine I had with dinner helps a little as I slip into the small library on the second floor with my phone in my pocket and a second glass of wine in my hand. Armani's words from our conversation earlier stuck with me all day, and the more I thought about his advice, the more confident I felt that it's time for me to formally withdraw from the Brunos' spy game.

It's time to finally tell Juliana no.

I figured a call would be easier than saying any of this to her face. I don't want to lose my nerve.

But when I bring up her contact, my anxiety gets the best of me anyway. So I down half of the wine I brought up here for moral support—a lovely new red blend that the Bellantis are launching next season, named after baby Liliana—and then wonder why I feel so panicked.

I guess it's like Armani said. I'm not accustomed to saying no to Juliana, and I've spent most of my life disregarding my own needs in favor of others. It's second nature for me to just say yes, go with the flow, and avoid rocking the boat.

The thing is, I can't go on like this. I'm done spying, or pretending to spy, on the Bellantis.

She picks up on the third ring, sounding a little distracted. "Hey, what's up?"

"Hey! Are you busy?" I blurt, my voice unnaturally high-pitched.

"Nope, just sitting on the couch. Is everything okay? You never call this late. Is it...him?"

It's barely past nine, but it's been a while since we've had an evening chat. And now that I'm thinking about it, I realize that we never talk like we used to. Before Armani, we'd call or at least text each other almost every day. We really have grown apart over the last few months.

"Um, no. That's all fine. I thought I should check in. See how things are going."

She pauses. "They're going the same as they were yesterday. I'm not calling off the wedding."

"Right. Of course not! I just figured I'd...see if you wanted to delegate anything."

There's a rustling sound in the background and I wonder if she's flipping through bridal magazines without me. The thought makes me a little sad.

"Okay, Candi. What is up with you? You're acting kinda...off." More rustling.

"What's that noise? Are you marking up that marriage contract? Make sure you put in a clause that says he has to bring you breakfast in bed every morning and give you a foot massage every night."

She laughs, and it calms my nerves a little.

"I'm actually going through a box of samples for wedding decorations. I never even thought about most of this stuff. Tablecloths, napkins, bunting for the chairs, table place cards. I went to a wedding expo today—it was really last minute, or I would have asked you to come with—and brought home a literal *carload* of stuff. And of course I have, like, forty-eight hours to pick everything."

A wave of disappointment washes over me. "Oh, no worries. I get it. Maybe I could come over tomorrow and help you go through it all?"

"Oh, no, that's okay. The wedding is coming up so fast, I decided I'd better choose everything myself and get it over with. Plus, the vendors were super nice when I explained my short time frame. I've already made all the right connections. They're basically waiting on my call so they can get cranking."

"Sounds good," is all I can think of to say.

I get a sour taste in my mouth, and it's not from the wine.

"So, I wanted to talk to you about something..." I start, my heart starting to pound again.

She makes an exasperated sound. "Look. I know you're worried. I know this is super rushed. And yeah, I don't really know the guy. But it's a business arrangement, Candi. And it's temporary, so—"

"It's not about your wedding," I interrupt.

Though it should be. I should be talking her out of the mess she's about to get herself into. But who knows? Maybe she's right, and she and Mr. Orloff will have an amicable divorce in a few years and nobody will end up worse for wear. Or maybe they'll end up legitimately falling in love, and Jules will be telling the funny story about how they got married for the rest of her life. Who am I to judge?

"O-kay...then what is it?" she prods. "I'm kinda crunched for time here."

Taking a deep breath, I close my eyes and blurt, "I think you're wrong about the Bellantis."

I spill the words quickly and then gulp down more wine to fortify myself for the reaction I'm about to get. But she doesn't even respond, as if I've actually stunned her.

Finally, a huff comes through the line. "Are you serious?"

Shit. Now I have to explain myself. I'm so glad I'm doing this over the phone, rather than face-to-face where I'd have to witness the sight of her frowning disappointment in me.

"I am. Look, I've gotten to know them and understand them a lot more since moving in here. The pieces just aren't adding up, and—"

"Jesus, Candi. Are you listening to yourself? You've been snowed by good dick. It's making you think you have feelings for this guy and blinding you to what's right in front of your face."

Pinching the bridge of my nose, I remind myself to keep my voice down, so I'm not overheard. Armani and his brothers went to have some kind of meeting at the Bellanti offices after dinner, but Karina is still somewhere in the house. She and Marco have been out of town a lot, but he's got some time off from the racing circuit this week so they've been staying in Marco's rooms here at the Bellanti estate.

"It's not that, Jules. It's that all the terrible things you've said about them, like the trafficking and the drugs and the arms deals...the executions...I've seen zero evidence of anything like that."

"Of course you haven't—these are professional mobsters. It's not like they're going to bring their dirty work home with them and talk about it around the dinner table! The Bellantis are cold-blooded killers, Candi. And Armani tortures people! Did you forget about that dungeon on the property?"

"No, I haven't forgotten."

"Good, because there is a very fucking dark side to that man you're catching feelings for. He hurts women. He treats them like disposable goods, like...like *commodities*. He's not a nice person."

My lips tingle. I'm clutching my wineglass so hard, I'm surprised it hasn't shattered.

"What are you talking about?"

"I've told you this before," she snaps. "You've seen it yourself on the yacht! The Bellantis use women as bargaining chips for their allies and business partners. They pass them out like party favors and trade them with each other like baseball cards! How else do you think they take in such consistently high profits in a volatile market? They're a small family winery. There's no way they're raking in millions of dollars every year solely because they make good wine. The cops are probably in on it, too."

This phone call was a bad idea. I've never heard such vitriol in her voice. She's absolutely livid, and I can't be sure if what's coming out of her mouth is factual or merely ammunition to keep me on her side. The problem is, when it comes to the mafia stuff, I have no idea what the Bellantis are involved in.

"Did you forget when their shipment of wine went up in flames on the docks?" she goes on. "Did you forget what else they were gearing up to transport that day?"

"The police didn't find any women. The fire wasn't even on the news," I point out.

"Which is so odd now, isn't it? Unless you consider the fact that we're talking about the goddamn mafia. These people can bribe their way out of anything, and they have the Napa police in their back pocket. The only reason there weren't any women there is because we set their shit on fire first."

Closing my eyes, I sink down into an overstuffed chair. Is she right?

"It's a good thing you tipped Uncle Sergio off about that shipment when you did, by the way," Juliana says. "Remember, the whole reason we're doing all this is to stop the Bellantis from getting away with these heinous crimes. With all their money and their friends in high places, they'll never stop trafficking women until *we* make them stop."

My throat tightens. Her voice lowers, taking on the sweet, even tone I know so well.

"*We*. Meaning you, and me, and everyone else that's working toward this goal to stop the Bellanti reign and all the sick shit that comes with it. I need you, Candi. I need you to stay in the fight. I know you want to believe in the fairy tale, but come on. Use your head."

"I don't know what to believe anymore," I whisper, my voice wobbling.

"Of course you don't. It's called Stockholm syndrome.

But you need to get it together. You're picking the wrong side of this battle. You married a *sociopath*. I'm sure he's very charming. That's why he's so dangerous. But he doesn't give a shit about right and wrong; he doesn't know what human empathy is! He destroys women for money. You can't forget who he is and what he's capable of."

Memories flash in my mind—the smell of blood and bleach in the Deep Cellar, Armani cuffing me to a chair in Vegas and getting so rough with me that I cried, Armani torturing the tattooed man, not a shadow of remorse in his eyes, the hard bulge of Armani's guns under his jacket every single day, his—

"Get me the names I need," Juliana commands, interrupting the whirl of my dark thoughts.

I'm still wavering. There's more to Armani and me than sex, I know there is. But what if he's truly as bad as she thinks? What if he is a sociopath and I'm just a toy for him to play with? And I've known Juliana for years. I've always trusted her. There's no benefit for her in lying to me about this.

"I'll try," I murmur.

"You need to do better than try, Candi," she says, sounding for all the world like her uncle Sergio. "Get the information I asked you for, and stop fucking around!"

She hangs up on me then, leaving me stunned. Pulling the phone from my ear, I stare at it like there must be some mistake. But no. The screen says Call Ended.

Slipping it into my pocket, my heart thumping hard in my chest, I toss back the last few sips of my wine and decide to get a refill. I'm going to need it to process that conversation.

In the kitchen, I find a fresh bottle of zinfandel. It'll do. After I uncork it, I bring it with me to the back patio. The swimming pool glimmers under the moon, solar lights glowing prettily around the yard. The air is warm and makes me instantly sleepy when I slide into one of the chairs surrounding the fire pit.

It's not until I've poured a glass and taken the first sip that I allow myself to mull over my conversation with Juliana. She made a lot of solid points. And if the Bellantis really are trafficking women, I need to know. I need the truth. But who am I supposed to believe? Armani will deny it. Juliana will insist she's right. And then there's me, caught in the middle, loyal to both even though I can't be.

I don't know what the hell to do.

The back door opens, and I whip a look over my shoulder. It's Karina, wearing a bathing suit with a bathrobe over it. She freezes when she sees me with my palm over my chest.

"Sorry, I didn't know anyone was out here. Didn't mean to scare you," she says. "I'll go."

"No, don't. You're fine," I tell her, waving my hand. "Seriously."

She hesitates, seeming to debate her options. I bet she's going to leave, though, because she hates me as much as the rest of this family does.

"Hey, um—would you like some of this wine?" I say hastily, my inhibitions muted by the amount of alcohol I've consumed over the last hour or two. "It's so nice out, and I just opened the bottle..."

Karina glances quickly behind her, and then shrugs. "Sure. Why not."

She walks over and takes a seat across from me. I refill my empty glass and go to hand her the bottle, only to realize—

"Oh. I only have one glass. Do you want to drink out of the bottle? I didn't bring another."

She laughs. "I'll just grab one from the pool bar."

She gets up and goes to the other side of the patio, where there's a full outdoor kitchen, complete with a fridge, grill, pizza oven, and cabinetry loaded with dishes and glassware of all types. An excellent use of Bellanti money if I ever saw one.

I pass the zinfandel over once she's back in her chair. She sips from her glass and looks at me with a brow raised. We haven't talked in a while. We were friendly when she first married Marco, mostly because Frankie was the leader of our pack...but then Karina and Marco started traveling nonstop for his races, and once the Bellantis found out I was working for the Brunos, Karina basically stopped acknowledging my existence. Along with everyone else in the family besides Armani.

"So..." she says, breaking the tension. "You came out here to look at the stars?"

"Something like that." I take another drink of my wine. "Actually, that's not true."

But I can't say, *I came out here to get drunk since I just realized how totally fucked I am.*

"What's wrong? Is it...Armani?" she asks.

"It's a lot of things. But yes, he's a big part of it. And... I'm also stressed because my best friend is getting married to someone she barely knows. Which I don't approve of. And now we're fighting."

Karina's eyes widen. "Oh. Gosh. I'm sorry."

"It could turn out okay, but I just feel like...arranged marriages have such a huge potential for disaster. And she's acting like it's no big deal, but it might ruin her life. You know what I mean?"

Her brows shoot up again. I wonder if she thinks I'm referring to her and Marco, or even Frankie and Dante for that matter. Or if she's aware of how my marriage to Armani went down.

"I was talking about my own experiences," I clarify, taking another chug of wine. "I wasn't throwing shade at you. Honestly, you and Marco seem really happy now anyway. So that's a plus for marriages of convenience, right? That they can turn out good in the end? And Frankie's pretty much living her best life too, so...I don't know. Maybe I'm worrying for nothing. It's just happening so fast."

All that word-vomit has me suddenly very self-conscious. If Karina had any suspicions that my elopement in Vegas had nothing to do with Armani and me being in love, I've just confirmed them.

"Your friend shouldn't be upset with you for caring about her," Karina says thoughtfully, turning the stem of her glass between her fingers. "Even if you're coming across as unsupportive, she has to realize it's because you genuinely want what's best for her."

"Yes! Exactly. And a quickie marriage ain't it. Unless it is, but that's quite a gamble," I babble.

Karina nods. "She's probably getting defensive because she knows, deep down, that this is a risky move. Which is scary. I bet she just doesn't want to have to admit it."

"It *is* risky," I agree. "And yeah, she's definitely the type to play the tough guy. More wine?"

Karina holds out her nearly empty glass and I give her a generous pour. Then I refill mine. I've lost track of how many glasses I've had now. Including the drinks I had at dinner and during my phone call with Jules, this is either my fourth or fifth. I do feel warm all over.

As we sip in contemplative silence, I wonder…is Karina truly happy? Or is she just pretending to be? Maybe she feels like she's locked into her marriage and has no other option but to live with it.

"Do you think you made the right choice?" I ask. "About marrying Marco?"

She laughs. "Oh, yeah. He's the best thing that ever happened to me. But honestly, when I look back out how starry-eyed and naïve I was going into it, I realize how badly things could have turned out. Someone else could have really taken advantage of me. Especially with the way I grew up. I didn't get a great sense of what healthy relationships are supposed to look like. I got really lucky."

"You are lucky," I slur softly. "When did you know for sure that…that he was the one?"

"Let's see…we met at a party. It sounds so cliché, but the moment I saw him, I felt…connected to him. But you're asking about when I was sure about him, and I definitely wasn't sure that early on."

"Was it when he said he loved you for the first time?" I ask. Because if it is, maybe I'll never have that with Armani. He can barely even admit that he likes me.

"No. It wasn't our first kiss either. Or the poetry."

"Poetry?" I gasp. "Marco?"

"I know, right? Not that he wrote it, he just transcribed some of the Italian classics."

"Wow," I breathe. "I had no idea he was such a romantic. A flirt, yes, but..."

"Yeah," she says. "There's a lot more to Marco than you'd ever guess."

Sounds familiar. Frankie told me the same thing about Dante—about all the Bellanti brothers.

"I'd probably have to say that I knew Marco was the one when he snuck into the dressing room during my wedding dress fitting. I was engaged to someone else when I met him, and the dress was all wrong. The groom was all wrong. Everything about it was wrong. But with Marco, everything felt right.

"That damn fitting was breaking my heart, and then there Marco was, and I just...instantly felt better. I knew in that moment that I loved him. That he was the one I wanted to be with. I was sure of it. I've had ups and downs with him since then, and plenty of temporary doubts, but...I've also had faith."

"I wish I had that kind of faith," I whisper. "I'm just so confused. About everything. And now my best friend is going to become Mrs. Orloff, and meanwhile I haven't even decided whether or not to be a real Bellanti."

My voice cracks and I look away, expecting her to get up and leave me to my drunken whining. But instead she leans over, takes my hand, and just...holds it. She doesn't say anything, but she doesn't have to. She's here for me. That's all that matters.

And I'm grateful.

26

CANDI

"There you are."

My head jerks up. Karina quickly pulls her hand away from mine as Armani steps out of the sliding glass door and makes his way across the patio.

"Hope I'm not interrupting," he says, folding his arms as he towers over us.

"I was actually just about to go," Karina tells him, popping up from her chair. "Thanks for the wine, Candi. Good night, you two."

She leaves, taking her wineglass with her. Armani leans over and picks up the bottle.

"It's just a zin," I tell him. "You can have the rest."

He turns it upside down over my empty glass, revealing that there are literally only two drops left.

"You're drunk," he says.

"Just a little?" I mumble.

"Cute. Let's get you to bed."

To bed. Those simple words instantly send a shiver of

want down my spine, even as all of Juliana's accusations about the Bellantis still ricochet around inside my head.

If she's right, my husband and his brothers are very immoral, very disgusting, very evil men. But my heart and my mind are still at war, and despite the alcohol muddying my thoughts, my body is screaming for me to let Armani take me upstairs and show me exactly what kind of man he is.

"I didn't drink the whole bottle all by myself," I insist as Armani takes my hands and lifts me up from my chair. "Karina helped."

"I see."

Once I'm on my feet, I stumble a little, right into his rock-hard chest.

"Whoa there, cowboy," he says teasingly, gripping my upper arms in his warm, steadying grasp.

Looking up at him, I realize his hair is damp and he smells like clean shampoo and soap. His tight black T-shirt hugs his torso so good, it's all I can do not to blurt out something awkward about wanting to be that shirt right now. Or about how much better that shirt would look on our bedroom floor.

"Mm, you smell good," I whisper.

He barely suppresses a laugh. "A shower will do that."

"Maybe you should put me in one of those too, then, yourself," I attempt to flirt. "Except with both of us. At the same time. In the shower, I mean."

This time, he lets out the laugh. "I'll see what I can do."

"You know what I'm saying," I insist, drawing him down for a kiss.

I close my eyes and try to lose myself in the reassurance

of his mouth on mine, but I can't. All I can think about is the fact that I shouldn't be attracted to a man who hurts women, and I sure as hell shouldn't love one that does.

Even as I pull back, the feel of his palms sliding down over my ass both excites and burns me. What is wrong with me? I need to get some real answers before I lose my head again. Before I allow the strong pull of desire to blot out the direness of the situation I've ended up in.

"Let's go upstairs," he says softly.

Lust, panic, uncertainty, my heart saying yes, my inner logic saying no, the echo of Juliana's scolding—all of it has me freezing up until I realize I'm already letting him walk me toward the house.

He's gentle as he leads me inside and then locks the door behind us. Patiently, he helps me down the hall, up the stairs, and into our room, supporting me as I trip, giggle, find my feet, and trip again.

Once the door is shut, he scoops me right off my feet and throws me over his shoulder. After he carries me through the sitting room, then into the bedroom, he tosses me onto the bed.

"Hey!" I exclaim, rolling into a sitting position.

But he's on me in a second, pushing me onto my back, climbing over me and pinning my wrists above my head. Normally, I would love this. I'd lean into playing submissive, relishing the feel of his body weight, his domineering attitude, the demands about to spill out of his mouth.

Right now, though? I can't handle it. I'm suddenly a lot more sober than I was five minutes ago.

"I was serious about the shower," I say, struggling in his grip. "Let me up."

Instantly, he does, sliding off the bed and watching me. "What's wrong?"

"Nothing. I just need to wash up."

He follows me into the bathroom, then looks away and leans against the doorframe as I peel off my clothes and step into the shower. My head throbs and my eyelids feel heavy, but my adrenaline is racing as I soap up and close my eyes under the hot water.

"Why was Karina with you tonight?"

Ah, there it is. The first question of the evening. He's never this quiet and observant unless he's preparing to interrogate me.

"She came out to swim, but I was already sitting there so she joined me for a glass of wine."

After a moment, he says, "Interesting."

I look at him through the steamy glass door of the shower. He hasn't moved. "I know, right?"

"What did you two talk about?"

"Oh. Nothing, really. Basically just how much she loves Marco."

"Hm."

He doesn't push me for further details as I shampoo my hair, condition it, wash off my makeup...it's been at least fifteen minutes now, but he's still standing in the door. Obviously, he's not going anywhere. I turn off the water and push the shower door open. Armani wraps me in a towel.

"Thank you," I say, not meeting his eyes.

"I'll go get your robe."

"I'm fine," I say sharply.

Armani takes a deep breath, but he doesn't move. And I can't just run out of the bathroom. It's a large enough space, but he's standing right in front of me. Blocking me. When he raises his hand to touch my face, I instinctively flinch back.

"Hey. What's wrong?"

"The wine. I have a headache."

He snorts. "You have a headache? That's your excuse?"

I look up with a glare, about to go off on him about how I don't need an "excuse" to not want to be touched, but he's on me in a millisecond, tugging my towel off, slipping his hand between my legs, his finger tracing the wet line of my pussy as his tongue laps the beads of water on my shoulder.

Gasping, I scramble for the towel and hold it over myself as I push past him. In the bedroom, I rifle through my drawers until I find a pair of sweatpants and a tank top, getting dressed as fast as I can, even though I'm still soaking wet from the shower. My hands are shaking, my breathing shallow and fast.

From behind me, I hear Armani say, "You don't have to run away from me. I wasn't trying to force you. That's not my thing. If you don't want to—"

"I do want to!" I yell, whirling to face him. "That's the whole problem."

"Then why are you so on edge?"

"Because I don't feel safe," I blurt, before I have time to consider my words.

His face changes, his eyes immediately darting to the window, the perimeter of the room, as if he's expecting someone with a gun to leap from the shadows. "What happened?"

"Nothing."

"I need to know, Candi. Was there someone outside? Did you see something? Hear something?"

"No." Shaking my head, I whisper. "It's you. I'm afraid of *you*."

"Why? Did Karina say something?"

"No. It's just—I can't be feeling like this about you." My lower lip trembles. Tears sting my eyes, but I blink them back. "You're not a good person."

All the breath seems to go out of him. "That's true. I know I'm not...good. But I'm the same person I've always been. What changed? I shouldn't be any scarier to you now than I was yesterday."

"You traffick women!"

His whole body goes rigid. "I do *what*?"

Searching his face, I try to determine if he's just trying to play innocent, but I can't tell. He looks genuinely shocked at my accusation, but he's also the absolute king of poker face and deceit.

"I know all about it. I know what you and your brothers were planning that day at the docks, the day of the fire. You weren't just exporting wine. Women were supposed to get added to the shipment."

He crosses his arms, glaring at me with fury in his eyes. "Is that what you really think?"

"It's what I was told! You were more than happy to give me a tour of the warehouses, even teach me how the shipping process works, but I didn't know what you were *really* shipping until—"

"Until Sergio told you. And you believed him. Jesus Christ. You *were* the one who told him about the shipment going out that day from our private dock. Jesus, fuck, Candi!

My brothers were convinced it was you, and I defended you! And yeah, I had my own suspicions, but then someone else confessed to leaking that intel and I actually thought—I thought we'd judged you too harshly. I should have known all along that it was you who stabbed us in the back."

"I did what I had to do. I did the right thing," I insist.

A harsh laugh escapes his throat. "Jesus. Wow. I am honestly shocked at how easily my headstrong wife was manipulated by goddamn Sergio Bruno. But apparently that kind of accusation is enough to override your common sense, or any need for actual confirmation! Did it never occur to you to simply *ask me if it's true*?"

"You would've just lied about it anyway."

Advancing on me, he grabs my shoulders roughly. "All Sergio has to do is plant a seed and you just let it grow! You eat it right up, all his lies, anything he tells you about my family. Did you even once *consider* that he might be lying to make you think you were doing the right thing by spying on me?"

The more he talks, the more I have to consider the possibility that I've made a terrible mistake.

"I didn't know what to believe," I admit, looking up at him with tears in my eyes. "I've been going back and forth about all of this since the Brunos first hired me on. I never know what's real and what's not. What's true and what's bullshit. Which family is the good one, which is the bad one. All of you are mobsters, so how the fuck am I supposed to know?"

Armani lets go of me.

Slowly, gravely, he says, "This family has never—*never* —been involved in human trafficking. Not even when my

269

piece of shit father was in charge. The Bellantis have never, and will never, partake in that kind of activity. Apparently my word means nothing to you, but that's the goddamn truth."

I see nothing but sincerity—and yes, indignant anger—in his eyes. And...if Armani and his brothers really were involved in trafficking, wouldn't Frankie and Karina know it by now? Would Karina be so in love with Marco if his family was trafficking women? I know Frankie wouldn't put up with it.

"I'm sorry," I murmur, my voice husky with emotion. "I'm so sorry. I've gotten everything so twisted. This has been an impossible situation since the beginning. Everyone around me is using me. I'm everyone's fucking pawn. Nobody tells me the full story, not ever. But...I believe you. I do."

Armani spreads his arms wide. "This is who I am, Candi. I'm not all bad and I'm sure as hell not all good. Take it or leave it."

Before I can say anything in response, he grabs my chin, lifting it so I have no choice but to look him in the eyes.

"But if you take it," he growls, "you take it all."

Without even meaning to, I instinctively glance over at the bed. When I look back up at him, there isn't even a glimmer of a doubt in my mind any longer. This is what I want. This is *who* I want.

A soft moan escapes me as I throw myself at him, lips crashing into his, my hands clawing at the hem of his T-shirt. Armani meets my desperation in kind as he leads me to the bed and pushes me down onto it. I watch him with bated breath as he peels his shirt off, drops his pants, and climbs on top of me.

Trapping me with one arm on either side of my head, he says, "I said if you take it, you take it all. All eight inches."

My eyelids flutter as desire pulses through me. "Yes. Give it to me. All of it. Please."

And then I submit completely as he takes control and claims my body, demanding an apology that I'm all too happy to give.

27

CANDI

Yes, I'm hungover. Yes, my head is pounding and I'm a tad queasy. But that's okay.

Because today, I have no responsibilities other than having myself a long, luxurious bubble bath and drinking ginger tea with honey and snacking on the box of saltine crackers that Armani brought me from the pantry. Nobody has to know that I didn't get out of bed until after noon. Nor that I'm wearing freaking sunglasses in the bathtub.

After I sink into the hot, sudsy water, I tilt my head back and let out a long, slow breath. I figure I might as well take advantage of this alone time and give some serious thought to the conversation I had with Juliana yesterday. It was easily the ugliest fight we've ever had. My cheeks still burn with humiliation when I think about the way she yelled at me and then hung up.

Was she lying to me about the Bellantis and the trafficked women? Has she been lying all along?

And why would she tell me something so completely horrible if it wasn't true?

I meant what I said last night when I told Armani I believed him. I do believe him. Not just because I want to, either. My gut says he's not bullshitting me.

Plus, there's the complete lack of credible evidence to support Juliana's accusations. They're nothing but hearsay. I haven't seen anything, haven't heard anything, haven't gotten any shady vibes from Armani's brothers or their wives. Even Google has turned up zilch, despite there being copious archived news pieces about Enzo Bellanti's criminal activities, none of which had anything to do with trafficking.

Money laundering? Yes. Illegal gambling? Yes. Selling guns, drugs, fixing races, extortion, blackmail, etc. Yes, yes, yes. And that slimeball was somehow acquitted every single time, lending credence to Juliana's insistence that the Bellantis have law enforcement in their pockets. But never has there been even a *hint* of trafficking, running brothels, or even being associated with escort services. I would have found *something* while I was up all night searching on my phone, battling a combination of insomnia and post-booze vertigo.

Juliana's story just doesn't hold water.

I've always trusted everything my best friend has told me. But apparently, the entire time I've been handing over information about the Bellantis, jumping into the fire for her, risking life and limb to do the right thing, she's been spinning a web of lies.

It's certainly possible that she was lying unintentionally —that her uncle Sergio has been lying to her all along, brainwashing her so completely that she never even thought to question his stories. Just like I never thought to question my supposed best friend. Except...it's hard to believe Juliana is just another innocent victim when she's been actively involved in some shady-sounding international business dealings with a Russian. A man she openly admitted was pretty rough. Who is, in all likelihood, a mobster. Who she now intends to marry.

Which is interesting, considering the fact that she has no trouble going out of her way to smear Armani for being in the mob. I guess it's perfectly fine for her to marry a criminal, but the one I'm with is the devil and has to be destroyed at all costs. It's also suspicious as all get-out that she never breathed the slightest mention of this guy to me before. Is it because she knew I wouldn't approve? Or because she thought I'd try to talk her out of it? Or did he really just pop up out of nowhere and she's just decided to throw caution to the wind? I don't get it. There's no excuse for her shifty behavior.

There's only one thing that makes sense to me about any of this—Juliana's prejudice against the Bellantis is rooted in the sad reality that they killed her parents. However, this was decades ago, so it was the work of Enzo Bellanti. A man I know very little about, except for what I gathered from the news articles I read and the bits and pieces of stories Armani has shared. I have no doubt that the former Bellanti boss was a tyrant. Violent, abusive, ruthless, egotistical. The list could go on. The point is, yes, Juliana may have every right to believe the Bellantis are pure evil.

But is it fair to lay the sins of the father upon his children?

I don't think so. Not at all, in fact.

Especially when those children have tried so hard to get out from under his shadow.

Has Juliana let her biases against the Bellantis cloud her judgement to the point where she's never considered that her uncle might be lying to her about the crimes that Armani and his brothers are allegedly involved in? Or has she been in cahoots with Sergio all along? What does she get out of any of this? Revenge? Power? Her uncle's approval? Is it a money thing?

Over the years, she's detailed plenty of heinous crimes that the Bellanti family has been involved in. So when Sergio asked Juliana to recruit me as a spy, it seemed like a no-brainer. The few times I met him, I thought her uncle was intimidating—and he definitely had a devious air—but Jules vouched for her uncle and I quickly agreed to help them take down their enemies. I had no reason to question the stories I'd been told about the Bellantis.

As far as I was concerned, the tales of the Bellantis' misdeeds had real weight, simply because I'd been hearing them for so long. Every time Juliana had a few drinks, she'd relay the latest sordid stories about what they had done recently. The Bellantis were behind the influx of fentanyl-laced drugs circulating in Northern California, responsible for the deaths of hundreds. The Bellantis were selling cheap weapons to African warlords. If a local restaurant or boutique went out of business, it was because they'd refused to pay the Bellantis protection money. A local politician got caught up in a sex scandal? The Bellantis were the ones who'd framed them. Meth lab explosion? It was the Bellantis' lab.

She rarely mentioned the same misdeed twice. It seemed like she had something new to report every time she went off on one of her diatribes. And I rarely pushed back.

The few times that I did, she'd turn her anger toward me for questioning her. I learned to simply be the sympathetic ear she needed.

Now, I just feel like a fool.

My best friend isn't who I thought she was.

Guilt pangs inside my chest. After all we've been through together, and all the help she's given me over the years, it feels traitorous to think of her in anything other than a glowing light. Yet...how can I trust her anymore? I've been played.

Juliana pushed me into agreeing to spy on Armani for her uncle. She encouraged me to sleep with a Bellanti, to move into the Bellantis' estate, to dive right into the vipers' nest, just to get information. And when I'd texted her to let her know about my surprise elopement in Vegas, she'd been over the moon. Not because she was excited about me getting married, but because she was thrilled to learn that I'd made so much progress weaseling my way into Armani's life, while simultaneously reminding me that I needed to gather more intel. To do more, more, more.

Despite the danger, nothing I did during my time as a mole was good enough for her, for them. It didn't even matter that I'd legally bound myself to a mobster, possibly for the rest of my life. I doubt if that even crossed Juliana's mind. Her best friend had sacrificed herself for the "cause," and she was totally fine with it.

Now? I'm not even sure anymore what the cause is.

There are plenty of other things bothering me, as well. Like, why hadn't she told me about her Russian fiancé before the sudden engagement announcement? We used to tell each other everything, and immediately. She'd call me with the smallest bit of news, no matter how trivial. Yet she didn't let on about this marriage deal until she was already preparing to sign on the dotted line. And I don't believe it was sprung on her so quickly that she didn't have time to tell me beforehand. What is she hiding?

Despite the warmth of the water, I shiver.

My head is pounding, and it's not just from the alcohol. All these doubts and suspicions have my head spinning. I don't have any answers. All I have are hundreds of questions, circling each other in my mind nonstop like a dog relentlessly chasing its tail.

I hate this.

I sip my tea, which has gone cold. Sliding my sunglasses on top of my head, I look out the window. It's raining, and hard. Fat droplets smack against the glass, driven by the wind. Tree branches bend and sway, their leaves flying around from the force of the storm. A perfect match for my mood.

With a shiver, I sink deeper under the water. There's an ache at my core that's both delicious and sore, and I recall how rough Armani was with me last night. As if he was desperate to mark me, reclaim me as his own, ensure that I gave myself to him wholly and with complete loyalty.

Obviously, I loved every second of it.

He had reason to be upset with me, to banish me from the bedroom, from his life. The accusations that I made clearly triggered him, and not in a way that I expected. He'd been shocked, angry, incredulous. Not only that, but also... hurt. Wounded.

But he didn't send me away. He defended himself and his family. Because it mattered to him that I stood there and listened to what he had to say. All of that just doesn't strike me as the reaction of a guilty man. And in my heart, I have no lingering doubts. Mafia family or no, the Bellantis live by their own code, and that code says they won't be involved in anything to do with the skin trade.

I think through my time with Armani, the things he's revealed about his family and himself that began to change my beliefs about them. I'd been groomed to see the Bellantis as the enemy, but the tug-of-war started when I realized that Armani is the man that he is for a reason. To protect what he loves, at all costs. It's just like the trifecta of Italian words that he has tattooed across his chest: *famiglia, onore, forza.* Family, honor, power. These are the things that Armani holds dear.

Swallowing hard, I get out of the tub and wrap myself in my robe.

I need to talk to my husband.

Urgency burns in my gut, but I'm not sure what to do. Run to him and tell him what little I know about Juliana's impending wedding? Confess that my best friend calls Sergio Bruno uncle? My rational self rejects these impulses. I can't go in, guns blazing, when I don't know anything for certain...

Except that I've been manipulated cruelly by my best friend. I feel sick at the thought. I still don't know what I'm going to say to her the next time we speak. How much trouble will I be in when I tell her I didn't get those names for her? I thought our friendship was bulletproof. Is it even Armani's help that I'm after, or am I trying to satisfy some dark urge to make my friend pay for deceiving me?

Either way, my instincts are telling me to go to Armani,

to get his help sorting this out. It's the only way forward I can see.

Hurrying into the bedroom, I shrug off my robe and get dressed. This is it.

No more secrets. No more lies.

It's time to tell Armani the truth.

28

ARMANI

"Do you have a name for us?"

"Better." With that, Clayton slaps three black-and-white prints on Dante's desk and crosses his arms, clearly pleased with himself. "I have pictures."

My brother-in-law has wasted no time flushing out another local Bratva member with inside knowledge of the Bruno deal. Dante and Marco lean over to look as I grab the photos and study them.

Each one shows an increasingly zoomed-in image of a square-jawed man with thick brows whose broad shoulders strain the seams of his black leather jacket as he orders from an outdoor café, waits for his order, and finally leaves with a coffee in his hand.

"Is this—this looks like downtown," Marco says.

"Sharp eye on ya," Clayton says.

He pulls up more photos on his phone and passes the device around. These are in color and show the man walking along the waterfront, at the racetrack, and entering Sergio Bruno's property with a couple of goons at his side.

The picture quality isn't great, but the man's tall frame and leather jacket are unmistakable. And the fact that he's visited Bruno on his home turf? Jackpot.

"Fuck, Clayton, you're good," Marco says, shaking his head in wonder.

Dante musters a tight smile. "Well done. You sure this is our guy, though? He looks a lot younger than I expected. A little green. Or maybe he just needs a haircut."

"What a crotchety-ass old man thing to say," Marco razzes him.

"You could use a haircut, too, *fratellino*," Dante retorts. "You look like a mook."

"A *mook*? Case in point, grandpa," Marco says, sweeping back the dark hair at his temples. "Nobody uses that word anymore."

"You gotta go after the young ones," Clayton interrupts. "They're more liable to listen to reason. Elders are more vested, more loyal. More scared to step out of line. And they don't need the money."

"Makes sense," I say. "If you say this is the guy, this is the guy. Nice work."

Holding up his hands, Clayton says, "Whoa, whoa now. I didn't say I'd worked out any kind of deal. I've nailed him down, is all. Haven't made contact. Just done the surveillance."

"It's the start we needed to get moving on this," Dante says.

I grunt in agreement. But as my brothers (and brother-in-law) start discussing our new potential Bratva contact, my mind keeps drifting back to last night. To the moment when Candi admitted she'd tipped off the Brunos about our private dock, essentially taking responsibility for the warehouse fire there. Even though Donno had copped to it when I interrogated him...

But maybe Bruno had been doubly emboldened to act when he received that same intel from two different sources. There's no way to know for sure if the arson would have happened if she hadn't played the good little mole— but regardless, her betrayal is weighing heavily on me.

Jesus Christ, I really went to bat for Candi when my brothers first blamed the fire on her, not because I was sure she hadn't been involved, but as an act of good faith. Yes, I was well aware that it could have been her who betrayed us, but I didn't want to believe it. So I gave her the benefit of the doubt. I'd defended her with passion and fire, with everything in me. That's why it felt like such a fucking knife in the back when she told me to my face last night that she *had* done it. Especially since my lingering suspicions about her involvement had all but disappeared after Donno's confession.

I had just begun to *trust* her. Just begun to let my guard down the smallest bit. In my mind, I had even *forgiven* her for working for my family's enemies. I'd been ready to leave behind all the bad blood between me and Candi, see what the future might have in store for us. But she'd been lying to me all along. And despite my reservations, despite the fact that I knew better, I'd let her get away with it. Right under my nose. God, I'm an idiot.

Maybe Marco's right. Maybe I am pussywhipped.

In my line of work, that's a terminal sentence.

How can I ever look at Candi the same way? How can I ever trust her again? I am aware that, as twisted as it is to say

283

so, her heart was in the right place when she leaked that intel to the Brunos. She was convinced that in handing over information about our shipment, she was saving women from trafficking.

Does that make her actions forgivable, though?

And how can I be certain my wife won't get brainwashed by the Brunos again?

"Armani? You coming back to Earth or what?"

"What?" The word snaps out of me.

Dante hands me the phone so I can look at Clayton's photos.

"He's made appearances at all the usual Bruno haunts," Clayton is saying. "He likes the racetracks, but not for business. He likes to bet and he's garbage at it. Either he's wealthy on his own, or he's digging into Sergio's deep pockets already, because he's out tens of thousands."

"What else?" Dante prods.

I slide the phone back to Clayton and give him a nod, trying to tune back into the conversation.

"He's got a taste for Italian food. Visits two, three restaurants a day and doesn't lay down a dime at any of them. He drives two different black SUV's. A Cadillac, and a Suburban he picked up brand new off the lot. I spotted a woman with him twice, but I couldn't get a good look at her, and she was never in the frame long enough for a photo. She doesn't hang around, but he seems protective—or maybe just controlling of her."

"He has a weak spot, is what you're saying?" Marco ventures.

Clayton shrugs. "Women always are, aren't they?"

The men look at each other and I resist rolling my eyes.

These three are protective of their women to a fault. If that's how this guy views his girl, too, she might be a good target for maneuvering him.

"Any idea who she is?" I ask. "Bratva too, or…"

"Don't know nothing yet," Clayton says. "But I'll find out soon enough."

Dante claps Clayton on the shoulder. "No doubt."

"That's not all. He was driving around with a group of men yesterday that I didn't recognize as Bruno's regulars. I've scouted and surveyed those properties enough to know who his standard soldiers are. These guys were all in suits, very official looking."

"Feds?" Marco says. "You think this guy could be a plant? The FBI trying to set Bruno up?"

"Doubtful," I say. "My guess is, more Bratva. Higher-ups. Any idea where they were going?"

Clayton winces. "No. Caught 'em by chance when I was out driving. Got one pic, but it's shit."

The phone comes back to me and I look at the photo, Dante leaning over my shoulder. It's an out of focus shot, a black Cadillac SUV with four or five men inside, barely visible through the tinted windows. The outlines of faces and shoulders aren't detailed enough for us to identify the men.

"I'm going to assume this group all have the same purpose. All Bratva, and all here for Sergio," Dante says grimly as he crosses the office and pours himself a drink from the sideboard.

Marco follows suit, then offers Clayton a drink but not me. He's still salty from our disagreement the other day. It's funny that it still bothers him and here I am, not giving a

shit. Or I guess just giving a shit about much more important things. Like my duplicitous, backstabbing, manipula-
tive little wife. She needs to be punished, needs to swear her
loyalty to me anew. I go through a mental checklist of everything I'll need: blindfold, handcuffs, a remote-controlled
vibrator. I have a few ideas in mind.

"Armani? You in with this plan?"

Fuck. Glaring at Dante, I ignore his irritated sigh. It's
the second time I've been caught with my head not in the
game, and it's pissing *me* off. I need to get my shit together.

"Clayton wants to infiltrate."

This pulls me firmly back into the present. "No.
Hell no."

Clayton spreads his arms. "I'll just catch one of his
henchmen on the side at the track, strike up a conversation.
Lube him up with some hard liquor and see what comes
spilling out."

"Sounds too easy," I say, skeptical.

"Sometimes it is," he says. "Worth a shot, anyway."

I think about it. Despite his former employment by
various other mafia families, and despite his success at
rounding up information (and lowlifes) for me, he's still able
to move through the underground with relative ease. It
won't always be that way. This, in fact, could be the gig that
finally places a mark on his back if he's found out. Unless
the Bratva don't think before they pull the trigger.

"I don't like it," I tell him. "If you're made, you're dead."

"Or the perp won't live long enough to realize I've
skinned him for info," Clayton says.

"We don't have a choice. We need information and we

need it now," Dante says. "Before Sergio Bruno makes a pact with the devils that will burn Napa to the ground."

Letting out a long breath, I get up and finally pour myself a drink. "Do it then. But be strategic. Not all men can be loosened up with booze and the Bratva don't cave to pain."

Clayton looks unruffled. "I've got ketamine in my back pocket, if necessary. It goes down easy in a double shot of whiskey."

"Nasty drug," Marco comments.

Silence fills the room.

Clayton shrugs. "What? Anyone object?"

"Nope," I say for everyone, stabbing my brothers with a look. "Just watch yourself."

Dante looks at the photos on my desk again. "So what's the name of this asshole, again?"

"Orloff," Clayton says. "Maxim Orloff."

A sharp inhale makes everyone turn toward the door. Karina has one hand on the knob, as if she was just about to walk in. Her brows are knit together with worry.

"Sorry," she says. "It was open. I couldn't find you guys at the house so I came here."

Marco immediately goes to her and tugs her gently inside the office. "What's wrong? Did you need something?"

"No. I wanted to ask if we had dinner plans, but, um, did you just say Orloff?"

"He did." Marco tilts his head at Clayton. "Why?"

Karina frowns as she turns to me. "You should ask your wife about that. Really."

"My wife?" It's my turn to scowl. "What are you talking about?"

The door swings open, and now Candi is the one standing there with her eyes wide and her expression uncertain.

"She's right," Candi tells me. "You should ask me about Maxim Orloff."

Every eye in the room turns to her, my brothers tensing up as if they're expecting her to fight or flee. Needless to say, trust issues run deep in this family—and she's at the top of their shit list.

Candi glances around the office, slowly taking in the stern and suspicious faces, the defensive postures. She knows she's surrounded, and not by friends. But instead of looking intimidated or scared, she lifts her chin and addresses all of us.

"Let's talk."

29

CANDI

THE SECOND I stepped into Dante's office, all eyes were on me. Glaring, expectant. The pressure was on. But before anyone could launch into interrogation mode, Armani came over to usher me out the door.

"We'll do this at the house in half an hour," he calls over his shoulder as he leads me away.

"The home office," Dante says.

With that, the eldest Bellanti shuts the office door behind me and Armani with a cold finality that has me chilled to the bone.

I don't know what Armani and his brothers were meeting about just now, but it had to be about the Bratva—I heard the name Orloff loud and clear from the hallway. I also heard Karina implicating me. And although I'd gone in search of Armani specifically to talk to him, I hadn't actually decided what, or how much, I would reveal. The only thing I was sure of was the fact that Juliana's betrayal had burned down a wall, and now my secrets were going to come tumbling out.

This will be a good thing, I try to convince myself as I walk with Armani down the gravel path between the Bellanti Vineyards offices and the main house. I'm sick and tired of playing both sides.

Once we step inside the house, we make our way down the hall to the large downstairs office. Armani guides me to the couch, saying, "Sit right there. And stay."

I feel like a dog being given such commands, but all I do is nod. Armani grabs a bottle of water from the minifridge and hands it to me before he leaves me there alone. The second the door clicks shut, the edge of panic I've been feeling explodes into a full-blown anxiety attack.

Mentally, I will myself to stay calm, but it's impossible. Something huge is about to shift in my life. I drink a few sips of the water, sorely regretting the amount of alcohol I consumed last night. I'm doing a lot better after my bath, but my stomach is in knots and I still have a lingering headache.

The office door opens, and I expect to see Armani, but instead it's Marco and Dante followed by Karina and Frankie, who is holding baby Lili. No one looks at me as they shuffle around, grabbing desk chairs and side chairs and finding seats anywhere except the couch. They circle up around me, like lions corralling a zebra they're about to rip to shreds.

Just then, Armani reappears with a mug of hot tea. He sets it on the side table next to me, giving me the slightest nod before he drags a chair front and center and sits. He's directly across the circle from me. The perfect place for an interrogator to do his dirty work.

But this time is different. I have nothing to hide. Not anymore.

His expression softens, as if he's encouraging me and reassuring me. *Tell the truth and nothing bad will happen*, his face seems to say. He clasps his hands together. A beat of silence falls. Even the baby is silent. I look over at the tea.

"Eyes on me. Do not look away," he barks. "Tea is for after."

I do as he says and am acutely aware that his command has caused everyone to stare at me, too. I might as well be tied to a stake with a pyre at my feet.

"Orloff."

Armani drops the name coldly, already knowing it means something to me.

Keeping my gaze steady on his, I say, "Is the name of the man my best friend is going to marry."

"What else do you know about him?"

"Nothing. She told me the marriage is a business arrangement. A green card thing. He's Russian."

He doesn't blink. His face, impassive. "How well do you know this woman?"

"Like I said, Juliana is my best friend. From college. I know her well." My throat suddenly goes dry and I take another sip of water and add, "Or, I thought I did."

"This is the best friend you never mentioned to me until your brunch the other day."

"Yes."

He pauses and my pulse picks up. I can't tell if he's trying to make me even more nervous, or if he's actually puzzling over the whole situation in his mind.

"Why is that?" he asks.

"Because I thought I was doing the right thing by keeping her a secret. Now I'm not so sure."

One dark brow raises. "What changed?"

Everything, I think. Absolutely everything.

Regardless, even though I'm unhappy with Juliana right now, there's no way I'm going to throw her under the bus. For all I know, she might even be desperate for a way out of this wedding arrangement but knows she can't shirk her familial duty—or risk the wrath and punishment of her uncle Sergio. Her happy chatter about wedding planning and the ring and the dresses could just be a front. She's clearly an expert at hiding things from me, which probably includes her feelings. What if she needs my help?

Acutely aware of everyone in the room, I'm careful to focus on Armani so I don't lose my nerve.

"Maybe I should start at the beginning—"

"How is your friend connected to Sergio Bruno?" he interrupts.

I clear my throat. "She calls him her uncle, but I'm not sure if they're actually blood related. She lost her parents at a young age. He's taken care of her ever since. Sent her to fancy boarding schools in Europe, provided her with a monthly allowance, offered her a job at one of his consulting firms after she got out of college...he bankrolled her life, basically."

It dawns on me then. Had Karina and Juliana ever crossed paths? Sergio is Karina's uncle, flesh and blood, and Karina grew up in Sergio's sprawling mansion. Surely they at least knew about each other, even if they never met...? I glance over at her and realize that everyone else is, too.

"I don't know any Julianas in our family. But that proves

nothing. My uncle's middle name is shady. I believe what Candi's saying."

Armani nods. "Okay. So your friend and Sergio are working together."

"Yes, though I'm not clear on the exact...role that she plays. Other than being unofficially in charge of whatever I'm supposed to be doing here."

"Is she sleeping with him?"

I can't help my knee-jerk reaction, cringing in disgust. Sergio Bruno is an intimidating, pushy, hideously over-bearing man with a perpetual gleam of violence in his eyes. I've never felt comfortable around him. The feeling that something bloody and terrible is about to happen follows that man like a stench. Besides, Juliana truly thinks of him as her uncle, legal relation or no. She'd never sink that low.

"No," I say firmly. "Of course not."

Except...Jules has never kept a guy around for long. Is it because she "belongs" to Sergio? Is this just one more dark secret she's kept hidden from me? Suddenly, I can't be sure.

"Even if she's Bruno's niece by blood, what makes her important enough that she'd be married off to seal a deal with the Bratva?" Dante interjects. "She's nobody."

"I really don't know," I say miserably. "She said she'd worked with Orloff before, in a consulting capacity. Possibly she seemed like a good match because they built up a rapport or something."

Marco frowns. "Sergio has no daughters of his own. Maybe she's considered the next best thing. Daughter of a kingpin is pretty impressive, no?"

"Or maybe her parents were high up on the Bruno

ladder," Armani suggests. "It'd give her a pedigree. A bit of clout she didn't earn for herself."

I shake my head. "Why don't I just tell you everything I do know, that way you can ask better questions? You're just going in circles."

"Good idea," Frankie interjects. "Otherwise we could be here all night long speculating."

Armani nods at me and I finally relax a little. I'm ready to give a full confession, but I'm hoping I can exonerate Jules in the process. She's not a villain. She's a product of her circumstances and the horrible thing that happened to her parents. Yes, she wants her revenge. But Sergio is the one pulling all the strings. And hell, if anyone understands the need for revenge, it's Armani.

"I first met Juliana at UCSF," I begin haltingly. "We were roommates, starting freshman year. I wasn't aware of her involvement with the Brunos initially, because she never talked about it. And she never mentioned how her parents died. The topic was off-limits. But then, maybe two or three years ago, she told me out of the blue that she was working with someone who was going to help her get revenge."

"For...?" Armani prompts.

Taking a breath, I hold Armani's gaze even though I'm trembling. "Her parents' murder. She said the Bellantis are the ones who killed them."

A beat of silence fills the room.

"Our father might well have done that," Armani says, turning to look at his brothers.

"I'm not discounting it," Dante says. "We are not in the business of killing women, but our father wasn't above it.

294

There could be a record of it somewhere. A dollar amount, a name."

"What was the mother's name?" Armani asks.

"I—I don't know. Like I said, Juliana's last name is Guerra. That should be her parents' as well."

"I'm not familiar with it." Armani frowns. "Continue."

"Okay. So...when she asked me to help her, I said yes. After everything she'd done for me over the years, it was the least I could do. I didn't know who the Bellantis were at that point. Back then, you were just a name on a wine label."

"What did she ask you to do, exactly?"

I take a deep breath. "She encouraged me to start working for the winery, because it would give me access to the inner circle. She...wanted me to befriend Dante's wife, too, because she knew Frankie and I went to high school together, and that we'd had a passing acquaintance. But I would have tried to be her friend anyway, because Frankie is kind and funny and warm..."

My voice breaks. Shame burns in my cheeks. I glance at Frankie, but she looks away.

Armani draws me back to him. "So she asked you to spy on us. And you agreed."

"Yes. All the terrible things she and her uncle had said about your family over the years just compounded in my head and I fully believed them. Until...I started not to. And now I know...even if your father was as ruthless as the Brunos made him out to be, that's not who you and your brothers are."

"He was despicable," Dante says dispassionately.

I add, "You shouldn't have to pay for what he did just because he raised you."

295

Marco just nods. Armani's face is unreadable, but his jaw is clenched. I've struck a nerve.

"Having met you all, lived with you, spent time in your grapevines and around your dinner table, I have to say, things look a lot different from the inside than what I'd been led to believe. And I'm so, so sorry for what I did but I really, truly thought that I was helping Juliana. I just can't stop worrying that she's been lied to as well. She might be in way over her head, too. Sergio is...forceful. And scary."

"That's putting it mildly," Karina says dryly. "He's a snake."

"If it makes any difference, I wasn't much of a mole," I say. "I couldn't go through with a lot of what they wanted me to do. Even so, I am deeply sorry for what I did do and the damage it caused."

Dante waves his hand in the air, dismissing my words. I'm not sure if it's because he doesn't give a shit about my pathetic apologies or because he doesn't think I need to apologize for myself.

The last thing I say is, "I don't want Juliana marrying this Russian. She's so focused on getting revenge that she's willing to sacrifice herself just because Sergio says so. But I have a bad feeling about this Bratva guy, and I don't think she's telling me everything about the arrangement."

Armani says, "Sounds like we find ourselves in agreement. This marriage needs to be stopped. The Bratva can't unite with the Brunos. If they do, there won't be anyone left after the smoke clears."

"They'll take out all the other mob families one at a time, and they won't stop until they're the last ones standing," Marco says. "At which point, I'm assuming they'll turn on each other."

"I've heard enough. We'll move on this right away," Dante says. "Candi, thank you."

He's not smiling, but having the leader of the Bellantis give me a verbal sign of gratitude is enough to instantly fill my chest with warmth.

"I'll help however I can. Please, let me help," I plead.

"If you want to help," Armani says, "your loyalty needs to be one hundred percent with us."

"It is," I say without hesitation.

"Then you're in," Dante says.

And it's really just as easy as that. Standing up, Armani crosses to me and picks up the tea from the side table. It's still hot when he nestles the mug in my hand.

Frankie looks at me and for the first time, it's not with condemnation. "Looks like we have a wedding to bust."

30

CANDI

Ever since my confession, I've been walking on eggshells.

Earning back trust takes time—I know this—but it seems like none of the Bellantis know quite how to treat me now. Except for Armani. He's the same as he's always been. It's a comfort, honestly.

Still, it's awful being in limbo while he and his brothers figure out how they're going to use me in their master plan to stop Juliana from marrying Maxim Orloff. Whenever I ask Armani about it, he says they're still strategizing, but every time he brushes me off, my anxiety creeps higher. Especially since I haven't spoken to Jules since she hung up on me. What am I supposed to say to her when she calls?

What if she never calls?

My stomach churns just thinking about it. One way or another, it seems I'm destined to lose my best friend for good. And in the meantime, the Bellanti family is far from accepting me. I've never felt so adrift. Armani is my only anchor.

I just want this to be over and done with. Wedding canceled, Sergio Bruno permanently neutralized (in whichever manner Dante specifies), and most importantly, everybody safe from the Bratva. Maybe then I can start fresh with Juliana. If she doesn't hate me for ruining her life.

I'm sprawled on the sofa scrolling through social media when I get a text from Frankie.

Are you working today?

A wave of guilt hits me. It's a weekday afternoon, but I haven't been putting in many work hours since Armani and I got back from our fake honeymoon. Things have just been too hectic. I've been monitoring my work emails, and responding to the urgent ones, but that's the extent of it. None of the Bellantis have brought up my lack of productivity so far, but I guess the dip in wine sales must be noticeable by now. Shit. I figured someone was going to start asking questions sooner or later.

I'm not, but I can be, I text back. *Do you need me to follow up with a distributor or something?*

Gripping my phone tightly, I watch the screen, wincing a little when the dots pop up that show me she's typing her response.

Not a work thing—just wondered if you wanted to come over and help out with the christening scrapbook?

I let out a sigh of relief, but almost immediately start to fret again. Is this craft session invite truly an olive branch from Frankie, or is it some kind of test? Am I going to think we're having a good time scrapbooking, only to realize later that it was a cover for an interrogation?

But the more I mull it over, the more I realize that it doesn't matter if Frankie has ulterior motives. Her invitation means the world to me, and I'd love to contribute to a scrapbook for baby Lili. Mostly, though, I don't want to miss the chance to start repairing my friendship with Frankie.

I'd be honored! I type back, adding a pink heart emoji. *Just tell me when and where.*

She responds in seconds, telling me to come over to her house whenever I'm ready. Excited, I jump up and switch out my sweatpants for jeans, brush the taste of stale coffee out of my mouth, give Mr. Sprinkles a chin scratch for good luck, and then lace up my sneakers. Since Frankie and Dante's house is high up on a hill on the neighboring property, I call Donovan to see if he's available to take the short drive and drop me off.

Ten minutes later, I'm standing on the front porch at Frankie's, debating whether or not to ring the doorbell. If the baby's sleeping, it will wake her up. Maybe knocking is better. Before I reach a decision, the door flies open.

"There you are," a smiling Mrs. Abbott says. "Frankie said you'd be over any minute. Come on in, Candi. She's in the dining room."

I smile back, grateful for the warm welcome. Frankie's mom has always been kind to me.

When I get to the dining room doorway, I hesitantly peek in. Lili is sleeping soundly in a bassinet. Beside her, Frankie sits at the head of the table, hunched over a scatter of photographs. I see sheets of colored and printed paper, a plastic box of stickers and fabric scraps and notions and embellishments. Glue gun, decorative scissors that cut different designs, double-sided tape. The invitation to the christening is set in the center of the mess.

"You didn't have to wait for me," I whisper.

Frankie looks up and lets out a quiet laugh. "I wasn't, actually. I'm just miserable at this. I don't even know where to start. It seemed like it would be a lot easier to do when I saw it on a blog."

"Famous last words," I quip.

"Have a seat."

I take a side chair and assess the supplies. They are plentiful.

"So yeah, I'm not very crafty," she sighs. "I didn't get the artsy gene from Mom. Charlie did."

"Why don't you show me the blog article?" I suggest. "It'll give me a sense of what you want."

She picks her phone up off the table and taps the screen a few times, then hands it to me.

"This is my Pinterest board of all the different baby books I loved," she says. "I didn't have one specific style in mind. I just want it to be…meaningful."

We look at the reference images together. The scrapbook spreads are perfect, of course, but they don't look that difficult to recreate.

"I'm seeing a lot of layering," I tell her. "And lots of different materials on each page."

"Yes! That's exactly what I'm going for."

Nodding, I poke around in the pile of printed paper until I find an ivory page with a border of pale yellow rosebuds. I set it on top of a sturdy piece of scrapbook paper and then set the christening invitation at the center, then move it a bit higher. Frankie nods approvingly and starts poking through the supplies. She positions scraps of lace around the invitation, digs out a sheet of Easter stickers with Catholic themes—a cross, a dove with golden light radiating from its wings, a rosary—and sets aside the ones she wants to use. Meanwhile, I've found a piece of cardstock ephemera with a church on it that looks similar to the one where Lili was christened, stained glass and all, with white doves flying above it.

When I hold it up for Frankie, she lets out a little gasp. "It's perfect."

Soon enough, we're pleased with the layout we've created and I start looking for the right paper to use on the second page. Once all the pages are ready, we'll glue down everything all at once. Better to give ourselves some leeway in case we change our minds or want to make adjustments along the way.

Frankie selects a few photos and lines them up beside the first page with the invitation on it. They're all from the day of Liliana's christening. She holds up one of her, the baby, and Dante.

"She looks so much like him," she says. "Not just the hair, but the set of her chin and the way she purses her lips. Don't you think?"

"Yes. She must have inherited the...Resting Bellanti Face, I believe you called it?"

Frankie snorts out a laugh and then claps her hand over her mouth, looking over at Lili to see if she's been disturbed. The baby makes a little fussing sound and then goes quiet again.

Sorry, I mouth silently.

You're fine, she mouths back.

Smiling, Frankie riffles through the photos some more until she has a stack, then splits the stack and hands me half.

"Let's cut mats for the photos with the fancy scissors.

You do yellow and I'll do cream, that way we'll have a double mat for each picture."

Silence falls between us again as we focus on making the mats. I do my best to cut perfectly straight, finding a kind of zen in the repetitive labor. When I find myself finished before Frankie, I pick through the plastic box full of fun bits and pieces.

"These are cute," I tell Frankie, holding up a sheet of tiny white satin roses with sticky backs.

"Those are precious! We need to use them. Maybe with one of the pictures of her in the gown."

Nodding, I sort through the pile until I find the perfect photo of Lili dressed in her christening gown, fists clenched at her chest, her mouth pulled up in a toothless grin. The roses match her gown perfectly. Frankie takes the photo from me and looks at it lovingly.

"I asked Dante if he had a baby book, but he has no idea. I looked through that entire house more than once trying to find mementos of when he and his brothers were small, but there's hardly anything. Their mother had the christening gown tucked away in a cedar chest, luckily. She had it professionally preserved, bless her. It was wrapped in archival tissue paper and everything."

She gives the photo of Lili back to me.

"I'm sure their mom had photos of them, at the very least," I say. "They must be somewhere."

"They got robbed of their childhoods. I agree, she had to have kept some sentimental things, but...I can't help but think their dad just got rid of everything after she died."

Frankie is probably right. How tragic. I'm glad I never had the chance to meet Enzo Bellanti.

We set the mats to the side and start pulling together the next batch of photos.

"Speaking of the little Bellanti boys, look what I *did* manage to dig up," Frankie boasts.

There's a small wooden box near her left hand that I hadn't noticed before. It's tied with a faded blue satin ribbon. The knot looks like it had to be pried apart, leaving the edges of the ribbon curled and sightly frayed. She pulls the ribbon apart easily and I wonder if she's the one who'd gone through the effort to open it in the first place.

Taking off the top, she pulls out a stack of snapshots and faded Polaroids.

The first photo shows two small boys standing in front of a Christmas tree in matching red sweaters. The taller one is holding a baby who looks like he's two seconds away from screaming.

"That's baby Marco. Dante is the tall one, and of course, Armani is scowling in the background."

I can't hold back a small laugh. Sure enough, he is. His chubby cheeks look too cute to hug a frown like that. The next two pictures are the same, but with the boys in different order near the tree.

Another shows a woman with her back to the camera. She's wearing a deep pink dress. Or maybe it's red; it's hard to tell from the faded colors. Her hair is styled in an elegant French twist. Most of her is hidden behind the tree. My heart flips.

"Is this their mother?" I ask.

"I think so. There aren't any more photos of her. I wish there were. I'm sure she was lovely."

"Maybe Dante has some?"

"I thought about that, but I decided not to ask him," she says. "He...doesn't exactly know that I found these. I'm not going to cut them up or anything, I'll just have copies made so I can use them in the scrapbook."

Too bad. I'd really like to see what Armani's mother looked like. Frankie hands me the entire stack of musty old photos to go through and I flip through them very slowly, taking time to study each one. I see so many nuances of Armani's childhood. The way he's dressed and how his hair is combed to the side with a perfect part. The same serious look he wears in each photo...except for one.

His arm is around a small girl. Older than Marco but shorter than Armani and Dante. She's staring straight into the camera. Big eyes, thick dark hair. The corners of her mouth are lifted ever so slightly. Just enough to make her appear as if she's up to something a tiny bit naughty.

Goosebumps rise on my forearms. My breath catches in my throat.

I know those eyes. That heart-shaped face. Even the smirk is exactly the same, despite the years of a life well-lived that separate the girl in the photo from the woman I know.

My hand trembles as I study the image, trying to wrap my mind around what I think I'm seeing. It can't be. Can it?

"What's wrong? You look like you've seen a ghost," Frankie says.

I shake my head, unable to give voice to my suspicion.

"She just looks so young and...full of life," I murmur, my voice choked up. "I can't believe she's gone."

"I know. It's really lucky I found it. Now Lili will have a

picture of the aunt she was named after. It's nice seeing all the Bellanti kids together, isn't it?"

"It is," I agree.

What I don't say is that this child…the Bellantis' sister… she's the spitting image of Juliana.

It's her. It really is.

Beyond a shadow of a doubt.

Juliana Guerra is Liliana Bellanti.

Armani and Candi's story concludes in Captive Heart…

Nothing lasts forever… except the Bellanti's hatred for the Bruno family.

My family prepared me to fight.

My best friend taught me loyalty.

My husband showed me who I am.

And now I'm caught between them all.

The thing about secrets is that they always come out.

The past is never gone.

No one expected it to explode.

I finally understand why my life led me here.

I was the only one who could uncover the truth.

And I'm damn sure I'm the only one who can prevent a war.

Men have pushed me around my whole life.

But I was built for this... I am Mrs. Armani Bellanti.

Find out what happens in Captive Heart.

PAIGE PRESS

Paige Press isn't just Laurelin Paige anymore...

Laurelin Paige has expanded her publishing company to bring readers even more hot romances.

Sign up for our newsletter to get the latest news about our releases and receive a free book from one of our amazing authors:

Laurelin Paige
Stella Gray
CD Reiss
Jenna Scott
Raven Jayne
JD Hawkins
Poppy Dunne
Lia Hunt
Sadie Black

ALSO BY STELLA GRAY

The Zoric Series

Arranged Series

The Deal

The Secret

The Choice

The Arranged Series: Books 1-3

Convenience Series

The Sham

The Contract

The Ruin

The Convenience Series: Books 1-3

Charade Series

The Lie

The Act

The Truth

The Charade Series: Books 1-3

The Bellanti Brothers

Dante

Broken Bride

Broken Vow

Broken Trust

Marco

Forbidden Bride

Forbidden War

Forbidden Love

Armani

Captive Bride

Captive Rival

Captive Heart

ABOUT THE AUTHOR

Stella Gray is an emerging author of contemporary romance. When she is not writing, Stella loves to read, hike, knit and cuddle with her greyhound.

Printed in Great Britain
by Amazon